NORHAVEN

NORHAVEN

An album of short stories

Mark Jackson and James T. Duthie

Matador
9 Priory Business Park,
Wistow Road, Kibworth Beauchamp,
Leicestershire. LE8 0RX
Tel: 0116 279 2299
Email: books@troubador.co.uk
Web: www.troubador.co.uk/matador
Twitter: @matadorbooks

ISBN 978 1803130 088

British Library Cataloguing in Publication Data.
A catalogue record for this book is available from the British Library.

Printed and bound in Great Britain by 4edge Limited
Typeset in 11pt Adobe Garamond Pro by Troubador Publishing Ltd, Leicester, UK

Matador is an imprint of Troubador Publishing Ltd

For James T. Duthie
(1942-2009)
Writer, Fisherman, Friend

NORHAVEN

EDITED BY EILIDH M WHITEFORD

'As Alan stepped out of The Drifter, biting in a burning cold breath, he stopped and stared across at the *Sans Peur* sitting safely in the basin. A sudden wild gust of wind buffeted him and checked his stride. Alan shook his head slowly as if trying to hear something or, maybe, clear the echo of a distant song or a long forgotten story. Something his grandfather had told him once, long ago, reached out and touched him, something he couldn't quite catch hold of. It was a tale about a woman and the sea, *of mermaids and magic.*'

Here are eleven stories, some uplifting, some dramatic, some sad. They are set in Norhaven, a small Scottish coastal town. A singular place, the home of fishermen, shop assistants, filleters, welders, ships painters, teachers and pupils, pensioners and surfers.

Their triumphs, disappointments, hopes and passions.

Cover Design: Alexandra Bartholomew

AUTHORS' NOTE

Although these stories are set in Norhaven, Scotland, the characters and dialogue are products of the authors' imagination. Any resemblance to living people is entirely coincidental.

This book would not have been possible without the commitment and support of the family of James T. Duthie.

CONTENTS

SANS PEUR

SANS PEUR

i.   org. (French) meaning without fear, no fear, fearless.
ii. Motto of the Clan Sutherland, northern Scotland.
iii. Norhaven-registered fishing trawler (NW208), built at Irvine's Shipyard, Peterhead, by Graham Sutherland Snr.

The *Sans Peur* was a real fishing vessel. She inspired and merited this saltwater fairytale.

PROLOGUE

The beach was a wide arcing strip of sand curving out into the North Sea.

It formed a spur from the town, Norhaven, a fishing port that clung to the rock that jutted into the bitter waves. Clung to it and defied it, an exposed forgotten shoulder of rugged coast on which the cluster of granite-blocked buildings formed a stubborn epaulette set against the cutting Norse winds.

A sea spray rose as gulls keeled harshly on powerful currents above a fishing boat as it laboured towards the harbour mouth. From a distance, it appeared to bend and push into the wind, as if this last leg of the trip might prove beyond it. Its destination was the narrow, angled mouth between two flat-faced, high, granite-grey breakwaters. The harbour's outer defences. These barriers were carved out in the sea with early Victorian conviction, when it had seemed even nature could be curbed by the power of the British Empire and the determination of the age – a delusion of progress and industry.

Norhaven was a settlement constructed inland from the harbour basins. One street had been built at a time during the early years of the 1840s' whaling boom. It withstood the sea, the cold, the wind. The ocean's bounty fed and clothed the town. For a while whaling had sustained the town, later herring had fed it and consolidated its early fortunes.

The beach rose slightly, running into the dunes. The slap-down clap of breaking waves produced the low notes, the cry of wheeling gulls the high notes. Marram grass swayed with the wind and the tide in an unpredictable rhythmic dance.

Gulls soared above the waves, catching high, sweeping currents. Forces you could sense but not see. The wind pushed and pulled the bruised grass along the rising curves of the dunes.

The wide curving beach reflected the icy Winter sun. Norhaven Beach was deserted but for a distant dog and his walker, wrapped against the wind that lifted sand in swirling waves up towards the dune banks. The promenade was closed to business; closed to anyone's business. Two sturdy four-sided beach shelters squatted next to a weather-beaten wooden tea hut, its original colour long since lost to the salted elements, with a creaking rust-blistered ice-cream sign swinging forlornly on rusted hinges. It slouched next to another taller wooden building, a former Lifeboat shed, gable-end on to the sea. Norhaven had been one of the first communities in Scotland to establish a Lifeboat, raised through public subscription with the blessing of the local laird. It said so on faded information boards erected by the council during more affluent times, harbouring the fading hope that visitors would bravely venture this far north and east.

Back to the bleached tea hut. The windows were boarded up with a sign roughly daubed with white wash to withstand the elements: 'Re-opens 5th January'.

At a sharp angle to the flat beach, a lone surfer was riding the waves, carving out sharp cut-backs, his motion fluid and powerful. A sweeping poised shadow.

The wind carried a cast of rain with it. The rainfall deepened the light across the sand, a reflected yellow-orange glow beneath a range of dark slow-moving clouds. The sky was immense, the waves and the beach pale strips beneath it. It could have been a template ready for Turner, except for its rawness and rebellion, the eye-stinging wind, and the sharp sea chill.

The black-clad figure emerged from the sea. He lifted his surfboard from the water. Alan pulled his hood off to reveal a rugged, athletic face with watchful eyes, blue-green that could stir like the sea in a storm.

Saltwater ran down his face, unnoticed beads formed on the neoprene wetsuit. His chest was still heaving from the exhilaration of life and the elements.

As he walked his footprints left no impression on the frozen sand. The beach and the waves were his on New Year's Day.

OCTOBER

THE SAME YEAR

The *Sans Peur* rose and fell, leaning against and then away with the North Sea. On the wooden deck two men were hauling in a net, the obsidian waves high beside them. Both men were sturdy, weather-beaten and in their prime. They had to shout to be heard.

"Keep the line tight, Suds!"

Suds eyed a rising swell of water. He pointed to it.

"Waves would be good right noo."

Alan scowled at him and tightened his line, bending into it. He gave the thumbs-up to another man, affectionately known as Potty, a rough-looking man, maybe in his fifties, perhaps older, who was standing at the winch. All three were in discoloured oil-skins that had been hauled on over heavy check shirts. Solid, thick-soled rubber boots, a form of oversized industrial wellington, completed the crew's unofficial uniform. The angry crosswind buffeted and slammed at them.

Suds tightened his line, but unseen by him a rust-caked pin began to give under the pressure. The net erupted from the sea, heavy, spilling mud and life. It arced high. The men watched it, on their toes in readiness, judging its wild, erratic swinging progress.

"Watch the line!"

Suds couldn't hear him. The catch lurched and the pin holding Suds's line felt the strain. The pin snapped, molecules straining, metal splitting and parting. The catch, a huge organic demolition ball, reared back towards Suds, who tried to back-pedal and dodge it. Alan leapt across to pull his brother out of the descending haul's path, taking him down in a rugby tackle to the deck. The spinning net thrashed above them, veering wildly in a violent swirling dance.

Moving with surprising and decisive speed, Potty drew a large knife and slashed down on the line.

Alan and Suds looked up from the floor of the deck, as the winch buckled and the net discharged some of the catch on the deck, vomiting the rest over the side. They rose slowly, breathing deeply, each letting the sweat-shock of adrenalin ebb away.

The trio considered the mangled winch. It looked as if it had been struck by a small car. The aftermath of a traffic accident. Alan looked at his brother with a rising tide of anger and disgust, but Suds matched it.

"Never your fault, like!"

They were of a height. Suds maybe owned an inch. It could have been the wildness of his hair. In build they were from the same pattern. Both were well-muscled with nothing spare, physiques hardened by graft on deck not gym work.

Alan looked at Potty and turned away to start to haul the half-empty ruined net back in.

Suds's anger had become a dance with practised, oft-repeated steps.

"Tell him, Potty! Boat's a bucket!"

Potty hefted his knife.

"At least you're in one piece for Arlene," Potty's voice was a low rumble, vocal chords dragged over the seabed.

A cruel knife took the side off a fish. A slim chainmail-gloved hand turned the fish over and filleted the other side. The fillets joined a stream on the conveyor belt. All this was done in a blurred, near-robotic motion.

The hands belonged to Arlene, a pale, slight girl somewhere in her early twenties. She was wearing a white lab coat with a wisp of streaked blonde hair poking out from beneath her blue hair net. Behind her in rows, women were filleting fish. Moving through the factory, canning machines were in rapid, repetitive production; metal and white concrete. Tins ran along winding rails. The tins were a speeding line of painted colour amid the factory's stark functionality. The mechanical soundtrack, a constant industrial techno beat in the chilled, fish-wet workplace. Plump fish arrived, carcasses were carried away, the remains falling off the end of the conveyor belt into square tubs, yellow or blue. These repositories added colour, but failed to add much warmth. In this concrete yard the filleters and charge-hands were the only sources of heat, their breath visible even when they were not speaking.

The girl facing Arlene from across the line leaned in to be better heard.

"When's Suds hame?" Joanne was small and dark with piercing intense eyes of Pictish blue.

"Twa days yet," said Arlene, turning over another wet silver fish, gutting it.

Their attention was caught by Chad, a sleek American inspecting one of the canning lines. His tan jarred against the cold white of his lab coat. Perhaps that was the point. As if sensing their interest, Chad looked up and smiled directly at Arlene.

Arlene went unnoticed by most. She always had. Except for her hair of deep fire, which she took pains to dye at every opportunity, hoping to change her character with each rinse: brunette, auburn, honey. Character washed in, genetics washed out.

Any colour would do to mask her heritage, deny her Celtic nature. She had always been ashamed of it and squirmed at the attention it brought. Her mother's pride in her daughter's primary school pigtails had only added to Arlene's desire to retreat from her redheadedness. For her, being a ginger had never been cool. It never would be.

Embarrassed by Chad's deliberate gaze, affronted by its brash confidence, Arlene sliced another fish, hardly glancing down to the flicking blade.

On board the *Sans Peur*, another knife flashed, deftly used by Reef, a sparse, hollow-cheeked man in his middle twenties, wearing a green woollen watch cap, the kind immortalised by WWII Commandos.

He had a cigarette in his mouth as he gutted another fish. He was at home in the stinking, shadowed, pitching hold, shifting his balance with the boat. It was done as if second nature.

Reef lived in his own world. A North Sea bubble. He shared it with you in the manner teenage mates share a drag, with whoever was there at the time.

With the Sutherland brothers, it was different. As a unit they had adopted him. Despite their roof and shelter, Reef remained a stray, a behatted, shaven-headed odd-ball, a surfer, and the creator of strange, almost hypnotically seductive art.

The cigarette finished, he spat the stub out and planted his over-sized yellow rubber boot on it. He paused and patted his chest pocket, then fished out another from a battered sweat-damp pack of Lambert and Butler, and looked up through the hatch, waiting for the net to come in. On the wall behind him in the gloom, illuminated in a block from the open hatch above, were stylised sketches of mermaids and dolphins interspersed with a distinctive wave motif. The square of light framed the artwork, as intricate as the scrimshaw of long dead seamen. Its unevenness and the boats rolling movement gave the sense that the drawings were alive, the mermaids swimming sensuously across the wall.

Reef was joined by a still scowling Suds. They worked quickly, fluidly, showing great balance. Reef mimed standing on a board and Suds served up a reluctant smile. It was then that the reassuring drone of the engine cut out. Silence. The duo looked sharply at each other in alarm. *Not again.*

On deck, Alan and Suds were standing amid the stillness. The *Sans Peur* was their life. It had been their father's boat. Now, it was one of the oldest in the Norhaven fleet. Wooden-hulled, it had been built in nearby Peterhead at Irvine's Shipyard. Launched in 1971, it was one of only two surviving wooden vessels still fishing out of the port. The other was the *HOPE*. And there wasn't much of that about.

Alan loved the way she handled; at 23 metres, powered by an upgraded 385 Kelvin engine, the *Sans Peur* possessed character and spirit. A vessel worthy of its name.

Despite its age and wooden build, it held its own against more modern metal-hulled craft – at least, in Alan's eyes.

Now, the boat and its crew were in trouble.

Without a working engine, the trawler, offering no resistance, was being bullied by the sea. The brothers looked at each other, then at the unending expanse of water. Waves slapped the boat's hull. A dull hollow thud of doom. Eerie.

At sea, when your engine dies, the seconds become hours.

In the dank hold, Reef exhaled a smoke. He looked up at the ceiling, light still spilling in from the hatch. The heavy claustrophobic press of the waves against the side of the hull was magnified in the cramped, dark space. He looked at his drawings etched on the wall. Reef could see and hear his own breath, his heartbeat thundering in his ears. He felt the pressure building. It was moments like this that he wished he'd become a joiner.

Potty climbed out onto the deck. The boat was adrift in the vastness. A sudden, sharp crack carried across the water. Alan and Suds swivelled around in alarm, but Potty was simply emptying his pipe on the rail. The older man raised an eyebrow at the brothers. Suds reached for the rail as the *Sans Peur* lurched, angling the deck further. Alan and Potty exchanged a moment's stare, bonded in urgency. Potty nodded and made to return below to the engine room. It was down to him. He was the boat's helmsman, the Driver, heavily muscled, with bleeding tattoos snaking down his hard forearms. Only two words still stood out, SCOTLAND and MOTHER. No one dared ask if they were somehow connected.

The grizzled engineer was using a wrench on the engine while Alan stood at the doorway.

"Same as last time, Potty?"

Suds appeared at his brother's shoulder, shadowed in the doorway.

In the gloom, Potty realised, the brothers were difficult to separate. Suds could have been his brother's shadow. There were those in Norhaven who said he was scant more than that. Strange how things work out, thought the engineer, but he wasn't one to dwell. He had an engine to fix.

"What do ye expect? That tight arse, Peter, wouldn't pay for the overhaul. Fuckin' arse. He disnae give a fuck if we sink."

Alan ignored the familiar grating voice at his shoulder and turned his attention back to Potty.

"Catch is poor. He'll nae be happy aboot an early landin'."

"That all ye care aboot?" hissed Suds. A voice like radio interference. Made to pick and provoke.

"Go help Reef grade the fish." Alan's tone was dead flat. A warning in it.

"It's deen." Disgusted, Suds stalked off.

Ten minutes later, a tense, simmering Suds was on watch in the wheelhouse, when Alan squeezed in to the narrow space. It was a curved shape, windows set to give visibility. The array of electronics dominated the wheelhouse. The furniture of navigation and communication had the feel of having been bolted on to a boat from a different century. In some ways, it had.

"He'll fix it."

Suds agreed.

"Potty can fix onything."

Alan gave a tired smile.

"Have you thought aboot it?"

"I'm nae goin'." Suds was definite, his stance shifting as he crossed his arms. Unspoken defiance.

Alan tried again. He even softened his voice for his brother. It was a wasted hope that Suds would give any ground. His brother made his decisions early, sometimes before he'd even been asked the question at all.

"It's only one nicht. Surely you can put up wi' Peter for one nicht?"

"You go to your fancy fitba' nicht, I'm gonna surf," came Suds's reply.

"What aboot Arlene, does she nae get a say?"

"She's cool," the reply, too quick. Something in Suds's hurried tone told Alan that Arlene was not cool with it. Not cool at all.

The Harbour Bar was always busy midweek. Arlene and the girls were having cocktails. Bold colours in voluptuous glasses.

Shore Wynd was Norhaven's strip. Bars propped each other up along the narrow road that ran beside the harbour. At one time there had been many more, two dozen perhaps. Even the Harbour Office was flanked by them, The Sauchen and The Duke, the latter named for Wellington not Cumberland, the newly painted office at attention, like an upstanding starched officer with two merry rogues for minders.

The trio of girls were settled in a booth, freshly showered and changed, the clinging, clammy scent of fish scrubbed away together with thoughts of work. Clocked off, lippy on. Their first port of call was Happy Hour, a midweek massive. A weekly blend of cocktails, shots and confidences. The room was long, the bar down one side, disappearing into the shadowed booths at the rear. The new owner, 'Fat' Fred Cumming had revamped the bar. The booths still smelled of faux-leather. The sticky burgundy velvet had gone. Arlene was grateful for that. The toilets still needed sprucing up, but you couldn't have everything.

Elton John ended and Peter Gabriel replaced him. *'Solsbury Hill'*. Arlene preferred the one with Kate Bush. The renovation had done nothing for the acoustics of the place either.

Joanne pointed out Chad at the bar, but Arlene merely shook her head. Monica rolled her eyes. It did not deter Chad as he walked across and placed a cocktail in front of Arlene.

"You should try it, Ma'am." His voice, even amid the bar's din, was like chocolate.

Arlene felt a growing uncertainty, panic rising, as Chad smiled and walked away with a cowboy's swagger. Joanne leaned forward and sniffed the drink.

"It's an orgasm!"

The girls shrieked with laughter.

"Twa days you said." Joanne's tone was a whisper, a conspiracy.

Arlene shook her head, but was still flattered. She knew that her friend would already have had the bronzed, exotic American if he'd glanced at her once. Joanne was like that; she enjoyed different flavours.

There'd been the Danish oil worker, the French exchange teacher, the Aussie who thought he could surf until the North Sea had confounded him. Arlene sometimes wished she could be more like her friend. Joanne had no hang-ups, no guilt, and only one rule: local lads, born and bred in Norhaven, did not get a sniff. Joanne was exploring the world from her bed. Or theirs.

Monica was of a different creed. She had Tommy. She called him everything, yet since they had been fourteen, they had been a match. He worked offshore, was rarely home. When he was, Monica disappeared off the planet. However, when she was around, she could be as bad as Joanne for trying to persuade Arlene to let her hair down. Among other things.

In the stale, shadowed hold, Alan and Reef were inspecting the catch. It was stacked and packed in blue or white hard plastic crates, the fish insulated by crushed ice which spilled from the boxes. Alan's words echoed in the stillness of the hold. They were used to making themselves heard over the low deep hum of the engine, the boat's effort when steaming against the waves.

Now there was no background noise. Just a feeling. A growing sense of helplessness. They were aboard a tiny wooden box surrounded by sea and sky.

"You've got to be neater, Reef. We need a good price,"

Reef's puny radio tried to fill the space.

"John Redman reports how the farming industry will have to adapt to new regulations coming into effect…"

"Fishing's the same. Always movin' the goalposts," said Alan sadly.

The fishing industry was under severe pressure. Quotas had been cut again. A Government sponsored decommissioning programme had been introduced to reduce the catching capacity, a scrappage scheme that led to boats making a one-way trip to Denmark to have their hulls smashed open and their souls torn out. Alan had heard that Norhaven Harbour was now bidding for some of this distasteful work. It sickened him.

Reef took off his woollen hat and scratched his shaven dome. What did he know; it was all fish to him.

A convoy of brightly coloured Kombi campervans by-passed the harbour and approached Norhaven Beach. Two BMX riders stopped to watch the caravan roll past them. Fish workers on their tea-break had done the same. The slow-moving rainbow had drawn spectators as it rolled through the town as though the circus had arrived. Norhaven was not accustomed to such cheerful declarations.

The vibrant painted colours caught and warmed in the mellow dusk glow. There were four in a slow-moving bracelet, each one with panels of designs, each distinct and bright. The models spanned the decades, like a production line charting the evolution of 'the People's Van'. German-built order challenged by artists' curves. Spectrums of moving street art. One had poetry stencilled on its doors – Yeats. And lyrics – Van Morrison.

Reaching the rise above the line of parked cars flanking the promenade, one of the distinctly painted Kombis stopped with a judder and a small figure jumped out. The vehicle was powder blue with small delicate flowers discreetly placed across its bodywork. A graceful woman followed him. The small boy was Jake. He pointed out the glinting traffic of fishing boats at the harbour entrance to Abina, a stunning, wild-haired woman. She was studying the surf as though memorising it, tracing the lines of the breaks in her mind. It was a rough sketch, but it pleased her. She shaded her eyes and took in the angle of the waves, the receding beach and dunes. She thought she could make out another settlement, probably just a small village, in the distance, before the headland curved back on itself and joined the horizon.

They'd heard good things about the waves at Norhaven; maybe they were justified. It looked as though it would prove worth the trip, she thought.

Alan was at the wheel of the *Sans Peur*, when Suds pushed the door open, wrestling against the rising wind to close it behind him. Rain pressed against the angled windows. It added to the vessel's sense of vulnerability. At least Potty had coaxed the engine back to life.

In the tight confines of the wheelhouse, Alan and Suds were encased by an arc of electronic equipment ranged beneath small, curved windows. Alan took the tea being offered. Suds placed his in the lipped catch to stop it rolling with the motion of the boat. Behind Suds were charts, pinned up with a postcard showing a surfer in action in Hawaii. The noise of the radio and other electronic instruments was an incessant buzz.

Suds delivered the bad news to sweeten the tea.

"Sixty boxes."

Alan pursed his lips in dissatisfaction.

"For four hours work."

"Winch's badly buckled, Alan."

Alan's face tightened, but when he turned to his brother his expression was kinder.

"Will it work, brud?"

"Aye, just aboot."

Alan nodded slowly. Neither was happy with the other. They had been at cross currents for the past few years, at least, since Alan had wed. The fact was, Suds had never understood why. As for Alan, he understood less with every day of his marriage.

"We'll move on, try off Cromarty." Alan's voice was more hope than intent. Suds shook his head.

"Be just a waste o' time. We've only four days left on the quota this month. Movin' would just eat up it up," he pointed out.

The radio crackled into life.

"Alan, are ye aboot? Klondyker on 2182."

Alan picked up the mic. Klondyker was the by-name of his friend Petr Renko, another surfer, who had a choice berth aboard the 'Graceful'. He owed his name to his Russian grandfather, a tiger of a man from Murmansk, who had arrived aboard one of the Soviet factory ships and somehow remained in Norhaven. A minor miracle during the Cold War.

"Aye, I'm here, Klondyker. Go to 2345."

Suds raised an eyebrow as Alan moved the dial.

"Alan, the Open's on. This weekend. Waves should be juicy man. Have to bring it forward, like."

"Shit." This from Suds, as he took in Klondyker's meaning.

"Will we see you there, like?" asked the disconnected voice across the water.

Alan looked straight at his brother, who stared back.

The visitors had set up a small surfers' village, a tight cluster of tents and campervans overlooking Norhaven Beach. The vans were drawn up like a wagon train. Inside their circle, tents were pitched sheltering against the Kombis. Towels and wetsuits were pegged on lines that stretched between the gaudy vehicles. The wind had risen, with the clouds being shunted across the bay.

The waves were coming in beneath the layers of fast-moving clouds, their outlines rimmed orange at the edges against a bold blue sky.

Abina was surfing. Other figures bobbed on their boards waiting for the right wave to come in. She stepped out of the water and pulled off her hood, her wet hair catching the winter sunlight. Lighter, ruby notes in the damp tangles.

She was joined by a towering figure. Erin was a surf warrior, long-limbed and long-haired, sun and salt bleached. He made to speak to her, seeking her eye, but Abina concentrated on the sea. Erin was poised to speak, but she turned away from him and carried her board to where Jake was drawing in the sand. Erin watched her go, his words trapped in his throat, only to slide back into his chest. *Words unsaid wither or fester.* They were tight in his lungs as he heaved his board and stepped into the water, immersing himself in the icy cold saltwater. All his attempts to talk to her had floundered, run aground on his clumsiness and her remote coldness. It was her distance that frightened him, even more than had her past passion. He was discovering that he was undone by both. He was a fearful giant, an emotional coward.

Aboard the *Sans Peur*, Potty sat on his haunches in the engine room. His face was almost wood-grained in the low tinny light, but he was nodding gently as he listened to the engine gently shuddering. It was the music of his life and he had revived the old girl once again. He could feel the *Sans Peur* making steady progress, steaming.

The wheelhouse seemed small with just Alan and Suds in it.

"The biggest meet o' the year, Alan," persisted Suds.

"No. We're here noo."

"For Christ sake! Seven in a row. Do ye nae want that?" Suds exploded, spilling his tea.

Alan's dominance of the Norhaven Open Surf competition was something that Suds struggled with. It was just one of the hinges in their relationship that irritated him, but it was the most obvious distinction, the scab he kept picking at. He had been runner up a handful of times. His own desire to claim the crown remained undimmed. Yet the contradiction of being a brother was that his pride in his sibling was a badge he also wore. Nor was it merely reflected glory, but a quiet acknowledgement, in simple tribal terms, that his younger brother was the Sutherland clan's champion. It was a mantle that Suds scorned, yet reluctantly respected, while for Alan it was a crown he felt increasingly uncomfortable wearing. A poor fit, for an ill-made knight.

It was Alan's view of his abilities that his brother could not fathom. Confusion clouded him, his voice already unsteady and uncertain. As usual when understanding eluded him, Suds turned to anger, a more familiar prop.

He was in Alan's face.

"No." Alan's voice was solid.

"Awa' an' fuck!" Suds had met this wall before.

Alan tensed. Suds was ready as the engine died. Again.

Alan's anger grew as Suds could only look pleased. He couldn't hide it. Didn't bother to try.

"Now we'll have to heid hame."

Alan took a step closer to his grinning brother, but checked himself, fighting to control his anger and the overwhelming need to connect with Suds's jutting, taunting jaw. Alan's control held. Just.

At the end of a long line of seafaring Sutherlands, captains of the sea, was Suds. If there was such a thing as diminishing evolution, Suds was the proof.

It was Alan, who steered the ship. *When the engine worked.*

In the dark, hot, airless, oil-fumed, bowels of the boat, Potty was working on the engine. It died on him.

His working life had started on deck as a boy, running messages between the fishing boats, the Drifters, tied together in the harbour, leaping from one vessel to the next, from one end of the port to the other.

School had failed to hold him, and he had drifted naturally to the sea.

First, he was a cook, then a deckhand, graduating to a share, that prized unseen pip on a fisherman's shoulder. The system in Norhaven was common place across Scotland. After each trip, costs were deducted and the Skipper's share, with the remaining bounty divided between the crew members, depending on whether they were on a full share or a fraction of it. In many ports this manner of allocation was being eroded, but, to date, in most cases, Norhaven Skippers were still the boats' owners and the system endured.

Then, one trip, thirty years ago, the Driver, the boat's engineer, Victor Forsyth, had failed to appear, too inebriated after his brother's wedding. The Skipper, Auld Russell, had put to sea anyway, promoting the young Potty in the process.

So, in this quiet way, the affair had started. As it had happened all over the world: man and machine. As Potty grappled to understand each gauge, each turn and component, every metal bolt, the fundamentals of temperature and pressure, so his absorption and fascination grew.

This engine was his darling, his life-long frustration, his one true love.

He struck it with a hammer in pent up annoyance as Alan joined him. Sweat covered the engineer, lending a sheen to his heavily-muscled forearms and blurred tattoos.

"Potty. Fit's going on?"

"It's nae jist the engine, Alan. She needs an overhaul," rasped Potty as he patted the engine lovingly, "And an owner that cares for her."

Alan's fist hit the metal bulkhead.

"The winch is broken too, down to Suds's carelessness."

"It's years o' neglect."

"Always sticking up for him."

Potty straightened up.

"Somebody's got tae. Spik tae Peter."

"When has that ever worked," Alan already sounded defeated.

Potty laid a heavy oil-stained paw on Alan's shoulder.

"Offer to buy in – tak' a share, ma loon," he urged the younger man.

"Fix her," Alan turned away.

"She'll get us hame," promised the older man, but Alan had gone.

Overlooking Norhaven Beach, Chad stepped out of his brand-new gleaming Volkswagen Beetle, the latest model, christened with the number plate 'C5AD'. His surfboard was stamped with stickers more colourful than visas from all over the world, announcing a global surfer. He struck a contrasting figure in Norhaven: tanned, confident and athletic. Streamlined would have summed him up.

The local canning factory, MacNaughts, was now American-owned. The takeover had been front page news for the *Norhaven Courier* and had even mustered a narrow column of paragraphs in the *Scotsman* and the *Fishing News*.

Most of their rival fish yards remained locally controlled. Some of the more successful skippers had bought in, ploughing in cash, contracts and influence. Fishing dynasties were always looking for expansion, seeking a greater return, or, perhaps, a role for a family member less suited to life on deck. The plus side for the workers at MacNaught's Yard was that they were paid every two weeks, office and floor workers, whatever colour overall they wore.

The filleters now saw a few Americans as a result, sent over by the parent company to set targets and conduct audits. Rumour within the factory was that Chad was the son or grandson of the US company's president. His manner did nothing to dispel this legend; he was relaxed, confident, entitled.

He noted the make-shift surf camp and its followers, the Irish number plates. Unlike the Norhaven natives, he'd seen it's like before. Basic ingredients from California to Bali. He hoisted his board and headed to the waves. He hoped they'd hold for the contest this weekend, for he had high hopes of kicking ass.

The shelter, nestled on the promenade, was newly painted, this season's coat, with graffiti etched above the bench level: SW luvs Dik. Celtic FC. Norhaven sucks.

It was the boldest signage that defined the shelter and assigned its place in local parlance and legend. 'Scottish Parliament' daubed roughly on one side, white writing across dark council blue.

Two gnarled old fishermen, Watt and Hendoo, were sitting in the shelter. They were both in their seventies, weather beaten, wrapped against the wind in old cable-knitted sweaters, known locally as ganseys, and macs.

Watt had a bonnet crammed on his head, tufts of coarse grey-white hair sticking out beneath it. Their expressions belied their age; sharp, bright eyes. They were watching the sea. From their position perched in the shelter they had a panoramic, almost wide-screen view, from the dunes right across the bay to the red and white beacon jutting out into the sea. Hendoo was rolling his own smokes, tobacco tightly pinched from a small worn tin by stained fingers criss-crossed by old scars. The badge of a lifetime of hauling nets.

The pair had appointed themselves as the surfing community's unofficial commentators. Neither had ever surfed. Watt couldn't swim. But they could judge. In that, they were true parliamentarians, interweaving Norhaven myths and long dead grandfather's traits to explain a surfer's technique and mental fortitude – or the lack of it. Neither suffered fools, unless it was their fellow commentator.

They were studying Chad's progress. The American was surfing, his style smooth, crouched, strong.

Their thin blueing lips pursed.

"Nae bad," mused Watt.

"For a Yank," Hendoo sat hunched in judgement.

Where the beach ran into the dunes, Abina and Jake were donning wetsuits when Chad strode from the water. Spying them, he changed the angle of his path towards them. He smiled at Abina, brilliant American white, as he passed them, and ruffled Jake's sun-bleached hair. Displeased, the boy grimaced and swept his unruly hair back in place.

A fishing vessel was approaching the towering red and white beacon at the end of the long harbour wall, progressing in troughs. Peering at the boat, Watt looked quizzically at his colleague, who had the sharper eyes. Hendoo shook his head, passing Watt one of his homemade tabs.

"It's nae them."

Hendoo and Watt took a drag as Chad approached, drawing in the comforting nicotine warmth. He nodded to them.

"How you doing, old timers?"

The pair considered him through their smokes. Chad tried again as he rubbed his rubber-encased arms against the raw, biting wind.

"How do guys surf here all the time?"

"We're hardy," from Hendoo.

"Hardy?"

"Aye, tough," growled Watt.

Chad nodded, accepting this truth, as he tugged the draw zip of his wetsuit.

Encased deep inside the airless heat of the *Sans Peur* engine room, Potty was wiping his hands as the ancient engine grumbled resentfully. To Potty's ear it purred.

"That's ma girl."

Satisfied, Potty drew out a worn, slim silver Horner mouth organ from the chest pocket of his grease-smeared boiler suit. He wiped his mouth with an oil-stained paw and began to play '*House of the Rising Sun*'. A slow, sorrowful rendition.

Disconnected notes reached the hold, where Reef was drawing on the wall. The lithe curved figure of a woman surfer with a flowing mane of hair was taking swirling, sensual shape. A Mermaid, a Siren, *Die Lorelei*.

Alan and Suds were sitting facing each other like aggressive chess Grand Masters across the galley table. Potty's head appeared from the engine room hatch. The craggy Driver looked between the two of them. The small table and their hostility separated them.

"A'right," conceded Alan.

"Safety first, brud," Suds was trying not to smirk.

"You tak' the wheel."

With that, Alan got up and stalked out. Suds flashed a grin at Potty, who shook his head. Potty knew where Alan was heading. He'd known the lad all his life.

Alan was standing looking out at the sea, to where it knitted with the sky, his hands gripping the starboard railing. Wind buffeted him, although he hardly noticed it, hardened and insulated against it. His deck-earned familiarity with the cold chill bred a degree of imperviousness in him.

His eyes were on the clouds pulling across the horizon. The forecast was poor. At sea or on land, he admitted to himself.

Alan Sutherland was solid.

Everybody said so. A Topper. The boy in the class others wanted to be. Not the best, but good enough for others, his peers, to aspire to be.

He was a gifted fisher with seawater in his veins. He was a coming man. Except that he had been that all his life. Like a promising footballer tipped by all to play for Scotland, but who had somehow never won a single cap. Now they were heading home. To Norhaven and all that waited to ambush him there.

The wind helped to clear his head and cool his anger. Between Suds and Potty, he could only take so many truths in one day.

It was pre-dawn as the fishing boat negotiated the mouth of Norhaven Harbour, turning past the tall beacon with red collar. As it the entered the port, it swung round defying the angle. The name *Sans Peur* painted dull white on its blue bow. Its registration number *'NH208'* was a faded and flaking giant barcode, slanted black digits on a white box.

The vessel manoeuvred to a berth on the quayside directly alongside Norhaven Fish Market. This was a low granite stone building with wide wooden double doors on rolling grooves. As they came to within two metres of the pier, Reef leapt from the boat to the quayside. Hanging in the air like an oil-skin clad

Bob Beamon, he landed nimbly and turned to catch a rope thrown from the deck by Suds. Reef wrapped the heavy rope around a stanchion, damp with the early morning cold. Steam rose off the gaunt young fisherman as he toiled. Sparse to the point of being skeletal, he moved as if every joint in his body was doubled. Or maybe his entire frame was elastic. His gait was the most recognisable in Norhaven; a man with extra hinges and no sensible path. He lit a cigarette, the action a reflex to fill the stillness.

On the boat, a compact squat winch lifted two boxes of fish and ice from the hold. Suds was standing on deck steadying the pallets as they came up and guiding them with an attached line. Behind him stood Alan.

The harbour was washed in a low haze, giving a soft glow to their faces. Yet, their breath remained visible in the clear early light. Alan drew it in. He loved the dawn. On days like this, its light and its promise. The lyrics to the Elbow anthem 'One Day Like This' came to him and rose around him. He smiled to feel the sun on his face.

"Fish!" Suds voice carried in the still dawn chill.

The load arced juddering upwards and across. Reef, on the quayside, lined up a trolley for the fish boxes as they landed. He unhooked the grapple hooks and tossed them back. A young boy was working with him. Paul Pesic was a harbour fixture. Brought down to the quayside by his Dide, his Grandfather Buchan, when aged only seven, he lumped fish boxes, collected orders for Agnes at the Harbour Café, and acted as watch on trucks of fish. A harbour veteran at eleven, the stocky boy hoped to go to sea as soon as the law would permit. School rarely claimed him, but the entire Fishmarket knew him and had come to expect his presence. Many among them had started the same way. The pull of the sea was strong in some families. Saltwater in the blood.

The pair broke off to have a mock boxing match. Rosehearty rather than Queensbury Rules: strike first, mean it, and apologise after. After you'd won. The smaller figure was trying to duck under the advantage of Reef's greater reach.

Reef ran his rubber-gloved hand across his narrow unshaven face, leaving a signature of sweat and grime. The men were working at speed.

"Prawns!"

Reef quickly waved for the trolley to be moved. Young Pesic obliged, pulling the low trolley with two long metal hooks. His job today was to line the boxes on the market floor and to be neat and quick about it. Four boxes came up and swung over this time. Reef quickly undid the hooks and hauled the boxes onto a half-stacked pallet a few feet away.

From the deck of the *Sans Peur* the two brothers watched his labour.

"Get someone to give the man a hand, brud, afore he kills himsel'. He's nae wise!" said Alan.

"He's doin' alright. Fish!" hollered Suds, as he sent another haul across. "Pull yer finger oot Reef!"

Reef turned and raised the finger at the two brothers, his face splitting into a wide uneven grin.

"He's alright, ye ken," said Suds, underlining his point.

"Aye, I ken." Alan's eyes drifted to the tall dark grey buildings that ringed Norhaven Harbour. Reef bedded down in one of those foreboding tenements. Windows like black eyes peered malevolently over the harbour.

Alan gazed out across the harbour basin, the low golden

sun catching the boats' painted hulls. The fleet had shrunk. He thought back to his days down here with his Grandfather.

Smaller boats, yawls, still went out all day, laying creels to entice lobster or the far more common brown crabs.

In the main, the port was split between white fish and prawn boats.

Alan and his crew went out for the white: cod, haddock, ling and monk. A mixed fishery and, often, he thought sadly, a mixed bag. It was a volatile market; prices rose and slumped, while other costs such as diesel and insurance grew every year. Debt could sink a boat as surely as the sea. Alan could hear his father Graham senior saying it.

The most recent decommissioning scheme, incentives from the government of the day to step out of the industry, was looking increasingly attractive to many families.

Some vessels had already suffered that fate. Broken up for scrap and an HM Government cheque in the Norhaven Shipyard.

Their rusting, hollow, unhinged hulls lay like dead iron carcasses, picked over by seagulls and scrap merchants. Involuntarily, Alan's eyes shifted towards the shipyard which now resembled a graveyard. He felt a chill fleet across his shoulders.

It wasn't merely the older vessels, just those with families under pressure. A fishing skipper had to be a seafaring captain and a businessman. In some cases, increasingly, it felt as if the Bank Manager had become a needy extra crewman.

Another load of fish reared up, turning slowly as it swung across to the skinheaded deckhand. Suds was right, Reef was working out fine, despite early reservations.

Sometimes, Alan knew, Reef slept on the boat. He didn't object. He'd once picked Reef up from his grimy dispiriting flat and the experience had depressed him. Dingy, unfriendly stairs, impregnated with the rank residue of urine and poor plumbing, walls darkened by years of damp. *Count your blessings.*

Reef was renowned for his wardrobe of hats. He had started with his Grandad's trilby. He had been thirteen when the old man had died. The hat had been his meagre inheritance. He had been presented with a detention for his refusal to take it off in class. The hats multiplied; so did the detentions, earning Reef an unwelcome reputation for rebellion with the teachers, and a cult following among the pupils. It was his way of honouring an old dead fisherman.

Reef's lopsided grin evaporated as Peter, a stocky, powerful man, the other side of fifty, appeared in the entrance to the Fish Market. He was smartly dressed, in contrast to those labouring in the cold market, and looked almost deliberately out of place. Alan suspected that was his intention; he wanted to emphasise how far he had risen from the Fish Market floor, with his long dark coat and maroon cashmere scarf. Peter evidently did not like what he saw, in particular, Reef.

Alan and Suds spied Peter too.

"The Dark Lord," muttered Suds.

Peter was standing staring at them from the quayside, his hands thrust into the pockets of his Crombie, an air of menace about him.

"Sixty boxes," Suds's words were a grimace.

"Nae enough for Peter," Alan knew what was coming. The calming beauty of the dawn had been too good to last.

Regimented rows of blue and white plastic boxes crammed with fish and packed with ice lined the cold concrete floor.

More boxes were being hauled into single tiers by men with iron hooks – the lumpers. These were the market porters: the muscle, the grafters.

Men in gumboots and heavy insulated jackets were treading over the boxes, inspecting the fish, mobile phones in one hand, burning cigarettes in the other. Ice was swept away to get a better look as men talked into their phones, comparing prices from other ports, Peterhead, Fraserburgh or Buckie.

A group gathered at the head of one of the lines of boxes as the salesman stepped astride a box of fish.

Peter, Alan and Suds were standing watching the sale, while Reef was dragging a couple more boxes to the end of the row. He stopped to light a warming cigarette and eyed Peter cautiously from a safe distance.

A man standing among the buyers' huddle looked up and nodded to Peter. A cold acknowledgement.

"Bob Muirhead, the thieving whore," muttered Peter, his eyes black, narrow slits.

Alan and Suds said nothing.

"That bastard would rob his own mither."

The brothers remained silent, although their expressions, quickly masked, showed that they thought Peter could be referring to himself.

"Is that the best ye could do?"

He toed one of the boxes with his shiny shoe. He favoured a black brogue.

"It's shite. You're all shite. Especially him."

Peter pointed his cigarette at Reef, who was standing out of Peter's range. Reef gave Peter his best staged smile, but Peter scowled back.

"Alan!"

Peter walked and Alan, with a worried glance at his brother, but ignoring Reef's anxious look, dutifully followed. Peter stopped and stepped onto a fish box to make himself taller. It was an old trick. Alan's old PE teacher had done the same thing when he'd handed out a bollocking. Mr Mackie he'd been called. A good teacher, but short.

"They're both useless," Peter waited, but Alan did not rise, "and you, too, for havin' them wi' you. Things are not good. You think your Dad would put up with this. Graham had more balls."

Alan's face tightened. Peter always raised the spectre of Alan and Suds's father, Graham, who had been the Skipper of the *Sans Peur*. Peter's friend and captain. A Norhaven fishing legend.

"Back for a good reason? To spend time wi' yer wife?"

Alan's eyes narrowed further, but he knew what was coming.

"Surfing disnae pay the bills. Yvonne has expensive tastes, I know…"

"She's your daughter."

"She's your wife."

They both cut each other a little. And bled.

The two faced each other.

"Remember that." To emphasise his point, he flicked his tab at Alan, who tensed then relaxed. Peter gave him a strange look of contempt and sympathy as he turned away, as if there was something else he would like to say. Maybe he wanted to impart some wisdom or, maybe, simply some compassion. Peter didn't know which himself.

Increasingly, Alan frustrated Peter.

He feared his son-in-law was too deep, as though much

of the young man's effort and time was spent looking inwards, questioning himself and his place in the world. It held him back, yes, but also it was an aspect of his nature that marked him out, gave him an unknowable quality, hinted that behind the practical solidness there lurked an unpredictability, hinted that a sudden move could and would undo you if the wrong buttons were pressed. Even Peter knew he had to show some care with Alan.

In looks and manner he was Graham Sutherland's son, his obvious heir, but Bella had borne him. Those nine months counted.

As Alan watched him go, Suds appeared at his elbow.

"At least you're nae married tae *him*." A cold crumb, that failed to comfort either of them.

Alan's smile was a small sad one. It was Yvonne he was married to and he knew it.

Alan looked across at Reef, who was standing astride a crammed fish box. He grinned and mimed keeping his balance on a surfboard. Alan shook his head, but inside he was agreeing with him. The mischievous sprite.

The quayside bar was a dark warm watering hole, situated fifty strides from the port's main basin. It was called The Drifter. Named for the style of boats that had shaped Norhaven's history and paid for its expansion. To most, that name had been adapted to the Zulu. A fisherman's play on words. A kind of Drifter. As in all the towns ranged along the jagged Northeast coast, by-names were earned and awarded. For both people and places. Sometimes none too kindly.

The velvet seat covers were worn dull under yellow strip lights, one of which flickered above the pool table. A photoframe of curling blurred smiling faces looked down from the wall. History in polaroid. The lino at the bar's entrance was marked and torn. The bar itself was long, extending right along one wall, a common style in Norhaven. Horse-shoe bars were for the city. Bar stools leaned unevenly along its length. The lunchtime trade was just arriving; regulars drifted in towards noon on a Friday, men who had grafted all week, and some who hadn't, but couldn't resist the pull of the weekend and the promise of different company. Some would dig in for the long haul. Others were in for that famous 'just the one'.

Inside, the crew were gathered along the bar. Potty was recounting a story. This time it was one they hadn't heard before, or had simply forgotten. The first of Reef's jukebox selections kicked in – '*Californication*' courtesy of the Red Hot Chili Peppers.

"Graham was canny though. There was no one on board. He threw a line across."

Alan and Suds laughed, but Reef looked blank. Potty noticed this and sought to explain, a mite annoyed that he had to do so. He washed his irritation away with a mouthful of whisky.

"Graham claimed salvage. Good bonus for us all that year."

Reef nodded slowly. Most of Potty's stories featured Alan and Suds's father, Graham senior. For Reef, Graham Sutherland had become a formidable fishing ghost; in Reef's mind he occupied an iconic status, somewhere between the Ancient Mariner and Popeye. He raised a toast.

"A tenner says Alan'll make it seven."

"You've nae cash, ye arse," pointed out Suds.

Reef was undeterred.

"Talking of arses, I wish he'd hurry wi' ma coin."

As if summoned, Peter stalked in and stared at them. A

gust of cold air with him. He tossed four small brown wage packets onto the bar.

"Piss it away – arses."

Reef looked into his beer, hiding beneath his hat, a small-brimmed trilby. A hitman's hat.

Peter had one last sally.

"Mind aboot tomorrow night, Alan, and dinna forget your wife."

Message delivered, he turned and left, his black flapping coat escorting him out. An unwelcome crow.

Suds turned to the barman.

"Let's have a round from you, Thomas."

The barman, slightly stooped from his trade, nodded as Potty leaned across the bar.

"A small glass an' all, min."

The landlord brought four. The empty stubby glasses were sitting on the bar, laid in front of each fisherman. Suds opened his wage packet to pay for the round. He peeled off some extra worn notes and deposited them in his glass. The others followed suit, all except Alan. The other three turned their attention to him until he relented and did the same. The landlord ripped off small pieces of paper, scrawled names on them and put them in with the notes. They all lifted their nips while Thomas hoisted the glasses. They joined a small train of glasses all with rolls of notes inside on a high shelf.

"Here's to us, min," declared Reef.

"Here's to us," intoned Potty.

"Fa's like us," Alan entered the ritual.

"Damn few," added Suds

"An' they're a' deid," they all joined the chorus before they downed their drinks.

"Another round, Thomas!"

"Not for me, thanks, Reef," said Alan.

Suds raised his glass at Alan.

"Up for a swally, brud?" A challenge in his brother's voice, but Alan was already pulling on his coat.

"Hame to Yvonne. A proper lapdog. Peter's poodle," Suds jeered.

Alan swung round. Reef stopped drinking, as Potty prepared to intervene. Reef had learned early not to find himself between the warring brothers, even when waters were calm. A closed eye and a loosened tooth had been the price he'd paid thus far. Potty, though, had no such concerns. He'd never been shy that way. He'd handed out hidings for Christmas in his youth.

As Suds slid off his stool to face his brother, Arlene and a handsome, tired-looking older woman, Bella, pushed open the stiff front door and stepped into the bar.

"Mama Bella!" cried Reef in welcome and relief.

Alan turned away to the bar as Arlene gave Suds a quick peck on the cheek. Bella looked between Alan and Suds, tasting the atmosphere. Suds handed over his wage packet to Bella. Almost an act of atonement.

"It's a bittie light, kind, Mam. The engine broke down," he explained, as Reef shrugged in agreement.

Bella looked at Alan, who stared back levelly.

"Winch is shot an' all. Peter went off his heid. You'd think he caught all the fish himsel'. Miserable bastard."

Bella looked back at Suds. This was old ground. Well-trodden. Muddy.

Nivana's 'Smells Like Teen Spirit' seeped out of the aging jukebox. Another of Reef's shouts.

"He kept his promise, Graham, when … your faither, died."

Suds shook his head. He didn't like being called Graham. His name and the subject were too close to home.

"I heard another story," mumbled Potty, the words exiting the side of his mouth.

"There's lots of stories, Billy Cardno," said Bella, dismissing the engineer.

In her determination she remained in many ways the fierce young woman Graham Sutherland senior had first noticed and then set about courting. She had enjoyed the chase and, in time, the capture. But Bella had never been truly tamed. Her widowhood and loss were marked by refusal, a defiance that spoke of more than mere stubbornness.

But Potty was not one to be silenced.

"Only one's true."

Bella stared at him, daring him to utter more family blasphemy. Being Potty, he did.

"The truth is only what you choose tae believe, Isobel Sutherland." Potty had made his point.

He studied Bella as he slowly took a stubborn sip of his whisky. Alan avoided Suds's eye and tipped back his drink. *Time to go.*

As Alan stepped out of The Drifter, biting in a burning cold breath, he stopped and stared across at the *Sans Peur* sitting safely in the basin. A sudden wild gust of wind buffeted him and checked his stride. Alan shook his head slowly as if trying to hear something or, maybe, clear the echo of a distant song or a long forgotten story. Something his grandfather had told him once, long ago, reached out and touched him, something he couldn't quite catch hold of. It was a tale about a woman and the sea, *of mermaids and magic.*

Alan halted in the doorway to his bedroom, suddenly loath to go in. He lowered his holdall to the floor and his wife stirred in the vast chaos of their king-sized bed. Yvonne woke then, sensing Alan was there and touched her face, aware that she still had last night's makeup on. It had run and slipped. Her hair, a short, highlighted modern cut, was a flattened tangle.

"When did you get in?" her voice hoarse. Alcohol dry.

"Six."

Yvonne looked at her bedside clock – 11.30am.

"I thought you…"

"Engine problems. Potty's workin' on it."

Yvonne slid out of bed. She was naked.

Somehow, her bareness was a criticism, a snub. In a way that Alan only half understood, she was showing her disdain for him, for their marriage. For what it had become.

Moving quickly, she stuffed away last night's clothes, which were still strewn on the floor. A trail of layers from the door to the wide bed.

"Are ye wantin' to go oot tonight?" It was her peace offering.

"Potty'll need a hand." Alan rejected it.

Angry with her. Sore with the reaction she induced. He was cross with himself, and ashamed that he felt this way.

Annoyed by his immediate refusal, she jammed the clothes into an oriental-style basket. It matched the sparse functionality of the modern decor. White walled, metal and glass, a cold antiseptic match.

"Work, work, work," her voice cracked again with last night's drink.

"Spend, spend, spend." They had been here before.

Yvonne turned to face him.

"I'm oot wi' your Dad the morn's evening. The Football Club Dinner," Alan's tone was softer.

Alan put his holdall on the bed.

"One thing about being home early is that if the engine is OK, I might make the Open." It was said gently, but it cut Yvonne.

"Surf, surf, surf. Damn you. You set all this up. There's nothing wrong with the fuckin' engine is there?"

Yvonne's high-heeled shoe hit him as she dashed into the en-suite bathroom and the door was locked with a resentful thud.

Alan was left to talk through the bathroom door.

"Yvonne."

On the other side, Yvonne was sliding down the door.

"Sod you, Alan Sutherland. Go surf – it's all yer good for."

Alan's face tightened. He clenched his fist. His anger did not lessen the blade of truth in her accusation.

Norhaven's slipway stood at the north end of the port, and a small boatyard overlooked it. Morning sunlight warmed the tones of the half-painted boats resting on their high, raising cradles.

A new boat was under construction at the boatyard. Peter was standing with the Harbourmaster, Andrew Robert Salt, and his business partners, John Cardno and Andrew Milne, admiring the work.

Salt hailed from Buckie. Tall and commanding, he'd captained Merchant Navy ships throughout the world before stepping ashore at Norhaven. In 1940, his grandfather had taken his small fishing vessel and joined the flotilla of British boats that formed the rescue armada at Dunkirk. He and his younger brother brought eight men back. Salt saw himself cast in his grandfather's mould. His Dide was known as Pepper for obvious reasons. The grandson ran Norhaven Harbour, oversaw its market, slipway and small boatyard. Within the town he yielded considerable influence; in the harbour itself, he was the power, a natural bishop, whose flock were quarrelsome fishermen. A fractious, floating parish.

"She'll be ready in a month," the Harbourmaster announced. Salt enjoyed the gift of good news; a schedule being met.

This pleased Peter.

"We'll mak' the launch a week or so after."

"Peter, still some payments to mak' up," Milne reminded him, ever the cautious one.

To Peter's mind, Milne was a weasel of a man. He had inherited a small fishyard. It was an inheritance that consisted of a walled yard, benches, and an unruly, hard-drinking, hard-fighting workforce of filleters. A local solicitor, in the way of cautious notaries, had advised him to sell up quickly and get out, but Milne was nothing if not canny, and quietly ambitious too. With the assistance of grants from the European Union and the Government, he had modernised it and, in doing so, managed to secure choice contracts. More had followed. Now Milne was supplying high-end London restaurants and bespoke stores. His stock had risen, or it would have if 'P. D. Milne & Son' ever went public. Milne was the 'Son' in the above enterprise. While he lacked his father's graft and open nature, he owned more guile. Some would call it low cunning.

They say that weeds thrive. A non-entity at school, Milne had made the most of his birthright and was now one of Norhaven's inner circle, a group of golfers that increasingly called the shots in the town. Milne was rarely the shooter; he was, however, the man who could be relied upon to load the gun, or at least to hold the coats.

Peter nodded.

"I ken. I'll mak' them. When has Peter Innes McGhee ever failed to deliver?" he brought his hand to his chest for emphasis and challenge.

Peter was one of Norhaven's merchant princes, a man who could not step back. Everything, every aspect of life, was an arm wrestle, a test to prove and show he was the better man. Competition coursed through his veins. His pulse beat to win, to challenge, to triumph. To crush.

Peter gazed up at his latest victory. A new, gleaming future. Another incarnation of his driving dream. One that would take them all forward. *Dragged, screaming and kicking.*

As the group stared up at the gleaming new vessel and its possibilities, a young skateboarder whizzed past the group. Another flashed after him, wheels skimming the ground before takeoff and landing.

"Hey!"

The Harbourmaster rushed after the young intruders, but they barrelled away from him, leaping over workbenches in daring manoeuvres.

They twisted and turned, leaving the Harbourmaster trailing in the wake of their mocking youthful laughter. Its echoes reached Salt as he slowed, admitting to himself that the chase was a lost cause. *Cocky wee buggers.*

With the harbourmaster out-distanced, they passed Reef, this time in a different hat, a floppy Soviet number with ear flaps, with a paintbrush in his hand. Dark blue, globular paint dripped from the brush. He was standing back on the quayside to admire his handiwork.

"Sly, min. Sly," he smiled. Mission accomplished.

Spread out in front of him on the concrete, held down by chunky and rusty ships weights, was a huge canvas Saltire. Norhaven as art.

The small low granite house was pitched only metres from the sea, standing lea end on to it. The wind came in with the sea, dragging the temperature down a few chilling degrees further. Having the shorter wall take the brunt of the wind's cold made sense, and fisherfolk were by necessity practical.

Oblivious to the wind, Suds was waxing a surfboard outside his house on the shore. It was Bella's house, but would be his one day. Only a faded Billabong t-shirt covered his torso. Accustomed to working on deck, Suds had developed a fisherman's second skin to ward off the North Sea blasts. Washing was hung out between the granite cottage and the shoreline, including a battered wetsuit between shirts and pyjamas. Poles and lines ran along the narrow strip of grass that spared the homes from the sea.

Reef appeared at the low gate to the yard. He vaulted over it with ease. A natural gymnast. He could climb a rope like a lizard. At school, this ability had been of scant worth; aboard ship was another matter.

He wore a different hat every day, changed it twice on Sundays. From flat caps to afghans, tammys, trilbys. For weddings he affected a stetson bowler.

He adjusted his woollen pom-pom and studied the line of Suds's board.

"Yer off plumb, min."

Suds looked up at the interruption, straightened, and threw down his waxing block.

"You do it, maestro," as he stalked into the house.

He pulled out a worn frying pan and started to cook breakfast, a fry. Framed faces beamed down at him from the mantlepiece, a picture of his father Graham senior, and a younger Peter on board the *Sans Peur*. He could hear his mother Bella singing to the radio through the house. Bella and Amy Winehouse competing over the chorus of '*Valerie*', a competition in which the only certainty was that the song was the loser.

He cracked open an egg. He had always been Suds. Named after his father, he had never really filled the name. He was slighter, of frame, of thought, of deed. Instead, he owned his mother's impulsiveness, together with her ferocity.

Despite being the elder of the brothers, he had never been the leader. Butter in the pan, black with use.

The contradiction was that Suds followed no one. He had, thus far, loitered through life, revelling in it and resisting it in rough, equal measure. His only achievement was simply in being Suds. A plain badge, an unofficial clan motif.

For his friends and his detractors, it was both an explanation and an excuse. He was, would always be, plain Suds, as though a full Sunday name would be too much for him to handle.

He struggled enough with himself to be burdened further with a baptised title. Bacon strips hit the yellow-brown bubbling fat. The egg joined the bacon in the pan.

Suds served eggs and bacon to Bella and Reef as they sat at the small kitchen table.

"How are ye likin' it at sea, Calum?" Only Bella seemed to call Reef 'Calum'. Sometimes he forgot he'd ever had the name. A relic from the daily register at school.

"Fine, Mama Bella. Except for the Skipper, I mean the

owner, ken. Peter." Reef said the last word in a flat tone, adding the name to make it clear he wasn't badmouthing Bella's other son. Reef was Suds's friend, both graduating from skateboarding to surfing together. However, he respected Alan. Liked him, too. The younger brother was nearer his age at school, but Alan was a Skipper, a leader at sea, even if he refused to accept that mantle on land.

Bella nodded with a slight smile. Reef gave a grateful shrug in return.

"He could mean Alan. Some skipper he is. Lackey more like. Peter's echo."

Bella took a breath, as if counting to three. With Suds it didn't matter what number she counted to. Even when he had been wee.

"Graham, we've been o'er this. When your Dad was lost, Peter came with the news himsel'. I thought he was helpin'."

"He helped a'right. Himsel'. He got the *Sans Peur* though. If we still had the boat, we'd be coinin' it in."

"You still have berths. Calum, too."

"Christ, Mam, can ye nae…"

Reef tried to play the diplomat.

"Hey, Suds, Mama Bella, tak' a breath."

"Shut up, Reef," Bella and Suds's voices overlapped each other as they cut him off.

Reef pulled his hat off and scratched his skull in defeat and attacked his egg. It bled yellow.

The day shift was ending at MacNaught's Fish Yard.

It had been there sixty-three years, situated along a narrow lane across from Shore Wynd, at the northern end of the road that skirted the port's quays and jetties.

Tall mean looking warehouses lined Shore Wynd overlooking the main harbour basin, where once mighty whales were butchered and stripped to their frame.

Now, most of the narrow sea-damp buildings were rundown net stores, the luminous green and orange rope providing an abstract psychedelic rain of colour swirls against the drab dark grey stone.

The boats added colour too. Squat floating boxes of rich pillar box red, deep blue royally bold, and the strident yellow of an angry bee.

Each craft had its name and number painted on the eye of the bow. They hugged the quayside, berthed side-on to each other in ordered rows.

Vessels homed at nearby ports ranged alongside Norhaven's own: FR, PD, BF, and BCK in prominent capitals were common enough. Joined occasionally by a west coast interloper bearing OB or SY.

Women in white and blue overalls and caps were streaming out of the yard's gates. Arlene was walking along with Beth and Joanne. The trio had been at school together, Girls' Brigade, Highland Dancing, and now shared a shift on the gutting line. Beth was the only one wed, the others her bridesmaids. A triangle with tight angles.

Joanne cocked an eyebrow and pointed ahead to where Chad's brightly polished, sky-blue Beetle was parked. Her exaggerated mime was for Arlene's benefit. *Trust Joanne to clock that.*

The languid American was at the wheel. Arlene checked and quickly changed direction, crossing the road. Joanne's taunting laughter reached her as she angled away, but she didn't care.

Moments later, the Beetle cruised alongside Arlene, and Chad had the window down. He turned down the music, Disciples '*On My Mind*', to reduce the competition.

"Come on, Lady, give me a break," he implored, but Arlene fired him a dark shooting glance and speeded up. She stepped quickly into a small passageway and was gone. The harbour and Norhaven's main High Street and Square, were connected through a disordered run of tight alleys, smugglers' shadowed twists and turns that had witnessed Redcoats hunting down fleeing Jacobites.

Chad gunned the engine and the car flashed past Arlene's escape route, the brakes screeching rudely as he took the corner.

Saturday Morning and the annual Norhaven Open surfing competition was already underway when a battered mustard and olive van turned into the impromptu car park.

Layers of receding clouds ringed the bay, like the seats of an amphitheatre, as if straining for a better view. The intermittent clouds gave the light a fractured quality, a softer filtered haze.

Suds climbed out. He pointed out two parking spaces to Reef, who was at the wheel. Suds then stood back as Reef parked his van across both spaces at completely the wrong angle, almost 90 degrees.

"Reef!"

"Van's parked, dude."

As Suds and Reef joined the registration line, they nodded to a couple of fellow surfers, one using crutches. He would not be competing this year.

"Caught the back swell at Thurso. Snapped it like a twig," explained Suds. Backswell, like Surfer's Ear, went with the territory. Having your ears drilled was often the price of admission for coldwater surfing.

"Messy,' nodded Reef in sympathy, "Plumb waves, Thurso, mind."

As they reached the table to register, the tanned figure of Chad shouldered past them.

"Some jerk with a beaten-up van is blocking the road," he announced, his distinctive accent making his words carry further down the line of waiting surfers.

"Hey!"

Chad turned to face Reef.

"Your van? Learn to park it."

Suds and Reef pressed forward, but Chad was undaunted.

"Who the hell do ye think ye are?" growled Suds.

"The jerk has a friend. Go home, guys, you can't park and you can't surf either."

Suds was raging now.

"Answer the question!"

Confronted by the two hostile fishermen, Chad seemed surprisingly calm and composed.

"You think these waves are big. You don't know anything. Ever surfed Bali, Stateside? No, just a pair of stay-at-home, pale, Scottish wannabes. Safe surfers."

"I'm gonna kick yer…"

A figure walked straight past the confrontation to register for the event. Her presence distracted Suds, Chad and Reef.

"What a vision!" Reef was the first to vocalise his thoughts.

Abina turned and smiled at the dumbstruck trio.

"Hi. Again." Chad's charm failed once more and Abina turned away from him. Beside her, casting a large shadow, was Erin.

Abina turned back to the line. She and Erin made to move off, but standing in front of them, crossing their path, was Alan.

Erin and Alan acknowledged each other – surfing rivals, eyeballing each other like gunfighters. The first to blink. Abina looked between them, amused.

"I have to get ready for my heat, *boys*." The emphasis of her accent was on that one word – boys.

Alan watched her go. Erin pointed out the small figure of Jake skipping along the beach.

"Our son."

Alan nodded, meeting Erin's eyes and measuring his words.

The stand-off ended as the Judge's voice boomed out of a megaphone.

"Surf's sik guys, but due to the forecast, it's twenty-minute heats, best three waves count. Got it? Best three waves count."

Alan stood as if watching himself. Somehow, he had just challenged the Irishman. Trespassed. With the woman between them at the centre of a bizarre subconscious dual. *How had that happened?*

The unseen wave.

The sky dominated Norhaven beach, blending and reforming golden-tipped clouds like gigantic battleships steaming across the bay, changing shape as they merged and parted. Alan watched Abina call to the small boy, who checked when he heard her and ran to meet his mother.

The sky's canvas mirrored the thin strip of sea and sand beneath the vast expanse of mountainous clouds. Alan needed to clear his head. He had a surf competition to win.

Along the esplanade, surfers were pulling off clothes and donning wet suits. Suds and Reef were getting ready just inside the 'Scottish Parliament', their bone-white, hard bodies accustomed to the stinging wind. Both were zipping up full wetsuits. The North Sea demanded it. Hendoo and Watt were sitting in their customary perch on the bench, the judge and the jury.

"Who do yer fancy?" enquired Hendoo, as he took a draw on his tab.

Reef paused, and Suds, with his trousers around his ankles, turned to answer. He didn't get the chance.

"Yon Irish giant. Carries the wave wi' him," confirmed Watt.

Reef and Suds regarded the pair, then looked to where Erin was standing. Even at a distance, his size and long hair marked him out. Two far slighter figures were standing beside him, Abina and Jake.

The duo picked up their boards. Reef handed the remainder of his smoke to Hendoo, who accepted it with a nod, tapped off the ash as they moved down to the beach.

Taking a drag, Hendoo savoured the moment.

"They haven't a hope."

"Nope." Watt nodded and spat.

Jake, a small, brightly dressed, pied piper, skipped through the surfers on the beach, a splash of colour amid the black neoprene figures.

Alan was standing on the beach, apart from Suds and Reef. Jake caught his attention and handed Alan a flyer. Alan turned it over. It announced in Tricolour lettering the forthcoming Celtic Surf Festival in Ireland. Jake ignored the others. Alan looked up from the flyer and, by way of thanks, winked at the small boy, and Jake grinned back at him before trying a wink himself. Now it was Alan's turn to grin.

The Judges were calling the first heat, handing out the bleached coloured bibs.

Suds struggled out of the sea, dejected, shoulders slumped in defeat. As he dragged his board out of the water, he spotted Arlene walking towards him. She'd put makeup on and Suds smiled to see her. He was pleased she'd come; however, his failure in the competition overshadowed the moment and he rejected it. He walked to meet her, but turned away from her intended embrace and continued to walk toward the promenade.

"It was nae that bad. Just one of those days."

Suds was angry now. With every word, his stride became more aggressive. Halfway to the stone stairs, with Arlene trailing behind him, he passed Jake. Something in the boy's open expression checked him for a second. Arlene and Jake swapped smiles as the boy pressed a flyer into Suds's wet gloved hand.

"Thanks," said Arlene.

"A million," replied Jake.

Arlene was slightly confused, but smiled anyway, as Jake darted away. Suds halted at the foot of the granite steps. His anger was receding. His anger with himself, his lot, his failings. He looked back, out to sea.

Chad was surfing and, much to Suds's annoyance, doing it well. He took a wave, a long, smooth, commanding ride.

Reef was standing with Suds. Both were watching the American when Arlene appeared at Suds's shoulder. Sometimes, he could see her far enough.

"He's good, isn't he?"

Suds grunted. *Annoyingly good.*

"Dude's in the final, min," confirmed Reef.

Chad lifted his board from the water and approached them up the beach. He tugged off his hood and, spotting Arlene, he smiled, a flash of perfection.

"Hi Arlene. How are you doing?"

Arlene blushed, colour flooding up from her neck. Chad's smile widened as though he had scored a point and walked on. Suds looked at Arlene for an explanation, and did not like the one he got.

"He's at the factory. Doing an audit. He's American."

Suds looked ready to explode.

"Hey!"

Chad swung around on the sand to face Suds, ready for the anticipated challenge.

"Ah, the stay-at-home surfer. You should widen your horizons, Arlene. Travel broadens the mind."

Suds stepped closer to Chad. Still embarrassed, Arlene found her initial reaction was giving away to a peculiar mix of being both flattered and concerned, awkward at being the central cause, but slightly, and surprisingly, thrilled to be. A few paces in front of her, Suds was a simmering pot. She could almost feel the heat and threat in him. In his stance and his voice. Chad, however, seemed completely unfazed by the threat. He was relaxed to the extent of dismissing the fisherman.

"Why do ye nae fuck off hame."

Suds's words were meant to provoke, but Chad merely laughed. More provocation.

"I'm in the final, Buddy. You're out on your pale blue Scottish ass. You want to take me on, beat me there."

Chad pointed to the flyer in Suds's fist, that the fisherman looked ready to launch at the American. Suds looked at the damp, crumpled paper in his hand.

"Come to Ireland, if you've got the nerve. Or stay at home…"

Chad smiled again at Arlene as though inviting her to Ireland too, leaving Suds both raw with rage and humiliated. On his home turf too.

Alan came out of the water, shaking his head in frustration. The defence of his title over. No seven in a row now. Consigned to the *Norhaven Courier*'s dusty archives and Bella's scrapbook. Leaving his board, he walked across and shook Erin's hand. The Irish giant looked slightly surprised, but he took Alan's hand with grace. It had been offered in that spirit.

Overseeing the beach, Hendoo and Watt sat perched like commentators in the Scottish Parliament, hunched against the cold. Only the microphones were missing.

"That's baith Sutherlands oot," said Watt.

"Aye, Alan ower cautious and the older one ower reckless."

"Aye," intoned Watt again.

"Aye, one's got his mither's temperament."

"The other, the faither's, aye."

Below on the beach, Alan hauled up his board and walked across the sand. The waves were tailing off. He watched Chad. The American was preparing himself. The final featured Chad, Erin, and one of the visiting Fraserburgh surfers. The fourth finalist had withdrawn with a wrenched neck. Alan would have stayed for the showdown. It was one in which he had triumphed many times, but he had a big night ahead with Peter and his father-in-law's cronies for company. It might prove a difficult test. The American acknowledged him as he passed and Alan nodded back. They were of similar build and colouring, albeit that one was evenly, almost cosmetically tanned, while Alan was merely deck-burnt, his hair lighter at its edges. A surfer's tell.

Back in his bedroom, Alan pulled off his clothes and turned on the shower. Yvonne was standing in the doorway in a lilac t-shirt dress.

"Hi."

"Hi."

"How'd you do?"

"Crap. Must be getting old."

"No, nae yet."

Yvonne stepped closer and brushed his chest. She reached up and kissed him.

"What's that for?"

Yvonne kissed him again.

"Maybe I'm trying to say sorry."

This was unexpected.

Yvonne kissed Alan again and this time he responded. Yvonne pulled the towel away from him and led Alan to the bed. She pulled Alan down on to it.

"You're just awa' so often."

Even in his growing anticipation, Alan heard the criticism and felt his wife's hurt.

For Yvonne, it had always been Alan.

In primary school, as she first began to notice, he had intrigued her, only to infuriate her once they reached Norhaven Academy.

Surfing was his passion, her bitter barbed rival. While she delighted that it had moulded his figure into the physique of a professional athlete, she resented the time and commitment his passion demanded of him. She focused on that figure now, the hard muscle lines, as she drew him towards her.

Later, Yvonne was still sprawled on the bed as she allowed herself a small, satisfied smile. Alan stepped out of the en-suite bathroom and started to dress.

"I'm going to speak to your Dad," he said, towelling himself down in the doorway.

"Dad?"

Alan was putting on his kilt.

"Aye, aboot the boat. She needs investment. I'm going to ask if I can tak' a share. A proper share."

Alan waited for a reaction, but there was none. When he glanced towards the bed, Yvonne was studying her legs. Her indifference made him more determined. Alan picked up his shirt.

"I'm going tae ask him tonight."

"We could meet up later. I'm awa' oot with ma pals."

Alan looked from his wife, still examining her legs, back to his own reflection in the tall wardrobe mirror.

"Aye, nae bother," he said, speaking partly to himself. *Cufflinks – where were they?*

Downstairs, in his white dress shirt, he checked a small drawer for his cufflinks and Sgian Dhub. He hefted the small ceremonial blade and paused.

He carefully picked up a small wooden model of the *Sans Peur*. The miniature had been made by his father. Gently, Alan set the model down and clenched his fist, his mood clouding. *Aye, nae bother, married to Yvonne, wedded to Peter.* He could almost hear Suds saying it, but as he headed back upstairs to finish dressing, the only voice he could hear was his own.

In the warm dimly lit hole that was the Lamppost Bar, Suds and Reef were drinking. The cluttered array of empties marking the tail end of a steady session. A blurred exercise in problem airing and solving after which nothing really changed, but which offered a temporary, rented euphoria.

"It would be cool, Reef. Just one trip, that's all we'd miss," Suds stabbed his finger at the creased leaflet 'Celtic Surf Festival' that lay face up on the table in front of them. It had been carefully flattened in an attempt to preserve it and the message it carried. Laid out on the coarse wooden table, it had, for Suds, acquired the mysterious promise of a treasure map, a talisman that promised adventure, a chance of escape. More accurately perhaps, it was a declaration. A manifesto for rebellion.

"Plumb, min, plumb, but you gotta convince Alan, and yon Yank will tak' some beating, dude," Reef made his point, waving his drink for emphasis.

Suds slammed down his own glass and suddenly stood up, as if ready to fight some imaginary foe.

"I'll kick bricks oot o' him," Suds's eyes bulged, with the sureness of drink.

Reef was unconvinced by the claim. He'd seen Chad's composure under threat and it worried him.

"Gotta get there first, Suds," he pointed out.

Suds looked down at Reef, his decision made.

"It's aboot time Alan listened to some sense," he announced, hauling on his jacket and spinning for the door.

Reef watched Suds storm out. *Some things never change.*

Yet, Suds had fight. In fact, he was in constant conflict – with those he held in contempt, those he loved, and, above all, with himself. His rancour and resentment would have better fitted a middle child, or the runt of the litter, howling at life's injustices.

Suds was neither. He was Suds.

Reef reached across to the printed surf flyer and scanned it. On the reverse was a schedule for an old workshop and garage for sale in Ireland, near some place called Bundoran. Reef studied and, with care, slowly poured the remains of Suds's pint into his own glass. There was always an upside. *Glass half full.*

In the midst of the Victoria Hotel's ballroom, Suds pushed his way through the throng of groomed flush-faced men in kilts and lounge suits. He spied Alan talking with Peter, the Harbourmaster, and some other men. He knew most of them and their reputations, had even been to school or the Boys' Brigade with one or two. They weren't as bad as Peter, yet Suds, resentful of their success, viewed most of them as pricks. Just being at a function like this made them so, putting their hands in their pockets to buy the right to call themselves Norhaven FC fans. Suds put them in the same despicable bracket as plastic surfers, those who liked the image, but never tested themselves in the freezing North Sea. Yet, his younger brother was here somewhere, among this sea of dicks.

As he considered how to approach his brother, Alan spotted him and turned to face him. Standing at Alan's shoulder, Peter frowned.

Suds seized his moment.

"Alan, sorry. Just a quick word, a favour, like," Suds's nervousness made him rush his speech. It did not sound prepared. Just well-oiled.

"What?" Alan's tone was not friendly. First his brother refuses to join him at the event, then shows up in jeans and a t-shirt. Was he trying to be disrespectful? Alan could feel eyes on them.

"The festival. In Ireland," Suds's eyes were earnest, he meant it.

Alan smiled through his drink, despite himself. This was his brother; his wild, maddening, older brother. *Irresponsible arse.*

"What are you on?" he asked more gently.

"Yeah, but think aboot it. Ireland, surfing. Just one trip. We could both go. See if you can put one o'er on that Irish giant."

Erin had seen off Chad to win the Norhaven Open, much to the American's chagrin.

Alan held his hand up. Through force of habit, Suds stopped. Alan was the Skipper.

"Woah, hold on. The fish are good right noo, Suds," he pointed out, still gently, easing his brother down from his high idea. To Alan's mind, his comical crusade.

"This is important, brud."

"Not to miss a trip for. We canna waste the quota or the days at sea. No."

Suds shook his head.

"You're turnin' into him and you canna even see it. She's not even our boat," implored Suds.

"She could be if you were willin' to work at it."

"Ye ken yer trouble," Suds was close now.

Alan looked surprised.

"Old before you're thirty. That's when life's supposed to start."

"What happened to you then?"

Suds pushed away from his brother, bumping his way through the gathering. Alan watched him, the seawater in his eyes darkening. From a few paces away, Peter had witnessed the exchange and carefully swirled his whisky around the glass. Conflict was his entertainment.

Picking his moment, Peter steered Alan towards the bar, away from the rest of the company.

"Drink?"

Alan nodded as Peter signalled the barman.

"Time for some straight talkin', Alan."

Alan watched Peter as he took his drink.

"You've got to start lookin' ahead. Can't live for today, like your brother. He's dragging you down. Holding you back. You could end up running this toon. Think aboot it. Have something tae leave yer loon, yer son," Peter had prepared this speech, too, Alan realised. *It was an evening for them.*

Peter's speech depended on the stock of the man facing him across the table. Effortlessly shifting gear through the dialects of business to broker the deal, from boardroom to boatyard. Peter could flatter, dominate, dismiss, sooth, cajole and press. With one aim – to get his way.

Alan's eyes narrowed, subconsciously adjusting his stance as though on deck.

"Come. Meet some people. People worth talkin' to," his arm drawing his son-in-law into the throng.

Peter knew them all, the big shots, including the Harbourmaster, the local Minister, his business partners and, out of place, but quite at home, Chad. Alan felt uncomfortable with this. He had a sense of treading water, while others, Chad included, glided effortlessly past. He shook hands with them, then mimed getting in a round of drinks and moved to the bar. As he signalled the barman, Alan found himself staring at his refection in the mirror behind the rows of whisky bottles. Each of the multiple images looked different. *Which one was the real Alan? Could he step forward, please?*

An hour later, the group were seated, midway through

SANS PEUR

their meal. Alan glanced around the table. Peter was holding a cigar. For a moment, Alan thought he was going to light it. Alan looked around the hall. His eyes met those of Bob Muirhead. Alan realised that the fish salesmen was waiting to see if Peter would cross the line and light the rolled Havana. Alan shifted position to make sure the two didn't face each other. Peter, he knew, would break the law to make a point, even an empty one, to Muirhead. Just as Muirhead would then report him.

Taking a slow breath, Alan decided to take his chance.

"Peter, the *Sans Peur*, she needs work doing."

Peter studied the tip of the cigar and shifted his eyes to Alan. He nodded slightly for Alan to continue.

"A new engine, winch, other stuff. I've made a list."

Peter waved away the list and Alan, when it was clear Peter would not touch it, reluctantly put the piece of paper back in his sporran. Like an investment.

"I'm nae askin' you to put your hand in your pocket. I'm askin' for a share. I want to buy back in. To the *Sans Peur*, to Dad's boat."

Alan now had Peter's full attention. He loved the unexpected. The challenge of it. The opportunities it presented. Peter put his unlit cigar down. The extent of Alan's naivety thrilled him. He almost purred, setting the bait.

"There are two types of men in this world, Alan – those who have dreams and those who realise them. You're beginning to see that," Peter held up his finger. He wasn't finished.

He had spent his life seizing both opportunities and the crowns of others. It was the act of taking that drove him.

That moment of ownership, clasping the cup, slamming his opponent's hand down on to the hard wooden tabletop.

The signature on the deal, the wager won. The confirmation of rank. His due.

"I will consider, carefully, what you have said. It's a worthy notion, but I need to ken. What are you bringin' to the table? You, fine fisher that ye are – you are nae sufficient. You need to bring me a plan. You need to bring me security," Peter pinched a sip of the malt," Something tangible," he paused, casting his line, "like a fishing licence."

Alan shook his head.

"It's nae mine. It belongs to Suds as well," a hint of frustration in his voice.

Peter nodded slowly. He knew all this.

"Think aboot it. I'll gi'e you a week," another meagre sip of whisky.

Alan studied his hands.

"I'll talk to Suds."

Peter smiled as he stood up and patted Alan on the shoulder.

"That's good."

Alan was left alone amid the big shots. The expensive malt had changed taste in his mouth, turned sour and bitter like a bribe. He couldn't stay here.

Alan tugged on his jacket. He checked and looked back to where Peter was in the midst of his cronies; they were all laughing at something he had said. Peter met Alan's gaze and nodded, as if he was giving him permission to leave. At that moment Alan's disappointment in himself and his dislike of Peter both magnified. He had a sense of fleeing a battlefield, one he despised. Most of all, he sensed that he had lost more in the evening's exchanges than he had gained. With Suds and his father-in-law.

As he stepped outside, greeted by the iodine taste of the sea, he thought of another defeat. It had seemed a small one at the time. One of his many concessions. As he bent into the pressing cold wind, Alan was back at school.

The blackboard dominated the entire east wall of the square classroom, a flat matt statement against the dull pale sheen of the painted walls. Their tone was bland, a non-descript magnolia. A wash of municipal indifference. The room was a dull box, stifling in summer, stuffy in winter if the heating system obliged, and baltic otherwise.

A gaggle of pupils filed into the room, some, the keen or resigned ones, already had their books out. Alan, around twelve, was at a seat by the window. A thatch of dark hair, its ends curling into lighter tones. A generous face, nodding to his classmates as they trailed in. It was a reluctant flow. No one sat with him. He was both liked and respected, but in such a way that his peers knew enough to give him space.

He looked away from the almost illegible scrawl on the board. Somehow, he always knew his way north. He turned to it.

In the distance, the beach and the sea. Alan rubbed the murky glass. His actions painted a greasy wave, a cloudy abstract window on the glass. It was difficult to make out the waves of unfocussed blurred motion.

Maths was his least favourite subject. If he was pressed, he would have reluctantly plumped for Geography. *At least, you knew where you were with geography.* If he hadn't been stuck in the dreary classroom the thought would have made him laugh.

A low whistle, one he answered to, jolted him and he turned. An older boy, Suds, was at the doorway, signalling to

Alan to follow him with a cupped palm. He was marginally taller than Alan, his hair more unruly, but his movements and his colouring matched his brother's.

"Come on, brud."

A couple of the other pupils noticed the boys' departure, but they did not seem surprised. The Sutherlands bunking off was a common sight. A part of the curriculum at Norhaven Academy.

The boys trailed down the corridor, each subconsciously hugging a wall, bodies low, only to find themselves face to face with a young bespectacled teacher coming the other way. He recognised them instantly, and their intention, and he started to shake his head in objection. The boys exchanged a glance, speeded up, side-stepping him with ease. Suds started to run, but Alan, already well past the teacher hesitated and stopped.

"Suds!"

Suds glanced back at his younger brother, but kept moving, bouncing off the double-doors to freedom.

The teacher, Mr Holland, studied Alan as he stole back into the classroom. He returned to his desk to find Yvonne, a slight girl with a pout and a Bananarama-style haircut, chewing gum in his seat. She smiled at him, trying to make sure the gum did not mar the effect.

"No surfing today, Alan Sutherland." Mr Holland's voice was reflective, as if he too somehow respected the call of the waves.

Alan could detect the sympathetic note in the teacher's tone. Mr Holland, 'Dutch' to most in the town, was standing between his desk and the blackboard. He was a compact man, built to run long distances, to set the pace. His gaze, fixed on a point out of the window, was somewhat distant, an athlete assessing the challenge ahead.

Alan stared out of the window and nodded slightly. Suds, being Suds, would be bragging later.

The memory stayed with him as he approached The Makar, the largest bar on Shore Wynd. One small episode at school and it had travelled with him since. A summation of his relationship with his wayward brother, or a cowardly reflection of his own sense of self-restraint.

As Alan pushed through the crowded dance floor of 'The Makar', he was challenged by Heather Small's powerful voice urging him to *'Search for the Hero'*. Apt to the point of being a sick joke, he thought. He was looking for his wife in the bar, since she had extracted the promise that they would meet after his footballing dinner was over. It was a promise he was reluctant to keep.

Yvonne and her pals could have been in any of the shoreline bars. Half a dozen were tucked along Shore Wynd. Dark, warm watering holes. As he ordered a drink at the bar, he noticed the Irish contingent and a few other surfers in a corner. Erin acknowledged Alan. Alan also spotted Reef and Suds. Reef waved, but Suds ignored his brother. Suds had always sulked.

A hush descended on the bar. This was unusual. Abina stepped up to the microphone. It was a karaoke, but she needed no backing music. Abina started to sing. Alan remembered what it was called from school – acapella.

Alan stood transfixed by the siren's song. Abina's song.

The Irish singer was in a simple sheaf dress. Her hair tied back with a simple scarlet ribbon. Was she singing for him? Did every man in the room feel this? Wish for it? Her song closed round him as her glance held his. '*Some Surprise*'. The moment and the song.

Alan was still in a trance when Yvonne found him, as she had to tug him on the arm to get his attention.

"Hiya," Yvonne's smile was intimate.

"A'right," Alan struggled to match it.

"Is it a folk night or somethin'?" Yvonne inclined her head towards the Irish singer, dismissing her and the music.

Alan tore his focus away from Abina to his wife and her friends. It took an act of will. They were waiting for his attention.

"You for another?" Yvonne waved her glass at her husband.

"Aye. Sure," Alan agreed, "a nip."

Yvonne smiled at him and turned, emphasising her walk to the bar. He recognised it from wilder, happier nights, when everything had led to bed. A signal of her mood and intent. Alan followed Yvonne's sway as Abina's song ended. Alan turned back to look at the Irish woman, her shadowed gaze seemed to reach out to him from across the crowded room when Yvonne's friend, Fiona, cornered him.

"She's looking stunnin', isn't she?"

Fiona was standing too close for Alan's comfort. She always did. An unspoken offer. A many-layered trap. She was someone he put up with rather than had warmed to over time. *Some people you just didn't.*

It took him a moment to register that Fiona meant Yvonne not the beautiful Irish singer. He looked again at Yvonne poised at the bar, the shiny fabric of her skirt taut on her thighs.

"Aye. Yes, she is," he muttered in reply.

Yvonne was smiling as she arrived with the drinks. As Alan took his drink, Suds strode past his brother without acknowledging him. Reef walked past and shrugged. With a resigned sigh, Alan turned back to his wife. After this drink, he was heading home. The Makar had that sense of anticipation and caution when the night begins to turn wild and bad with it. Alan wanted none of it.

As Alan and Yvonne left the pub, stepping out into a brisk wind. Yvonne was unsteady on her feet, tottering and trying to cling to him. Behind them, the sign read 'FAITH Mission'. Alan stopped to look at it as his wife struggled with her heels. He'd seen the sign hundreds of times before, but now it held his attention.

Alan looked at his wife, then across at the *Sans Peur*, berthed fifty metres away.

Standing on the deck was Abina, hair long and wild in the wind. Eyes fixed on him.

Her song filled his head. More intoxicating than any drink.

Alan mouthed the words of Abina's song, as his wife tottered and reached for his hand and, at her touch, the last sense of the image and its promise disappeared.

Alan started as Yvonne stumbled. Alan steadied her and looked back at the boat, but the image of Abina had gone.

Lit by the dull streetlight outside, Yvonne was pulling off Alan's shirt. Urgent. She kissed his chest.

They kissed. More lust than love. Their hands were all over each other in drunken motion. The urgency was Yvonne's.

'A man in a kilt," she breathed, tugging at the wide thick leather belt and its heavy clasped buckle.

For Alan, there was a sense of detachment as though he was watching someone else with his wife. He realised with dull surprise that he was drunk.

"Too much surfin', nae enough shaggin'," she hissed with a hint of venom, as she helped her dazed husband to take down her dress. Even underneath, Yvonne was dressed to kill.

Yvonne pulled Alan on top of her.

"Give it to me, give it to me, rough," her voice hoarse with need.

Alan seemed surprised for a second, before doing as she urged and Yvonne responded. She was frantic.

The sun rose over the dunes. Crimson and ochre slowly reaching out between the giant tufts of grass, turning the sand from pale soft silver to deeper ruby gold. It was a clear morning. The light, the air and sea all felt fresh. It had brought with it a taste of hope. The kind of crisp, bold day that helped him think. He needed it after last night. The wild union with his wife had left him with a hangover.

Alan was looking at the surf, assessing the changing wind. It was still fairly flat, although the forecast for later that day was promising. A stone flew past him. It skimmed on the water. Alan turned in surprise; he had heard no one approach, lost in blurred recollections of last night.

The small Irish boy, Jake, was standing with Abina. She started laughing at Alan's startled expression. He raised a smile in return and bent to select a small flat pebble.

He weighed it in his hand. *You had to choose the right stone.* He could hear his grandfather saying it.

Alan, Abina and Jake moved along the water's edge, all were skimming stones now. Alan gently threw Abina a smooth flat stone, ideal for skimming. She weighed it in her palm. *A perfect fit.*

Mid throw Jake stopped and pointed. They watched as a drunken man staggered along the promenade, his movements the jerky uncoordinated lurch of the truly plastered. The listing silhouette bent to throw up against the skyline. They watched the man move on with his exaggerated unpredictable lurching stride. Jake mimicked the drunk and Alan laughed. Abina watched the man and boy laughing together and quietly pocketed the oval-shaped stone that Alan had just given her.

If Abina had a Gaelic meaning it should have been 'of natural grace'. That she was beautiful went without saying. It was more than that, than the merely aesthetic; it was deeper, more earthy, more essential, even primitive.

She was fluid. She flowed, her rich heavy mane of rebellious curls following in the wind. Yet her mouth remained too wide, her nose too long. Such striking imperfections crafted rare beauty.

Outside Saint Columba's Church, the Minister was bidding people goodbye as they trooped out of his service. The Kirk was a bleak temple with a threatening unfriendly aspect, built on one of the highest points in the town. So that God's servants could look down on its poor sinners.

He shook hands with Peter, his long dark coat lifting in the wind.

"Thank you, Peter. I was hoping to catch up with you about the Roof Fund," he said brightly. His tone matched the clear fresh morning.

"Could we leave it a while, a few weeks, Alistair?" replied Peter.

The Minister frowned then, detecting a note to Peter's suggestion.

"Things bad, Peter? It's just, I've been hearing murmurs. Nothing serious?" The Minister kept his tone light as if sensing a wound.

Peter forced a smile.

"Nothing serious," Peter turned away, angry and unsettled at letting his guard down. *Fucking Norhaven telegraph.*

The High Street was deserted, the shop closed. No shops opened on a Sunday in Norhaven. Supermarkets had yet to venture far enough north. The town councillors dug in to resist such colonisation.

Arms hugging herself, Arlene was standing looking in the shop window of Burns and Maskame. She bit her lip, the strengthening wind making her eyes water.

Slim and graceful of figure, clumsy and awkward in manner, abruptness masked her persistent shyness.

Sometimes she flouted her reticence, but it usually required drink and the encouragement of friends. Not so much Dutch courage as Dutch abandon. Hence, she and Suds had combined. Both drunk. After the event, she was besotted, he was bemused.

They had both remained in their respective states, plotting contrary courses around each other, occasionally colliding and retreating. A two year-long skirmish, an intricate dance of attraction and avoidance.

Inside the window display was a full bridal gown on a shapely mannequin. It stared blankly back at her.

The afternoon Sabbath sun was low and deep when Alan was led into the wide cultured garden by Mrs Eva Mason, the small and curved Chairwoman of the Norhaven Horticultural Club. From the house came the mellow notes of classical music piece, '*Spiegel Im Spiegel*'. Alan didn't recognise it, but it reaffirmed his feeling that Mrs Mason was a cultured woman, albeit a slightly scary one.

She pointed towards a huge newly stained wooden shed as a figure appeared in the doorway. John Mason, also a keen gardener, waved Alan on. He glanced at the immaculate borders and lawn, watching where he placed his feet.

Alan stepped cautiously into John Mason's pigeon loft. His other passion.

John Mason was a sparse, slightly stooped man. Dapper, even on his day off, in a buttoned woollen waistcoat and braces. Alan thought of him as the Last Real Bank Manager in Scotland.

"I ken it's a Sunday, John, I appreciate this," Alan started, respectful of the low hum of the birds.

John was holding a Racing Fancy. Its feathers glistened as the sunlight caught them.

"Twenty-four hour banking," John smiled at him, forgiving the intrusion and the interruption. He had been a friend and admirer of Graham senior.

The banker smiled as the bird cooed softly in his slim soft hands. Alan's own hands were calloused.

Alan watched John Mason reassuring his birds. His voice a gentle Highland lilt. He was from up Inverness way originally.

"They are nervy with strangers, but they're taking to you." John cleared his throat, "Peter's right, I'm afraid. You need to bring something to the table."

Alan looked at the caged birds. They seemed contented.

"It's not a matter of selling the licence. Merely having it as collateral. There you are, darling. Come to Daddy. You need Suds's signature, Alan. You know you can't use the house," the explanation was getting worse. Alan knew he couldn't use the house. It was Peter's paper.

Fishing licences had been handed out in the 1970s. the Government's gift. Written permission to fish. A piece of paper then. Now, they were an opportunity. An asset.

The *Sans Peur* was covered by Peter's licence. Quotas meant that was all that was required. Alan and Suds occasionally rented out some of their licence, catching capacity. It helped Bella out, and without the capital to buy their own boat, they tended to view it as an insurance policy. A pension of sorts.

Alan stroked one of the birds offered to him by John. The Bank Manager studied Alan and gave him a smile that carried a hint of sympathy for the younger man. He liked him.

Composed and considered, Alan was the guy you wanted on your team. First to make the tackle, first to track back, first to make the unselfish pass. He was a grafter.

Yet, and here was the rub, some felt that Alan was always within himself. Perhaps, too far so. John Mason was one. He sensed that the restraint of the young fisherman in front of him was self-imposed, a form of personal exile.

Alan nodded, accepting the position.

"I'll talk to Suds," the feathers were soft and warming beneath his coarse fingers.

Inside their Scottish Parliament, Hendoo and Watt were watching as Suds hoisted his board out of the water. The wind carried the rain off the sea, a gentle refreshment.

"He's nae a happy loon," said Watt.

"He's surfin' shite," chimed Hendoo.

Suds laid down his board beside the shelter. Still in his wetsuit, he reached into his worn rucksack. From a small tin he pulled out a roll up. The old men watched as he lit it and sat inhaling deeply.

Watt cleared his throat.

"A' men were created equal."

Suds took a moment then he handed over the tab.

"First thing the Parliament should ha' deen," said Hendoo.

"What's that, like?" said Suds, although he knew what was coming.

"Legalise this shite," as he took a puff and passed it along. A big drag from Watt,

"I second the motion."

Suds nodded and picked his board up. *Leave them to it.*

"Need the practice if yer goin'," said Hendoo.

Suds followed his nod at the weathered 'Celtic Surf Festival' poster clinging desperately against the wind to the shelter's dark blue wall behind them. Suds stared at the poster as Hendoo and Watt passed the smoke between them. Suds hadn't got the heart to tell them it was just tobacco. Why spoil their fun? Parliament was in recess.

A huge iron ball hung like gallows in the shadowed dusk. The view from above the breakers yard was impressive. Alan stopped and looked down on a broken dismembered fishing boat. On her splintered hull, like a headstone, her faded name could still be read:'HOPE'. After the *Sans Peur*, the *Hope* had been his favourite boat in the Norhaven fleet. Souter John had been its Skipper when Alan was a boy.

He looked across to the *Sans Peur* berthed in the next basin. He was determined she would avoid this fate.

His thoughts were interrupted by a soft metallic click.

He turned to find Abina, the Irish woman, armed with a camera, an old 35mm Nikon.

"Sorry. I prefer black and white. Your boat?" she cocked her head and smiled in sympathy.

Alan shook his head slightly, his thoughts elsewhere and not comfortable.

"Not that simple. Black and white," part apology, part hope, as he left her to the view. Her intrusion had unsettled him. She unsettled him. So, he fled. Part coward, part salvation.

Abina watched the Scotsman go until he had disappeared along the quayside. For all of her noticeable physical attributes, Abina was watchful, cautious. There was no swagger to her sway. As if, sometime, somewhere, in her journey from a remote village in the west of Ireland she had earned doubt.

Even fallen from grace, with a mother who still did not speak to her, she was still trying to figure out what her penance might be. Perhaps, her son was her price. Not outwardly, as they delighted in a shared ridiculousness. Still, beneath that surface, she feared he would pay the price for her sins, the folly that was the failed union with his father, Erin.

A love on the beach amid the dunes that had ebbed away.

His ring she had gifted to Jake. He was forever misplacing it, subconsciously trying to lose it, casting it adrift. In contrast, she kept finding the small slim band. Under a mattress, in the tangle of a rug, in with the toothbrushes. Confirmation, she feared, of her unconscious wish for Jake to have some link with his father through a small, nondescript heirloom bought in an African bazaar that she had once thrown into the sea. That was before she had scrambled on all fours to retrieve it from the clear azure of the Moroccan shoreline.

She had surfed half the world, a backpacker with a board. Trapped in a cycle of freedom, endless horizons and point breaks.

It was warm from cooking in Bella's Kitchen. Condensation washed the window. Alan and Suds were at the table, both tense and uneasy to be facing each other as Bella placed the Sunday roast in front of them. Her presence added to their discomfort. She was the last witness to their struggle for whom they would have wished. But some rituals could not be cast aside and Sunday dinner at Bella's was one. The brothers studied the food rather than each other.

"It's the only way forward," Alan said again, as he stabbed a slice of beef.

Suds picked up a potato and chewed it, deliberately nonchalant.

"This way we can get the *Sans Peur* back. It was ours, it can be again," he tasted the meat and waited for Sud's response. His brother did not disappoint him.

"The licence is ours," came the reply.

Bella looked sharply at Suds.

"Dad left it to us. So, it's my shout," Suds was still chewing, but there was no mistaking his hostility.

Alan leaned in.

"This way we all win."

Suds put more food on his plate and shifted back, but he was not giving any ground.

"You mean *ye* do. And Peter. He gets the licence. That's all he's after. You're just doing his dirty work, as usual," Suds waved his fork airily.

"Why do ye think ye are still on the boat! If the repairs aren't done! Can ye nae think of someone else?" Alan's voice was low and fierce.

"What are ye going to do? Sack me?" Suds bit back.

The brothers were on their feet now, nose to nose. Veins

were standing out in their corded necks when Bella's huge teapot landed heavily on the table between them, sloshing ruddy tea over their uneaten plates.

"Sit doon. They'll be nae fighting here." For a moment Bella towered over her sons, "I mean it."

Alan and Suds measured each other and the distance before violence.

Suds sat slowly, but Alan swept up his jacket and aimed for the door.

"You canna be a waster all yer life," he snarled.

"Watch me," Suds threw back at him.

Bella regarded her son as the door closed behind Alan.

"He was good tae us. He used tae read tae ye. You looked forward tae it," Bella was trying to draw Suds back, but he was having none of it.

"That was afore I grew up."

"Grew up?" Bella was lost.

"Before I realised how things were," Suds took another mouthful.

They both ate slowly.

"I kent. Alan just blinds himsel', but I kent," Suds was now in dangerous territory and he knew it, but he couldn't help himself.

"You ken nothing," Bella spelled out each word, speaking as though to a ten-year-old, as she took his plate away even though Suds had not finished his meat.

Then Suds was gone, the back door still open, the argument left unfinished. Bella sat in the void, framed by her sons' stubbornness. A sharp sea breeze gusted through the gaping door.

The death of her beloved Graham had battered Bella. In these parts, they called that kind of loss a salt wound.

Amid life's storms, that lighting strike had briefly capsized her. She had righted herself, but at great cost; she was a finely crafted vessel that refused to sink.

Fishing towns, like mining communities, collected solitaries of widows. Some receded quietly, washed pale by the outpouring of emotion and tide, but Bella refused to ebb away, her back straight, still handsome and challenging, keeping her hair long, like a memory.

They hadn't even exchanged a farewell. It was against her own code; she always bid her sons goodbye. It has been a ritual since Graham had been lost, but Bella was trying to avoid crying. She could sense the swell coming up from deep inside her, her long submerged hurt. *Do something practical.*

Bella marked a calendar, blocking in more dark blue 'Awa's', interspersed with a handful of 'Hames'. Behind her perched the picture of Graham and Peter aboard the *Sans Peur*, watching. *Friends and partners.* She shook the thought away. It wasn't worth thinking about.

The Beach Café boasted a ramshackle wood-panelled interior in a faded waiting room cream. It was dated in a comfortable 1950s style, matching the outside of the hut, a salt and sun-bleached wood construction. Suds was sitting watching the waves as Arlene unloaded the tray in front of him, but he did not acknowledge it or her.

"Nae good for surfing just noo," she said lightly to draw him back to her. Make him notice her.

Suds reached for his coffee and dropped in sugar, a mechanical action. His mind on the waves and the chances of surf.

"Will the waves be good in Ireland?" Arlene made another attempt to connect.

"Ah?" The word Ireland penetrated.

"Chad, him from the factory, he left yesterday. He was drivin' o'er."

The colour rose on Suds's face; she had his full attention now.

"How do ye ken?"

"He telt me. He asked me to go with him, but I said no, like," Arlene shrugged, making light of the American's daring and his trespass.

Suds's coffee cup hit the floor, startling Arlene and the other customers.

"Fuck it! I'm awa!"

A stunned Arlene gasped as Suds stormed out of the café, crashing through the doors. She cast an apologetic eye at the staff and fumbled for her purse.

"Affa sorry, I'll pay for the china," she said, bending down to collect the broken shards of pottery.

Suds was striding away from the café, gaining speed with each step when Arlene came out and started to run after him.

"Suds! Suds!"

Suds paid no heed. His pace quickened and he started to run. Not the reaction she had hoped for, but at least she had got one. Arlene slowed down. It was a pointless chase. Suds could run for miles. She stopped at the railings, reaching out for support and looked out to sea. She could never tell if the waves were coming in or moving out. *You idiot, Arlene.*

From the splendid vantage point of the Scottish Parliament, Hendoo and Watt watched Suds's retreating figure.

"Headstrong," muttered Hendoo.

"Like his mither," agreed Watt.

Their dining room was a clash of chrome and glass. *It had always been a cold room.* Alan could see his feet through the table. There was something absurd about it. He wiggled his toes and almost smiled at them.

He and Yvonne were sitting facing each other. Neither made eye contact. They sat at opposite ends, with the food on pristine plates set in front of them. Alan looked up to where Yvonne was nursing a glass of water. She was looking outside, through the French windows, both hungover and preoccupied.

How had they got here? So disconnected, their thoughts parallel with scant chance of meeting.

Yvonne had lived with jealousy all her life. Her father's ambition, wealth and growing influence in Norhaven, combined with her mother's overpowering glitz had fostered the resentment as she grew up. Throw in the fact that she was a 'looker' and all the ingredients were in the pot.

Then she had bagged Alan Sutherland. Married him. A huge show of a wedding to mark her triumph.

Yet recently, she had begun to sense a different vibe, a scent of something else, from the kettle of her resentful peers. It troubled her. She recognised it now, finally: the whiff of pity that the girl who had everything – wealth, looks, glamour, a Skipper for a husband – did not own her true desire. For all his eligibility, Alan had not given her the one thing she craved, the fulfilment of motherhood. More than that, the recognition, the place in the community that she believed it would bring.

She turned back to Alan. They considered each other as if not quite sure at whom they were looking. The glass table made an easier study.

The following morning, under heavy, rapid clouds that you could almost touch, Alan was working on the winch with Potty when Peter's car, a sleek powerful German breed, pulled up alongside the berthed *Sans Peur*. The boat sat high with the tide. Peter climbed out of the dark immaculate Mercedes and waved. Alan returned the wave, but not Potty, who just hawked over the side of the deck as Peter clambered aboard. The taste of the sea was strong.

"Potty's done a great job, she's runnin' like a gem. Nothing to worry aboot there," all this to Alan in a friendly greeting, before he switched his attention to the grizzled engineer,

"Haven't you got work to do?"

"Aye, got a man tae see aboot a drink," Potty spat again, set his pipe in his mouth and jumped down on to the quayside.

Peter strolled to the bow.

He went straight to business.

"It's good plan, Alan. Admire that you brought it to me, but I'm going to finance any upgrading that might be necessary mysel'," Peter held up his hand to forestall Alan's response. Alan noted the evasive 'might be'. It grated on him and served as a warning at the same time. This was Peter he was dealing with.

"Perhaps, when you become more accustomed to responsibility – as a father – we can speak again. You and I must look to the future in another way," Peter waited for Alan's interruption, but it did not come. Alan was looking out over the harbour at all the boats tied up beneath the knotted low threatening sky.

"I'm building a new boat, state of the art. I want you to skipper her," he stressed.

Alan's face betrayed his lurching shock.

"You're in on that deal?"

Alan and all of Norhaven knew of the new boat under construction. The local rumour mill had been doing overtime. It was a common rumour, and, therefore, an accepted truth, that a consortium was behind the construction, but the exact composition of the cartel had remained cloaked in supposition and wishful thinking. Now, Alan realised, too late, that Peter was in the mix, if not running the show. And he had other plans too.

"You'll have Potty wi' you. He may like a dram, but you'll nae get a better Driver," Peter continued.

"Suds and Reef," Alan's voice was steady, but he knew what was coming.

"They're finished, the *Sans Peur* too, she'll ha'e to go for decommissioning. The forms are drawn up," Peter finished his mission statement.

"Scrapped?"

"You need to toughen up. To hire and fire. I told you – you could own this toon," Peter's voice had fallen for emphasis.

"Na," Alan drew the line.

Peter studied Alan as the younger man turned to match his father-in-law's gaze. The older man paused a moment, then applied the pressure.

"The only other alternative is you and Suds putting up the fishing licence as security. He'd have to sign. Get me Suds's signature and I'll reconsider. Otherwise the *Sans Peur* is finished and so are the Sutherlands," Peter was almost savouring the words, but the threat was real.

Alan said nothing. His eyes moved from Peter to the Sutherland motto *Sans Peur* on the boat's wheelhouse behind his father-in-law. Peter patted Alan on the back as though, for him, matters were settled.

"Mind, yer part of my family now, Alan."

There is no such thing as a merger, Alan tried to recall who had said that to him. It was when the deal had been done over MacNaught's and the Americans had saved the fishyard. They'd called it a merger.

Alan watched as Peter stepped down off the boat.

He was left to stand on the deck of the *Sans Peur*, trying to find his own courage and chart a course.

As he stood with the worn, wooden deck beneath him, Alan felt adrift, his balance gone. More than just the harbour swell. How could he make Suds see sense? It would be a first.

From the deck, Alan saw Arlene approaching, scurrying along the pier. Would Suds listen to Arlene? Alan rejected that. Who was he fooling? Suds had never listened. He'd defy the weather. It was in his nature. Norhaven's Canute.

She looked up, saw him and hurried on. *Something was wrong.*

Alan swung down off the boat and met her on the quayside.

"Alan, it's Suds. He's gone. To Ireland," tears strained her voice. Her pale face stretched whiter. Scared.

Alan held her close to lessen his own shock and building anger. *Fuckin' Ireland, fuckin' Suds.*

It was quiet in the Schooner, a one-room bar hidden away from Shore Wynd through a warren of black murderous Victorian alleys. Reef was playing pool against a stocky young fisherman, who had been awarded the by-name of Cable on account of having started an apprenticeship as a Sparky. Cable was watching his opponent lining up a long shot.

Potty was on a stool having a game of cards with the barmaid, Ida, when the door opened and Alan strode in, every step a statement. Reef cocked his head and looked up from his shot; Potty turned from his cards. Alan considered them both and jerked his head towards the door. Potty did not hesitate, downed his nip and slid off the stool in one fluid movement. Reef looked uncertain and shrugged at his playing partner. Cable knew a force when he saw it and he knew Alan Sutherland. Alan let Potty by, before walking over to Reef. Reaching him, Alan picked up his crewman's drink. Reef moved to accept it, but Alan downed the contents himself in two long swallows. Disgusted, Reef pulled off his hat, a grey WWII patched German cap, and loped to the door. Alan nodded to Ida the barmaid on his way out. She was left to scoop up the cards, taking a quick pursed-lipped study of Potty's hand. She'd have won that game. *Fuckin' typical.*

The *Sans Peur* was leaving port with the last of the dusk, the dark blue hull shadowed as the last sunlight of the day fell away to earth.

Arlene and Peter were there to see them off, standing on different quays. Reef, still mourning his pint, was waving to them, doing a little jig on the deck.

Below, Potty was coaxing the engine as he took a swig from a steaming enamel mug.

"Tastes like dirt; it must be good for ye," he muttered as he finished the bitter dregs.

Alan manoeuvred the boat out. He had the Sutherland crest and motto '*Sans Peur*' behind him. Taking strength from it, he acknowledged Peter from the wheelhouse, then turned and gave a much warmer wave to Arlene.

His hands froze on the wheel. *It was Abina, the Irish woman, in Arlene's place, staring straight at him. The song that she had sung in the bar last night swirled around his head. On the deck in front of him, Reef was dancing in slow motion to Abina's Song. A siren's call.*

Alan tried to clear his head and looked again at the quayside. A gull screamed and Arlene's sad, slight face stared back at him as she waved the *Sans Peur* off. *An empty farewell.*

They were an hour out at sea.

Alan was at the wheel. Reef was with him, looking strained and, to Alan's eye, still the worse for drink. As Potty entered he passed Reef a tin mug. Reef sniffed it and blanched.

"Get it down, yer, min," said Potty.

Alan allowed himself a small smile as Reef sipped it in disgust.

"Cardno's Cathodic Cure," announced Potty proudly. His own invention and torture.

"Gnat's piss." Reef wiped his mouth, reluctant to swallow the harsh mixture. The reek was enough. "Is Suds still asleep?"

"Suds is in Ireland," Alan voice was quiet, a dangerous stillness to it.

Reef near choked on his stinking brew. He was close to gagging from its vile taste anyhow.

"No way."

"The Celtic Surf Festival," Alan pointed to the map on the wall, "South of Killybegs."

Potty lit his pipe and watched Alan through the heavy aromatic smoke.

"Sly, min, real sly," Reef was obviously impressed.

Alan was not. "We're going to bring my brother back," stated Alan.

"We gonna surf, too?" asked Reef, even more impressed.

Alan was firm.

"No. We are going to find Suds and bring him hame. It's business."

Potty exhaled slowly.

"It'll mean crossing the Minch. The engine. She's fine noo, but we'll ha'e to treat her wi' respect.

"It'll mean crossing Peter an' a'," added Potty, the emphasis on his concerns about the boat's owner and his reaction, rather than the perils of the notorious Minch crossing.

Alan nodded and pointed out on the map where they are heading. The nearest sizable port was Killybegs.

Reef downed the remainder of his hangover cure, trying not to gag.

"Beezer." He spluttered.

More than a hundred miles away, on Norhaven's bleak links course, Peter and the Minister were concluding their regular round. The light was fading on them, low lines of it were withdrawing, angled through the shrubs and wind-huddled gorse across the course, but the golf was only part of the game. They came off the last hole and entered the clubhouse. A building in need of investment, it remained Norhaven's unofficial board room, where deals were sealed, and businesses made and broken. Recent research conducted by the *Norhaven Courier* had proposed the club was among the oldest in Scotland. The letters pages for the following few weeks had become the battleground for a barrage of correspondence from local historians supporting or attacking the newspaper's assertions. The local Member of Parliament had even raised the matter in a parliamentary question, only for the Chairwoman of the Norhaven Historical Society, a widely feared battle-axe, to rebuff him for his careless assertion in yet another letter.

To those who conducted their unofficial business in a building now dogged by local historical contentions, this was bunkum. They were with Henry Ford on this. They had more pressing matters to deal with, and preferred to look forward not back.

The Harbourmaster and Peter's business associates were already there, settled with their warmers. The laughter stuttered with their entrance as the Harbourmaster Salt signalled for Peter to join them. Peter had the sense, that itch, that only moments earlier he had been the subject of their mirth. Him or his kin.

"Ah, Peter, how's the new boat coming?"

"Everything's on schedule, anyone for a drink?"

There were no takers; Peter's generosity fell flat. His earlier suspicions confirmed.

"And the payments?" Milne was always direct.

Peter went on the attack.

"On schedule. I'm more worried aboot my game," he said, as he mimed his swing. However, to Peter's ear, the other men's laughter was strained and hollow.

"Heard the *Sans Peur* needs work, more than a lick o' paint," Milne was a terrier.

Peter forced a tolerant smile at the small dog.

"Those Sutherland brothers still fightin'? Need harmony on a boat, Peter. Not much there, from what I hear. And catches are poor," Milne turned the knife further.

"Too busy surfing," chipped in the Harbourmaster ruefully. As if the act was a great sin and the Sutherlands were damned for it.

"Surfing's over. For all o' them," Peter's voice was firm. His eyes on Milne. *The wee shite.*

The Harbourmaster nodded, but the company looked unconvinced. They all knew Graham Sutherland's boys.

The *Sans Peur* was making good progress with Alan at the wheel when Potty joined him.

"Purrin' like a kitten," he said.

Alan nodded satisfied.

"You were right, Pots. Peter means to scrap her,"

Alan indicated the vessel. Potty pulled out his pipe and baccy tin. It signalled he was assessing this new intelligence. He could think without tobacco, but his pipe certainly helped clarify matters for the engineer.

"When Graham was lost, Peter stepped in. He took on the debts. Yer Mam was grateful – still is, but Peter got what he wanted." Potty tapped the wheel, "He got the boat." He patted the wheel again. An act of gentleness.

"All we were left was the licence. That's in Suds's name an' all, and I've spent my life chasing after him." There was tension and imminent defeat in Alan's words.

"Yer Dad was always cautious and nae as trusting as Peter thocht he was," Potty took another draw. The dense smoke hung in the wheelhouse. It came to Alan that the aroma of Potty's pipe was a memory he had from childhood when his Dad brought both boys down to the boat. It had stayed with him. So had the engineer.

"Now Suds has been an idiot again and done a runner. Peter's bound to sack him," Alan ploughed on, "Suds has to sign it o'er. It's the only chance we have. Suds canna see it," Alan's anger was growing again, talking as much to himself as to the older man.

"You think that will stop Peter? Wise up, Alan. The man's a whore, onything for money. How dae ye think he managed tae pay off the debt when your Dad died?"

"He's still our only hope," Alan's desperation showed in his voice.

"Hope? Look tae yersel, ma loon," Potty drew himself up and left the wheelhouse. His pipe smoke remained, fogging Alan's view.

In the hold, Reef was painting, heavy red smeared brush in one hand, a dripping yellow one in the other. He was stabbing strokes as he toiled, earphones in. Reef worked to the mellow vibes of Scott Main's '*Walk in a Huge Park*'.

The *Sans Peur*'s engine stuttered, but Potty coaxed her on, working in the dark hot engine room like an alchemist.

The longer he spent in the dark, stifling, fume-filled den beneath the waterline, the more he sank into his own world of grease, sweat and the twin towers of frustration and hope. The last a slim cord.

His fingers had thickened, his nails chipped and blackened with grime and bruising, a big man turned lean by the heat in the fishing vessel's fierce bowels.

His lined face was drawn with secrets he kept of engines, skippers and crews.

He kept them all afloat. Still.

On the *Sans Peur*, under Graham Sutherland and later Peter, he had become driver and cook.

He remained both. Plus, he had taken on another role, that of the unasked, unnoticed guardian and watcher of Graham Sutherland's two warring sons; they were two sides of the same tempered coin.

To every man, a penny.

Potty carried two pennies, both Sutherlands, and their ghosts with them.

On the wild Atlantic coastline, Suds was exploring Irish surf town, Killymarten.

He felt a kinship to it. Like Norhaven, it was an overlooked kind of place. Coastal towns often are; they are a secret that few ever stumbled upon, isolated and independent. Killymarten had known boom years and lean times. Young people left and the old spoke of their loss as if, in going, their lives were done. They were lost to urban dreams and their unreality.

To his initial eye it seemed like a small four street coastal village. It was larger than that, creeping inland to where a school and a small industrial estate looked down benignly. He'd been to Killybegs before, but its smaller neighbour was new to him. The sun gave everything an optimistic sheen. He felt its warming tingling glow on his bare arms. This was the place. He had a bounce in his step as he wandered through the colourful narrow streets. Many of the low cottages seemed to have been freshly painted. He paused in front of a green post box, wishing he had a letter to post. It was a strange thought. He hadn't written a letter in his life. Except to Santa and he couldn't remember exactly what he'd asked for. Well, there was one request, just after his father had been lost. Usually, thoughts of his namesake were layered with guilt and anger, but not here, not today, in this small Irish town. For all he knew, his Dad might have been here before him. There was a comfort in it, with the emerald post box standing sentry at the corner of the street against the white-washed stone houses. He could taste the sea here, too. Just like home, but as if the grey had been banished. As he stood there, two girls sauntered past him. The taller, a vibrant red head, smiled at him. He watched them cross the road, their swaying walks, an image of Arlene joining them. If only she'd stop dying her hair, hiding her gift. The shadow of his frustration returned and threatened to darken the day. He mustn't let that happen. This was *his* adventure.

Beneath a towering Norhaven sky, gulls were screaming, bickering over the carcasses. Arlene, with her arms folded, framed by the fighting birds, was looking over the knackers' yard, her face white and stretched. The stark yard, with its decaying mountains of fish carcasses, fell away behind the fish factory, MacNaughts. She needed the air, even with the tainted smell of fish and rot.

Damn him. Damn Suds. Damn his obsession with beating his brother. To Arlene's eye, Alan wasn't so special. If he was, he wouldn't have married that Yvonne McGhee. Why couldn't Suds see his own worth. Why couldn't he see me? *See us.*

The *Sans Peur* cut through waves, and Reef's gallery grew. With no fish to catch, he was intent on drawing a school of dolphins and a harem of alluring mermaids. He had always drawn. At school, he drew through lessons out of boredom. At home, he drew to freeze out the arguments: his father's menacing growl, his mother's pleading whine, and the sounds that ended them. When he was drawing, everything else was tuned out. They took shape to '*Dope Smoker*' by Sleep, pulsing in his ears.

The walls of his damp cramped flat were plastered with sketches. Somewhere else in the world the romantic tag, 'an artist's garret' might have been aired, but Reef's small hovel was a cold hole, a dank, stale cave for the overlooked. He often slept on the *Sans Peur* and had started etching aboard ship – small swirls, shells, and waves on doorframes, steps, the toilet seat.

That last choice of canvas had unsettled the normally stoic Potty, but the burly Driver had known Reef's errant, explosive father and that explained much. It was all in the genes. *Darwin and all that shite.*

He was one of Norhaven's own, and small towns accepted home-grown eccentrics, even though most just saw the hats perched on the loping gait. If Potty gave an impression of resigned tolerance, it hid a sense of adoption that he, along with the Sutherlands, had quietly extended to the perpetual stray that was Calum Sangster Duthie.

The hold was the centrepiece of Reef's private world, an ill-lit industrial gallery, where mermaids, dolphins and kelpies magically rode the waves.

Amid Killymarten's bustling vibrant Irish surftown, Suds jerked to a halt. *Shit, that's all I need.*

Parked in front of him was Chad's car. It almost smirked at him in the warming sun, its perfect paint work polished to reflect the American's faultless finish: tan and teeth. Teeth that Suds would have liked to have knocked out of his head. His fist itched at the thought.

A few metres away, Chad was talking with some Irish surfers, including the towering Erin. Chad turned and met Suds's gaze.

"She wouldn't come with you either!" Chad laughed. He seemed to find this very amusing and at Suds's expense. The Scot sensed that mockery was Chad's primary currency. Derision as a default.

Suds nodded to Erin and the other Irishmen and planted himself a few feet from Chad.

"Time she had a real surfer," pressed Chad.

Suds pointed to the motif on his ragged beanie hat *No Fear*. "Sans Peur!"

The two men squared up. The re-setting of their feet and the loosening of arms was subconscious. Both were primed.

"Save it for the surf, guys," Erin's shadow stepped between them, just sufficient warning to make them pause in their schoolyard foolishness and to realise that the powerful Irishman was unimpressed by either of their stances. His voice was casual, came from somewhere above them, yet his caution embraced them.

"No Fear!" Suds shouted in the American's face and tore away.

He watched Suds's retreating back and smiled. *It was only a matter of time.*

Alan was standing on the deck of the *Sans Peur* surveying Eire.

His gaze spanned a beach that joined a small Irish coastal hamlet. It had a pub, that looked to be resting on wide wooden stilts on the sea front, joined to a small jetty. White painted cottages completed the watercolour beneath a light wash of warm blue sky.

Moving steadily, the *Sans Peur* was approaching the middle of the bay opposite the beach.

He had checked the charts, but it was best to be cautious. Better that than be wise and beached after the event. Once they found Suds, he aimed to make a quick getaway.

People outside the pub gradually began to notice the fishing vessel as it came closer, the low hum of its engine coming in with the surf.

Buffeted by the wind, atop the wheelhouse, Reef was wrestling to tie a huge yellow flag with the red Lion Rampant roughly emblazoned on it to the vibrating cabling. It was a struggle, forcing the young fisher to twist and strain in contortion to fix the heraldic emblem securely. Just as well Reef possessed the flexible joints of a superhero.

Alan poked his head out of the wheelhouse door and looked up.

"What the hell are ye playin' at?"

"You gotta make an entrance, dude," Reef shouted back.

"We are nae here to surf,"

Reef ignored Alan and stood up, holding on with one hand, the other keeping his floppy safari hat held firm.

Above Reef, his home-made Saltire was already flapping furiously next to the Lion Rampant.

The pub crowd cheered. They would have paid good money for this.

Reef was still standing atop the wheelhouse, arms holding the lines, part crucified, his head thrown back, yelling a battle cry like a feted warrior in a chariot.

"No Fear! Sans Peur!"

Alan couldn't help getting caught up in Reef's enthusiasm. He started yelling too. "Sans Peur!"

Suddenly, Reef's hat blew off.

"Shit!"

Reef howled.

The crowd watched in amazement. They pointed in wonder at the figure on top of the wheelhouse, some started cheering. One of the young surfers turned to Chad.

"All you Scots that crazy?" the assumption of kinship offended the American.

His Scots heritage had always been a source of quiet pride for Chad, as it had been for his father and paternal grandfather. Arriving in Scotland had given him a warm reaffirming sense of that connection. However, increasingly, he realised it was the environment, the land, rugged mountains and the rough sea that he felt linked to. The people frustrated him. He found their horizons limited and hemmed in.

He recalled one of his college tutors explaining that as a socio-economic group, the Scots that had emigrated to the southern states of America had statistically been among the least successful arrivals in the New World. The Red Necks. This had offended him. It still did. Now here in this remote fishing town, he was struggling to reconcile his romantic view of his heritage with the contradiction of the people he had met here. Their resilience and toughness, their sheer graft, he admired. Their steadfastness. This was set against their general disinterest in the wider world, their refusal to acknowledge it, let alone challenge it. He accepted that he was a well-travelled American and something of a rarity in being so.

Increasingly to Chad's mind, as a Scots-American, his time in the old country was underlining his sense that he represented the improved model in *Homosapien Ecosse*. American evolution.

Chad had to resist the urge to swear and spit at the same time as the *Sans Peur* drew nearer.

The three-man crew of the *Sans Peur* were surveying the shoreline.

"Where we gonna berth her, dude?" It wasn't like Reef to be practical, so it must be an obvious problem.

Alan looked at Potty for inspiration, but the older man merely shrugged.

"Nae option, Alan."

A few minutes later, a bemused Reef was still studying the anchor mechanism. It was corroded with salt-eaten, gnawed rust. He signalled to Alan, who frowned when he saw it.

"We've nae option, Calum," he said, pointing to a rusted metal rod. To Alan, it was a symbol of Peter's contempt and neglect.

Reef pulled the lever and the anchor, groaned, grated, then fell. Alan pulled a similar block the other side of the boat. Another anchor ratched, clanged and dropped. Reef gave Alan the thumbs-up sign. Potty watched from the wheelhouse, slow plumes of smoke arising around him.

The *Sans Peur* lay at anchor off in the bay a few hundred metres from the beach, sitting like a man-o'-war.

The crew reached the shore in the bright orange automatic life-raft. Alan, in his determination to find Suds, used the paddle to get them to shore. Potty slouched like an old pirate in the stern, with Reef, like a small child, pointing excitedly from the bow.

The Engineer had adopted a weathered old navy seaman's cap, pushed back on his iron curls, headgear which Reef had noted enviously, casting several covetous glances at the worn canvas peak.

Reef, rope in hand, made the leap to the jetty ladder. He landed, caught hold of one of the old blistered rungs, and hauled himself up. At the top, he turned with arms aloft towards the pub on the rise, where the watchers were still cheering. Alan was tying up the small boat, gesturing for Reef to help.

The flamboyant Reef completed his full majestic turn.

"He came, he saw, he drank." His arms stretched wide, embracing and appealing to his crewmates on the orange liferaft.

Potty knocked out his pipe on the side of the stubby boat. "Vini, Vidi, Swally." A sardonic echo.

Reef grinned at them, then turned to follow their gaze.

Jake was waiting for them amid the crowd. He was clearly delighted to see Alan, who winked at him. Jake winked back with difficulty as Reef draped a dog-eared Saltire towel around the small boy's shoulders. Reef's diplomatic gift to the Irish nation.

Fellow surfers nodded their approval and offered hands of welcome to the Scots.

Jake led them through the crowd to Abina, who looked questioningly at Jake. Erin was standing off. He nodded curtly to Alan, who suddenly felt uncertain of himself faced with the contrasting expressions on the Irish man and woman's faces – his hostile, hers waiting. He detected a current here, a charge, a sense she expected something of him. Something vital. An undefined possibility rose in front of him like a wave, leaving him swamped and unmanned.

"We're here to find Suds. My brother. To bring him hame," Alan had not stuttered since he was ten years old, but his words were a reedy babble.

Abina studied Alan. She took Jake's hand and led him away, casting a look of disappointment and annoyance back at Alan, although Jake looked back and winked. Alan was left to face Erin, who was plainly darkly amused.

It was then that Alan realised he had made an utter ass of himself. He looked around for support from his crew. There was none, Reef was eyeing a surf babe and Potty merely raised a quizzical eyebrow. Alan pulled himself back on track. They were here now and all that meant was finding Suds.

The street running parallel to the sea proved to be a surfing metropolis, modern, magical, mediaeval, with stalls selling clothing, equipment, many creeds of street food, and music blaring out. Lloyd Cole's '*Lost Weekend*' from one t-shirt stall folding into '*Mr Brightside*' from the Killers at the next stall.

Bold, glaring colours were everywhere, Irish flags hoisted outside a couple of houses. Surfers and locals mixed freely in this winding exotic bazaar.

The crew were finding their bearings. Seafaring explorers in a new land.

As they walked, people in the crowd acknowledged the Scots who had come by sea. Reef gave them the thumbs up sign while the Irish surfers warily measured the newly arrived surfing rivals.

Reef stopped, eager to look at a stall dedicated to hats: caps, bonnets, beanies, even a flying hat, and straw boaters. Reef had arrived. The owner, an aging hippy, smiled encouragingly as Reef reached out and picked up a hat, a flamboyant floppy felt number in bold burgundy, and put it on before turning and smiling at Potty. The Driver shook his head as he lifted the hat off Reef's head and tossed it back at the seller.

Something else caught Reef's eye. In a narrow gap between the stalls was a small arched alley. The narrow-stoned passage led into an enclosed yard. Reef turned, drawn into the yard. Surfboards adorned the walls and a bearded, spare man in shorts and a ragged t-shirt, his nose and mouth covered by a dust mask, was smoothing a horizontal board, working it into shape. His smooth seamless planing matched the mellow tones of Sinatra that enveloped the yard: '*Fly Me to the Moon*'. A gentle craftsman. Reef was transfixed by the sight.

Reef turned to face an Irish girl, dark haired with a Celtic cleavage.

"Plumb," announced Reef.

"Clare," the girl smiled.

At the other end of the Killymarten's main street, Suds was looking at gear at a stall lined with wetsuits.

As he meandered past the shops and stalls, he spied a brief splash of blue and white. The small figure of Jake was walking across the road slightly further down the street. The ragamuffin still had Reef's worn Saltire towel draped across his shoulders like a cape.

Suds was curious. Could there be other Scots here? Some of the well-travelled Broch boys, perhaps? He followed, stopping only to note Chad's car, still parked near the pub. Jake, like a homing pigeon, led Suds straight to the crew of the *Sans Peur*, who were trying to find their bearings amid the exotic sounds and sights.

"Reef! Potty!" Suds moved towards them, shock and delight on his face.

"Suds!"

Suds turned to find Alan facing him.

"Alan!"

Alan pushed his brother on to his back foot.

"What do ye think you're doin'?"

"Ireland," was Suds's open-handed response.

"Ireland. Fuckin' Ireland," Alan's voice was a low snarl. A warning before a charge.

"Nae unless it's changed its name," Suds laughed, his joy at seeing his crewmates undiminished.

Alan's eyes flashed.

"You fuckin' selfish bastard!"

Alan laid a hand on Suds and finally got the reaction he wanted from his brother.

"And I'm the only one? Am I? No, else it'd be Uncle Suds, wouldn't it and you'd actually have a relationship wi' your wife." Suds swept Alan's restraining hand away, chopping it down.

Alan was poised to strike him.

"Instead, all you've got is a relationship wi' your father-in-law. 'Yes Peter', 'No Peter', 'Kiss my fuckin' arse, Peter'," saliva ran down Suds's chin.

The brothers stared at each other, their loathing for one another and the truth binding them.

Suds waited, ready. Alan was trying to haul himself back from the brink.

The Sutherlands had grown up sparring. Evenly matched, winning one tussle had never guaranteed a successive victory. Their last clash had been at Alan's Blackening. Alan had been caked in the grime the occasion demanded, a special mixture Potty had taken great pride in devising. Suds had been left with his share of the baked beans, oil, and fruit juice smeared over him after their clash, an exchange ended by Potty's intervention. Both brothers had been bruised and drunk, though Alan couldn't recall who'd had the edge, the taste of his blood and the vile inedible wash in his mouth, Suds's incoherent slurred apology for spoiling his night in his ears. His knuckles and cheek had been raw from blows, both received and given.

Alan's hostility towards Suds had ballooned since then, fed by every single inch of selfishness, all the short-sighted acts of petulance his brother committed.

"Come on, guys, think about it," said Reef conscious of the watching crowd.

"Shut up, Reef," a chorus from Alan and Suds.

Reef looked at Potty for support.

"Let's go and ha'e a pint, ma loon," decided Potty, airily

waving his pipe in the direction of the jetty bar like an absent–minded professor.

Reef stared in disbelief. Potty's indifference caused Alan and Suds to pause in their face-off.

"I'm in mind o' a Guinness. You comin' or no, loon?"

Reef nodded eagerly at Potty, like a distracted dog shown a favourite stick. Alan and Suds's arms dropped.

"We're headin' hame," said Alan with finality.

Potty glanced back at Alan with a grain of humour and contempt.

"Nae wi' that tide, young Alan. No till the morn."

Potty turned and sauntered towards the pub. Suds shrugged. Reef and Suds looked at each other then Alan, whose eyes flicked with uncertainly from Potty to the moored *Sans Peur*. Alan started to walk to the pub.

"Sly, min, real sly," Reef was almost skipping. *Ireland, Guinness, Ireland.* Someone should write a song. Perhaps his mate Scottie Main would pen one for him.

The bar was perched on the town side of the jetty, part of stone and sections of wood. Its whitewash was peeling, the woodwork more so. To Reef's artistic eye, it appeared to float. And that, to Reef, was the best kind of bar.

They all drifted slowly to the pub as Potty disappeared inside.

Inside the cosy wooden-floored bar, John Cronin, barman and brother of the Landlord, was serving a customer, old Cornelius Herbert, when Potty entered, climbed onto a stool and waited. Reef joined him and pointed to an old-fashioned Guinness pump as John set down a pint of black gold.

"The Scots boys." A hint of welcome in the label.

Reef studied the bar, his eyes alight at the possibilities.

"Two Guinness. What's the plural for Guinness?" Reef laughed, with a glint in his eye. He was amused by his joke, even if the barman was unmoved. After fourteen years of tending bar, Cronin had heard them all. Or he thought he had.

Cronin started to pour when Reef leaned in.

"Do you want some smash?" his voice only a whisper. A conspiracy in the volume.

Cronin froze, the pouring spoiled. The barman exchanged a nervous glance with the nearby Herbert. Old Cornelius crossed himself and turned a blind ear.

"Smash. I've got loads," Reef was unabashed.

The barkeep's concern grew. Cornelius edged down the bar, choosing a different seat, putting distance between himself and the dubious deal being proposed by the Scottish skinhead.

Undeterred, Reef dug into his pockets. A huge handful of coins spilled across the bar, none of it legal tender in Eire.

"Are you needin' it?" demanded Reef, losing patience with the idiot Irish bartender, as relief washed the other's features.

Time passed slowly in the Irish pub. In a haze of Guinness and Bushmills, Reef later claimed.

The crew were now inebriated. Waxed, oiled, wasted. Potty had wandered to the end of the bar, fascinated by the musicians preparing for an open mic session. Reef was at the bar talking to Clare, the girl from the Shaper's yard. Alan and Suds remained seated, separated by a table full of empties, sacrificed chess pieces in a messy battle.

"Think aboot it," said Alan for the tenth or eleventh time.

Suds simply sat back with his arms folded.

"A'right, I'll sign. I'll sign, if you beat me the morn," Suds had laid his palms and his cards on the table.

"Surfing?" Alan was incredulous.

"Beat me in the Open and the licence is yours," repeated Suds.

Alan was incensed.

"Typical Suds, everything's a game. No. No way," Alan dug in.

However, Suds was sitting back. He seemed calm, a moment of drunken clarity had descended upon him. Focussed.

He saw his solution, his proposition to his brother, as an appropriate offering; it was both a challenge and an offence. Putting his brother on the back foot pleased him. Such power was new to him and he decided to press his advantage.

"It's up to you, brud. Live to surf, surf or die," Suds was pleased with his speech until just that second Chad came in and soured it. Taking a breath, Suds refused to let the strutting Yank mar his moment and raised his Guinness to him in an exaggerated toast, mocking the American.

Chad frowned, sensing an insult in the gesture.

"Tomorrow, Sutherland."

Suds ignored Chad's threat. The American's frown grew. No one liked being irrelevant.

Suds leaned forward, meaning it.

"Tomorrow, Alan."

The brothers reassessed each other.

"Reef! Get a round in, min!" Suds hollered across the bar against a spirited, if slightly disjointed, rendition of the Waterboys' anthem 'Whole of the Moon'.

As the last notes died away, the musicians crowded around Abina as she joined them. Their star performer. They were clearly pleased to see her.

Alan watched Jake's manic dancing and noticed Erin watching Abina. The giant had positioned himself away from the bar. Alan looked around the room. He saw them all. A kaleidoscope of faces. Of choices: Abina, Jake, Reef, Clare, Potty, Erin and finally Suds. But Abina just looked straight at him, her glance brushing over him as though she were painting him, her eyes speculative and challenging.

Suds caught the Irish woman's eyes on his brother as he watched Reef with Clare. He glanced down at his own tattooed forearm with 'Arlene' inked on it in a flowing Gothic wave. He had been drunk then too, to dull both the pain and the commitment.

A few drinks later and Reef was trying to down a pint of Guinness in one. Alongside him another surfer, and down the line, two girls; all were in the same race. Reef struggled with the last mouthful and started to put the pint down on the bar to claim the prize, but another beat him. Reef turned and looked down the line, his face registered shock as he found Potty looking him straight in the eye.

"Yer roun', ma loon," came the deep Doric growl.

The phone box stood overlooking the back of the bar, surrounded by a nest of kegs, casks and barrels. Inside, Chad was making a telephone call. Beyond him lay the Irish Sea. The wind buffeted the call box. His mobile was pressed against his ear, but the phone box kept the call private. He wanted it that way.

"Hi, is that Peter Innes McGhee? Yes, Peter…"

At the sea's edge, the waves were coming in. Alan was standing on the beach watching them, bathed in moonlight, his gaze lifted to the stars.

"Counting them? Or seeing double, are you?"

Alan swung round; Abina looked him up and down and mimicked his sway. In response, Alan dug his hands further into his pockets and stilled himself.

"Too many." Alan might have meant the drink, but he was looking up at the sky.

"As long as you can reach seven," came Abina's soft reply. She meant the stars.

Alan was even more puzzled.

"Seven stars on seven nights and you will dream of your true love,"

Alan looked from the laughing eyes back up to the stars. He turned back.

"It's a charm. Something my grandmother spoke."

He nodded slightly, caught in the moment. Abina stepped forward and planted a light hand on his shoulder and a soft kiss on his cheek, gentler than the Atlantic breeze that cooled his skin. It warmed him.

"Good luck for tomorrow."

She pointed at the waves. Alan watched her walk away. Alone, he looked up at the constellation and, clearing his blurred thoughts, started to count.

Reef, still with his hat on, *a baggy dated cricket cap,* was asleep, twisted at an awkward angle in his cramped bunk aboard the *Sans Peur.* He was dreaming, perhaps, of a mermaid in a floppy exotic hat. The deckhand had fallen asleep to the seductive story of Best Girl Athlete's *'Join the Masons'.* A shadow fell on his face causing Reef to stir slightly.

Water showered him and Reef sat bolt upright in gasping shock. Rough hands reached in and hauled him to his feet.

Squatting on deck, Reef was pulling on his boots. He checked and staggered to the railing, before vomiting overboard. He looked up, wiping his mouth. Alan pointed to the life raft lashed to the side of the fishing vessel. Reef rolled his eyes.

"I canna, Alan," Reef protested, the hinges on his legs not working properly.

Alan reached to propel Reef over the rails.

"You want to swim."

The duo rowed to the shore jetty in silence. Reef was beyond speaking and Alan was consumed with his mission. Reef was struggling as he quelled the urge to puke, but Alan's strokes were purposeful.

Alan marched Reef along the empty main street until they reached the closed yard, down the short dark alley. Alan knocked on the door of the Shaper's yard and the sound reverberated down the deserted road. Alan stepped forward again.

"You're gonna do it. You're gonna take on Suds," Reef's thought processes were finally catching up.

Alan considered Reef's logic, but said nothing.

Just then, before Alan could reply, the door to the yard creaked open, a watchful crack. A tussled Clare stared blurry-eyed at them. Reef gave her a winning smile, as Alan pushed past her into the yard.

Alan wasted no time as he picked out a board for himself and one for Reef.

"Can he add a logo?" Alan asked the dazed girl.

Clare obviously thought these Scots were mad.

"Sure. But not today," she said as Alan frowned.

"The Shaper's out of it. Lucky if he wakes up this week," she said, pointing to a hammock. Rocking slowly, the Shaper was clearly zonked out. She looked to Reef for help to make his crazy companion understand.

"I'll sort it, Alan," said Reef.

Alan looked surprised and so did Clare.

"Fit for a final, Reef?" Alan hoped Reef understood what he was really asking for.

"Nae bother," Reef's resolve was growing.

Potty was mixing another ugly looking mixture in an enamelled pot on the stove in the *Sans Peur's* narrow galley. He looked to where Reef was sitting at the table. Potty was making breakfast.

"He's gonna surf, Pots," although excited at the prospect, Reef still looked rough. He felt it, too.

Potty pulled Reef's hat off and planted an enamel mug of ugly murky liquid in front of him. Reef looked at the mixture, then at Potty, who was cracking eggs. Reef worried that the raw eggs were destined to join the gooey concoction. The image of Rocky downing uncooked eggs flashed through his mind and he choked back a sour, acidic retch.

Potty indicated the mug.

"Vici, Vidi, Swally."

Reef pulled a face and took an exaggerated breath. Courage for the condition and the cure.

It must have worked, because fifteen minutes later, Reef was working on deck, marking Alan's board and his own with the distinctive curling wave-like scrimshaw motif, when Potty tapped him on the shoulder and passed him a tin mug.

"Cardno's Cathodic Cure," the engineer smiled cruelly at him, "The sequel."

Reef rolled his eyes. One dose had been enough. He feared his insides would fall out. Yet, his hands were steady, the scrolled lines clean and smooth.

Alan was standing on deck. He surveyed the small town, the harbour, the beach and the waves. He spotted Abina and

Jake, who were walking on the beach. They were casting stones.

Alan smiled, remembering her lips softly brushing his cheek and her words.

"Good luck for tomorrow."

Potty joined him at the rail. "Beautiful day tae be alive."

"Any sign o' Suds?"

"Probably suffering fae No Fear nerves."

He handed Alan a mug of his hangover remedy. Alan winced, but he drank it. Sips of reproach.

"Miraculous properties," confided Potty.

"Suds never gets nervous," said Alan, screwing his face up as he risked the evil potion.

In a small, tired, hotel room, Suds awoke, bile in his throat. He groaned as a painful consciousness muscled in. He felt drained of blood, pale and hungover. He had to move. Just a handful of steps to the bathroom.

Suds face was pained. He shook his head, but nothing could clear it.

Barefoot, he was on the pan. He lit up. Perhaps a cigarette would help. His head back on the wall, Suds tried to psych himself up for the competition.

Reef was waxing a board, lovingly making the finishing touches still clutching Potty's foul cure, having crafted on his own motif. He nodded to himself, satisfied; he called to Alan.

With quiet pride, Reef showed Alan his intricate flowing handiwork and Alan, despite himself, was impressed. Mighty impressed. Even Potty pursed his lips in ironic, reluctant admiration. *Plumb.*

The shift at MacNaught's Fishyard was an hour in when Peter, his long black overcoat flapping behind him, swept through the factory. Workers marked his progress. With everyone else wearing white, he was difficult to miss, like Lucifer gate-crashing heaven. He arrived at Arlene's empty station bench, midway along the line. He turned to the girl working opposite, but Joanna pointed her knife at him, holding it up so the keen edge was between them as if she were warding off an evil spirit.

"She's nae here, so fuck off," she was ready for him.

Peter was shocked and incensed. Arlene's work colleagues shook their heads, all their eyes were now on him. He might view himself as a big man in the harbour, but here in the bleak chilled factory, he was the trespasser.

As Peter stalked away, Joanne started to strike the hilt of her filleting knife against the metal work surface. Another woman joined in, and another, as the clanging chorus speeded Peter's exit.

Escaping the din, his reception outside was no better. As Peter stormed from the factory, a seagull swooped down and he was splattered by the screaming angry bird: white on black. Livid, he yanked the Mercedes' door open as his car was bombed by the gulls.

Yvonne turned to face her father, who still had his jacket on. She tried to help him clean off the seagull mess, but Peter shook her off. They were in her lounge and Peter was still trying to step back from his growing fury.

"Has he called?"

Yvonne shook her head.

"They're in Ireland. Surfin'," Peter was struggling between disbelief and rage.

Yvonne gasped and started to cry.

"It'll be a'right," Peter reassured her, but Yvonne shook her head.

"I'm pregnant, Dad," Peter stopped in his move towards her.

"I just feel so alone," Yvonne started to cry. Peter looked more confused.

"Alone? He's left you?"

Yvonne moved to her father's embrace. His face, framed over her sobbing shoulder, was granite.

A golf ball was placed on the ground. The club-head lined up, addressing the ball.

Peter's face was rigid with rage. The club swung back. The club-head struck the ball in a blurred arc, sending it disappearing over the new boat. Peter's new vessel, under construction, was on towering steel plinths.

Every town has a Peter. Usually more than one. Not necessarily the biggest fish, but one of the sharks.

If he had lacked build, he would have been graced with small man syndrome. But his stature matched his power.

In his youth, his hair had carried a hint of flame, reflecting his impatience and latent fury. Now, both his hair and his anger were cold white.

Peter watched it, club in his hand like a weapon. The boatyard spread beneath him. A baron on the battlements.

"I will crush you, Alan Sutherland and your surf shite of a brither." His anger thickened his tongue. The club shook in his clenched hand with the violence in the threat.

The Irish surfers of Killymarten were cheering Erin as he cut across the waves. Suds was watching intently. He turned to find

Alan standing a few feet away with a surf board. Potty and Reef watched the brothers anxiously.

A black surfing glove landed in the sand at Suds's feet.

Suds looked at Alan then bent to pick up the gauntlet. Both brothers straightened imperceptibly, accepting the challenge.

Suds hauled his over-smock off to unveil his new Saltire wet-suit to a mammoth cheer from the Irish surfers, a great white cross on his bold blue covered torso. Suds had had the wetsuit made almost a year ago, but had bottled wearing it. Until now. Ireland, he had determined, was the time. His time. *Cometh the hour, cometh the wetsuit.*

"Real plumb, dude," Reef was impressed.

"Where's the noughts?" Potty less so.

"Got to show them we're Scottish, ye ken," explained Suds.

Chad laughed harshly, his mirth and disdain unnecessarily loud across the sand, designed to ridicule.

"Looks like a Scottish condom," he mocked.

Suds moved towards him, but Reef intervened.

"Let it go, min."

"You're a waste of space, Sutherland," Chad jeered, determined to goad them.

"Spaced Man, that's me," acknowledged Reef, deflecting the American's focus away from his friend.

Chad turned away still chuckling.

"Hope your board breaks, ya fuckin' prick," Reef muttered the curse softly.

An hour later, Reef was sitting on the sand with his bowed head in his hands, legs splayed wide apart.

"Shit," his fist struck the sand. Suds crouched beside him, Alan bending down on the other. Each held a portion of Reef's board.

"Shit, min, shit. Outa hand," Reef muttered.

Suds laid a hand on Reef's shoulder. It was then that Chad's laughter reached them. The trio all looked in the direction of Chad's merriment. The trio's eyes met over Reef's shattered board.

Alan and Suds both stood up slowly and gave each other the merest cold acknowledgement before they hoisted their own boards.

Reef was left nursing his broken board.

"Cool design. Sik," said Clare kneeling down beside him on the wet sand, her hand running over the board's swirling monogram.

Reef shrugged. "I could get into it."

Clare, encased in a wetsuit, passed Reef his hat, a small-rimmed Pork Pie. He cuffed the sand off it and crammed it onto his dome.

The surfers remaining in the competition were waiting while the judges conferred; Alan, Suds, Chad, and Erin were all standing apart from each other amid the other uncertain hopefuls.

A judge stepped forward with a yellow megaphone. Conversations trailed away in nervous expectation. He was known as Bandstand. A natural showman, part DJ, sometime stand-up, he was a well-travelled surfer. Tall, he leaned on a cane to spare his wrenched ligaments, a recent surfing mishap. In his other palm rested a megaphone, on his crown, a stunted top hat. He could have been Reef's long-lost cousin, except that Reef had no relatives living. Just the Sutherlands and his zoo of headgear.

Bandstand cleared his throat theatrically.

"The finalists in the Celtic Open Championships are," another pause here, dramatic effect and all that, "Chad Hamilton…"

The American smiled confidently straight at Suds, who remained uncertain as to how well he had fared. Suds began to feel the familiar cold pangs of failure deep in his gut.

"Alan Sutherland…"

Alan was more relieved than pleased. He looked across at Suds, who avoided his eye and then to Abina, who returned his gaze. Alan still sensed that she was assessing him and his qualities. On a level that he didn't really fully grasp.

"Erin O'Callaghan…"

The Irish surfers and followers went wild at the name. Reef admired their celebrations, then recognised a very tense Suds. His only friend, he realised, and, in response to that simple revelation, took half a step towards him.

"And Graham Sutherland."

Suds looked to the sky in gratitude and relief, then across at Alan. The brothers stared at each other. The challenge was still on.

A slim, blue-veined hand reached across and eased the megaphone out of Bandstand's grip. The judge had the grace to allow it.

"On you go, Graham Sutherland!" Boomed the megaphone with a warm Scots lilt.

Reef and Suds stopped celebrating and turned to the voice.

Arlene was standing in jeans and simple jumper, a small carry case at her side, with the megaphone dangling at her wrist. Suds was dumbstruck. In a daze, he walked towards her.

"Outa hand, lady," muttered Reef in admiration.

Suds and Arlene faced each other and both started to smile. No one marked Chad turning away in disgust.

Bandstand, the judge, had more news.

"The final will start at 10am sharp tomorrow, waves permitting, pray to the God of Swell," he announced grandly.

That was the nature of surf. It was down to Mother Nature. Like life, it was in her gift. A season could pass with scant blessings and no waves.

A pack of cans clinked as they were carried over the shadowed dunes. The remains of the day were reduced to a fine line of dark reddish gold on the horizon. Reef stopped to take a draw and looked down on a fierce bonfire. Below, surfers and party-goers were ranged around the leaping fire. A couple of smaller camp fires were dotted nearby. Music was playing, laughter, discussions, and the flat slap sound of the surf shrouded out of the bonfire's radiation.

Jake was squatting a few feet away, watching him. The Scot laid the smoke aside and turned to the small boy. Jake's mouth opened in wonder as Reef gave him a fierce grin. Reef was transformed into a Pictish warrior, one half of his face blue with pigment.

Reef was standing above the party, tins in hand, wearing a big floppy hat. The flames danced on one side of his face. It cracked into a wolfish smile before he threw back his head and howled.

All of the faces surrounding the huge blaze turned as Reef's call rose above the dunes. Alan and Suds exchanged a worried glance.

Another high echoing howl followed.

Then Reef came bounding into the fire's light, his face split down the middle, the dark and the light. His movements were elemental as he leapt, pivoted and twisted. Spinning around, he tossed Alan a tin, then in a fluid action, sprayed another in Suds's direction. Suds took a half-hearted swipe at him, but Reef was away, dancing like a shaman around the fire. Abina clapped her hands with delight; everyone was fascinated by the demented swirling Reef.

Potty took a long swig from a bottle of dark spirit. Then he leapt up, pulling the tartan rug up off the sand and started doing a wild jig. Others started to join in.

Among the first up was Jake, who was joined by Abina. Together they coaxed Alan up too. Alan couldn't help but notice that Erin was watching them closely across the flames, his eyes coal pits in the twisting firelight reflections.

Suds and Arlene were sitting with their arms around each other. No wild dancing for them.

The fire had lessened as Alan headed back across the beach towards the *Sans Peur*. He had lost track of his crewmates, but had a final tomorrow and he had to win. *To beat his brother.*

He angled towards the small jetty and came across Reef passed out with Clare, her head resting on Reef's chest. The Irish girl had Reef's hat on. Alan left him to his fate.

He glanced back at the bonfire to see Potty Highland dancing around the fire, naked except for a Tartan rug as a makeshift kilt. God knows where his brother was, although Alan had a good idea. Arlene was right for Suds, if only he could see it. *But what did he know?*

As the sun rose, Alan was sitting on the beach, gathering himself for the surf final.

Abina was walking towards him, wrapped in a patched homespun blanket set against the stiffening wind. She elected to sit a few steps away.

"Penny for them," Alan turned and was met with her stunning smile. He returned it, conscious that his own lacked her brightness.

"They're nae worth it."

"Not even a penny."

Alan shook his head slowly.

"You live here." To that Abina shook her head.

"We move about a lot. Following the waves, I guess. Me and Jake. Sometimes I worry about it – for him. School and things, you know," her smile dimmed a little.

Alan considered this.

"And Erin." Alan made it a statement.

"He comes, too. Sometimes. We've our own vans now. Jake's with me," she shook out her hair to emphasis the point, the warm gold dawn rays caught in her tangles.

Alan digested this. Abina looked across at him.

"He hasn't, you know, grown up. Everything is a game to him," she went on.

"I ken someone like that," Alan conceded, thinking of his brother.

"It's a common condition."

"And you?"

"A bird rests on a tree of her choice," her wide smile again, but now slightly uncertain.

"Your Grandmother?"

Her smile grew into a laugh, rich, deep and salty.

"It's from Africa. Heard it somewhere, sometime."

Arlene and Suds were walking down Killymarten's main street. It had yet to wake up. She reached to take his hand. Suds hesitated, then relaxed and squeezed her fingers.

"You should help him, Suds." It was a bold opening gambit from Arlene. Suds dropped her hand.

"If he beats me," he repeated, as they stopped and faced each other.

"He's your brother. The *Sans Peur* means a lot to you and yer Mam."

Suds was already shaking his head.

"Leave her out o' this. No. If he beats me," with that he walked away from her.

Arlene watched him go.

"He always does." Too soft for Suds to hear. She took a breath and followed him. She always would.

The Celtic Surf Festival finalists were pulling on their wetsuits. Suds and Alan gave each other cold nods over the keen wind. Erin was stretching nearby. Each competitor was going into his own private routine. Their own worlds.

Abina stepped in front of Alan, demanding his attention. "Good luck."

Alan nodded his thanks, pleased, yet uneasy. Erin's face creased, a sudden chink of hurt, as Abina walked away. He and Alan measured each other, acknowledging that in some bizarre dance their positions had changed now.

The flamboyant judge stepped forward and the crowd drew in.

"The waves are falling away, guys. Forecast is not too promising. So, it's best wave, one wave, one shot. That's all you've got." It was that or no final.

"Sudden death," breathed Suds, finishing the sentence for him.

The surfers and the crowd took this in, their faces tensed with excitement and relish.

"Sly, real sly," Reef wagged his finger reprovingly at Bandstand.

Waves buffeted Alan and Suds as they paddled, stretched out on their boards. Paddling was the building block of a surfer.

The ability to get back to the waves was vital in a waverider's armoury, particularly in a competition. Alan and Suds matched each other stroke for stroke. The pattern of their lives.

Behind them the beach and spectators faded away from them, becoming smaller in scale and significance with every stroke.

They hauled themselves up to sit astride their boards. They took in the distant shore, then focussed on the incoming swell at their backs.

The flag went up – the final had started.

Alan watched an approaching set of waves. *Sudden Death.* Then he made his decision, sliding into position, muscles burning as he paddled, and took one, standing quickly onto his board with powerful, fluid movements. He was in control, riding the wave. A strong, steady ride.

When Alan ploughed out of the water, drawing a deep breath, Jake ran up to him

Alan's expression was fixed, intense, but pensive. He halted in front of Jake, who winked at him then shrugged. Alan couldn't help smiling. He ruffled the boy's hair with a wet hand, but Jake didn't mind.

Alan turned back to the action unfolding behind him. He was committed now. It was done. His points were on the board.

Chad was converging on a wave, he climbed up and mounted the wave, cool and confident.

Reef's agitation showed as he watched Chad balance on the top of the wave.

He pushed his hat back and clenched his fists.

"Yes," muttered Reef, willing the shithead American to fail.

Suddenly, inexplicably, Chad was in the water, swamped by the unexpected collapse of the wave he had chosen, spitting salt and disappointment from his mouth.

Reef's hat spiralled into the air in slow motion, held by the wind, its colours catching the sun. Beneath it, Reef had his mouth wide open, his fists held high.

"YASSS, min!" his prayers had been answered.

Chad staggered out of the water. He stared across at Alan and the celebrating Reef, who was churning the sand up in a delighted circular jig. Chad threw down his board and glared at the duo, stalking off.

"Jerk!" Reef shouted after him. Although not quite loudly enough to reach the American.

Alan ignored all about him; his eyes focused on the last two surfers in the bay.

Erin was sitting astride his board. From here, he looked across the beach, his gaze sweeping the coastline. He swept his wet, wind-dragged, hair from his face, but his expression did not change. He was here to win.

Alan was looking back out from the beach; there were two surf warriors separated by their arena, the sea.

Erin switched his concentration from the beach to the incoming high swell. He was still, waiting for the kill.

Erin chose his wave, but a millisecond later checked back, taking the second one.

Reef was at Alan's shoulder, his palm shadowing a frown, disbelief on his face. Alan remained stony-faced.

"What's he doin', min?"

A small signal from Alan cut him off.

"He's blown it," Reef could not believe it.

Alan looked almost sad. He admired the giant Irishman.

Reef was jumping up and down with a huge megaphone, the kind that lifeguards use. He had purloined it from Bandstand, who discovered his loss as Reef's song spilled across the beach to greet the Irish giant as he emerged from the sea.

"Erin is a womble! Erin is a womble!"

Alan's black stare made Reef stutter and his chant ended lamely.

Erin was beaten. He lifted his board like a shield and stood straighter. The megaphone fell to Reef's side, shame and nerves getting the better of him.

Erin turned towards Alan and strode towards him. Alan, in turn, stepped to meet him. Erin stretched out his hand and they clasped forearms. Erin nodded to Alan conceding defeat. They all turned to watch as Suds moved across to catch a wave. When Alan had gone early, Suds had almost picked a wave then. Been panicked into it. That chance gone, his nerves had tightened as first the American, then the giant had gambled. Alone, Suds could see the risk that his nerve might fail him. He'd set up this bet, this game, to humble his brother and thwart Peter. *You prick Sutherland, just do it!*

Suds took the wall of water, arms outstretched, a moving, sweeping human flag. A dynamic, arcing, glorious saltire.

People on the beach were urging him on, Reef and Arlene both rooting for him.

Suds, flipped over the turning wave, as he followed it along the tube. It was a long smooth curve, then his arms went aloft as he completed the run.

Suds emerged from the water for Arlene to run up and embrace him. He was still getting his breath back. The sting of saltwater and adrenalin buzzing in him.

The finalists all acknowledged each other, even a gutted Chad, still struggling to accept his unfortunate floundering wave. Even his tan seemed to have faded in defeat. With matted hair, Suds was still drying himself. He'd never been tanned in his life.

The judge was looking for his misplaced megaphone. Reef came to his rescue and sheepishly handed it over. Bandstand took it from him with a scowl.

"Waves weren't great, but the surfing was," proclaimed the tall Bandstand to cheers from the crowd.

Alan and Suds measured each other. It came down to the two of them. Erin's misjudgement and Chad's misfortune had undone them.

The judge cleared his throat. He liked the theatrics; Bandstand was a gameshow host in the making.

"The winner of the Celtic Surf Championships," an actor's pause, "is Graham 'Suds' Sutherland."

Arlene wrapped her arms around him. Suds was stunned, putting his hands to his head. Alan looked at the sand, then the sky, trying to contain his disappointment. It threatened to consume him. The *Sans Peur* was finished. Sunk. Scuttled by his brother's childish challenge and his own foolishness. The one time it *really* mattered, meant something beyond the surfing and he'd blown it.

Reef let out a howl, before patting Suds on the back. Alan took a breath and stepped forward to shake his brother's hand. The last time that Suds had bettered him in a surf competition, he had been twelve. Suds hardly noticed his brother's presence, such were the chorus of backslaps he was receiving. In his daring bold wetsuit and victory, he had become a cult hero in Killymarten.

Erin shook Suds's hand, but Chad turned away in disgust and anger. Through the crowd, Abina gave Alan a sad smile and turned away. He watched her go.

A wide marquee had been erected on the area next the bar balcony.

The hostelry was busy. Suds was sitting with Arlene, his arm about her. Alan was sitting across from them, with drinks and empties strewn in front of them. A couple of surfers arrived and nodded respectfully towards the Scots, to Suds in particular. The Celtic Surf Champion. Arlene was radiant. Music was playing, Potty was with the band, jamming with them. He was in his element playing his old Horner to Van Morrison's *'And it stoned me'*. Reef carried over a new round, a teapot drawing with the words 'Make Tea' on the front of his t-shirt. Suds looked up, noticed the design and shook his head.

"You can an' all, Reef."

"Fit's that?"

Suds looked at Arlene, then towards his brother.

"Come to our wedding."

Arlene's smile widened and she gave Suds a quick kiss.

"Sly, min, sly," Reef downed his drink, "More drink!"

Reef walked to the bar. On the back his t-shirt read 'Not LOVE'.

"And you, brud. Job for you though. Best Man. Even though I was today," Suds's voice still carried a dig.

Alan looked up from his beer mat.

"Fit you for, Alan?" Reef called from the bar.

Alan turned and held up his drink, but seemed sober by comparison to everyone else. Defeat can have that effect, allied to the reality of its consequences.

Reef turned back to the barmaid, it was Clare. That made Reef smile.

"You always workin'?"

"Always on the job," laughed Clare, with a glint.

"A Guinness," Reef pursed his lips as he watched her bending down to select a glass. He waved along the bar at Potty. Mid-song, Potty held up his empty pint glass.

"Make it four," Reef instructed.

Clare smiled and Reef leaned in.

"Tell me."

Clare smiled expectantly, with teasing eyes.

"What's the Irish for blow job?"

Reef gave his rake's smile.

Reef sat down with the others. He was covered in Guinness. He spread his hands in defence.

"She disnae even speak my language," he shook his head sadly.

He pulled off his t-shirt and started to dry himself with it, but seemed unperturbed.

Alan returned with the drinks. Reef turned and waved at Clare, but she simply tossed her ink-black hair and made a point of ignoring him.

"You've no said much, brud. Takes some gettin' used to doesn't it?"

Alan came out of his reverie and met Suds's gaze.

"Winning," Sud's words cut across the table.

Reef and Arlene looked between the brothers.

"You'll get used to it," Alan replied, taking another mouthful of Guinness.

Reef and Arlene relaxed, but Suds was perplexed. It was not the answer he had expected.

Potty's voice filled the microphone.

"This one is for Graham and Arlene. God Bless!"

Suds raised a glass in Potty's direction and Potty raised his in return.

"Here's to us. Fa's like us," Potty's voice reverberated across the marquee.

The crew toasted each other.

"Damn few," Alan echoing Suds.

"And they're all deid!" finished Reef. Potty's makeshift band charged clumsily into The Proclaimers '*500 Miles*'.

When Abina and Jake arrived, Potty waved frantically, coaxing her up to sing. Jake planted himself next to Alan. Arlene smiled across at the small ragamuffin.

Abina started to sing, with Potty accompanying her. Morrison's '*Brown-eyed Girl*'.

Alan watched her, transfixed. Jake got up and began to dance. A bizarre, uncoordinated hop.

Reef stole a glance across at Clare, but she made a point of turning her back on him again. He looked down at his ruined t-shirt.

The atmosphere became warmer. The group were laughing at a story from Suds. Patting Suds on the thigh, Arlene got up and squeezed past him to buy a round. It was bad timing, because as she reached the bar, Chad, obviously worse for drink, appeared at their table.

"That the best you could do," he sneered.

Suds looked up at him. Chad nudged Reef and indicated his t-shirt. Alan came out of his reverie, to find Chad pointing at him.

"You should have won today, buddy."

Alan looked bemused and embarrassed, but Suds was livid. Chad's barb struck and burrowed deeper. The American snorted and turned away with the group watching him.

Arlene was paying for her drinks, when Chad draped his arm around her.

Suds was outraged. He jumped up and went straight for Chad. *Bastard American.*

Suds reached the American in three rapid strides and swung Chad around, but his punch failed to connect. One thing about Chad was that he was quick, dodging Suds's lunge and sending Suds sprawling with an angled push. As Suds struggled to get up, Alan stepped in. Chad smiled with the invincibility of drink, but he had met his match. Alan's anger from the last few weeks, his frustration over the *Sans Peur* and the shackles of an unhappy marriage, erupted.

In a none too gentle fireman's lift, Potty hauled Chad out of the Marquee, across the dark sand to the sea and dumped him into it.

In shock, spewing saltwater, a drenched cold Chad crawled out of the water and hauled himself shivering to his feet. In his disorientation, the American didn't know if the shaking was from the cold, the shock, or the humiliation.

Back in the marquee, Alan put his drink down. He frowned and lifted it up again. A beer mat was stuck to the bottom of his glass. The beer mat had Reef's monogram sketched on it. He held it up, catching Reef's eye. The other man shrugged. Alan looked at the design again, studying the beer-soaked cardboard. An idea slowly formed. The grain of a wild possibility.

A little later, hidden in the darkness of the pub car park, a brush was dipped into paint. The paint was being liberally applied, thick, globular, oily strokes. Soon all the surface was roughly covered; the painter sniggering and humming as he worked. A large spliff was sparked and Reef stepped back to admire his handiwork.

"Modern Art, min," the smile of a satisfied workman. Reef added the final flourish of a true artist. "Sly."

Ranged on the slopes of the beach to the south of the village, the party had shrunk slightly where Reef was holding court.

"It's a matter o' perspective. Taste," Reef sounded almost sober, but his eyes were a giveaway. They reflected the abstracted glaze of the truly smashed.

Alan laughed only for Reef to offer him an indulgent, arched look. Reef reached for his tin mug. He poured out a slug from a bottle. The others offered up their mugs and Reef did the honours as he continued his lecture.

"It's all aboot complexity, ye ken, smell, colour, taste, the notes, the hit, the aftermath. But mellow, min. Depth, substance, min. Irish!"

He raised his glass in a toast. The others follow suit.

"Sláinte!" said Erin.

"Irish!" laughed Abina.

"Cheers!" from Alan, not sure where this was heading.

Reef savoured his. They all ran the liquor around their mouths, but Reef was not finished in his dissertation on Irish whiskey.

"Like. There's just too much there. Subtlety sucks, min. It's the E's, min," he said in exaggerated fashion, sucking in his already hollowed cheeks for emphasis.

"Nibbles the gums, like," admitted Suds.

Abina's smile was full of challenge.

"It's got spirit, you just can't handle it." This fired at Reef, who shook his head. Drunkenly defiant.

"No, it's the E's. Too crowded in here," he said, tapping bottle. Potty held up his tin again. Reef blinked at him, but still poured.

"See, with Malt, Scottish Single, you can taste where you are. Where you were. Who was with you." This was deep. Especially for Reef, pissed as he was. But he was not finished.

"There are layers, min, colours. You can see them, taste them, feel them. They stay with you, like," Reef's speech subsided.

Abina shook her head at him.

"Irish whiskey is a man's drink."

Reef raised his tin in salute.

"Min." He looked sadly at the gathering in an exaggerated fashion, "See, it always comes down to it, trial by testosterone."

Annoyed by this, Abina's tone changed. From playful to hardball.

"Erin!"

Erin frowned, but reached into his sack and pulled out a clear bottle with no label. Abina took it off him. The flames were reflected in the clear colourless liquid. Abina was standing in front of Reef, hands on hips, looking down at him. For the first time, Reef looked slightly uncertain, he was also mesmerised and curious.

"This is the Irish. Poteen," she waved the bottle in Reef's face.

Reef looked amused and disconcerted, but Potty was eager.

"My kind o' drink, MAN!"

The latter was aimed at Reef. Abina smiled as she poured it out. Reef and Potty touched tins, crewmates together, and drank. Reef's face exploded as the fumes scorched his larynx, before the pure spirit hit his innards. Then, he was gasping, hands to his throat, as tears were streaming down his face.

"Tatties," he gasped, his breath burnt raw.

Abina was trying not to laugh, the others too.

"Too many E's in poteen for you?" she challenged, lengthening the word deliberately.

Potty savoured the liquor and finished it in one smooth accomplished swallow. A working lifetime spent inhaling diesel and worse had enhanced his immunity.

"Nae bad," decided Potty, as he held up his tin for a refill, "Affa fine, ma quine!"

Abina threw back her head in full deep-throated laughter, while Reef stared at Potty in horror. His definition of toughness torn up and redrafted. Alan looked at Reef, as the deckhand used the previous Irish whiskey to wash his mouth out to douse his scorched vocal chords. Reef pushed back his hat, a stunted Trilby, but was still reeling.

"Sly, min, sly," he gasped.

Alan and Abina grinned at each other. By unspoken agreement, they both rose and walked towards the sea. Abina kicked off her sandals and smiled at Alan. Challenged, he pulled his trainers off.

The tide came in. Abina laughed as the water washed over her feet and put her hand to keep her balance; it was their first touch. They both looked at her resting hand on his arm then made eye contact. Alan stepped back and Abina regarded him slowly as they moved apart. A silent, moonlit, distant dance.

He woke up in the near dark. The headache joined him on his second waking breath. The cramps followed, gate-crashing the day-after party. He tried to move, his clothes rustling, and groaned loudly, a response to the pounding head and his cramped muscles. He felt a moment of panic in the stifling darkness and fumbled for the door handle, his hand struggling to find it. His palms were slimy.

The door burst open and Chad, dishevelled and unkempt, tumbled out onto the ground, poised on his knees in the pub car park.

Unsteadily, he tried to stand, buckled, then made it. Upright, but uncertain, he stared at his light blue beautiful Beetle, its windows and paintwork now daubed with dark thick blue paint, with only a couple of chinks that Reef had missed. On the bonnet, with his fingers, Reef had crudely drawn his surfing emblem.

Leaning suddenly on the bonnet, Chad vomited and again. The number plate has been doctored too, now it read 'CAD'.

Alan was sitting amid the dunes, both Reef's homemade saltire and a tartan blanket wrapped around him. He was tired; sleep had eluded him, warded off by his growing unease, a sense of lurking disaster. He had lost the Open and with it the licence. He must face Peter and Yvonne, his father-in-law and his wife. His jailors. He looked up and across the beach. He finally dozed as he sat.

Lying across from him, Suds and Arlene were asleep in blankets on the beach.

Potty and Reef were crashed out on benches in the marquee bar. Reef stirred as Potty sat bolt upright on an opposite bench.

Alan, wrapped in blue and white, pushed himself to his feet sensing something amiss. He moved towards the sea. He speeded up across the sand as Reef and Potty came stumbling down onto the beach.

To their left, Abina climbed out of her brightly decorated powder-blue camper van, with a tussled Jake beside her. She pulled a jersey over his head.

Suds was helping Arlene up.

Alan was staring out to sea, hard-faced. The others joined him. Surfers were emerging from tents and Kombis scattered along the beach.

They were all looking out to sea and that was all they could see. The *Sans Peur* had gone. *Vanished.*

They all stared at the empty sea, scanning the horizon for the missing boat.

Reef peeled his battered hat off, a green US tank driver's cap, and scratched his head.

"Fuckin' no way, min. Outtahand."

Suds was standing close to Alan.

"What noo, brud?", but Alan was at a loss. Abina studied Alan's face, searching for his thoughts, but all she could sense was a strickened bewilderment. He walked to the sea's edge and she followed, walking towards him. Stooping to pick up a skimming stone, she tossed it to him. He caught it and looked at it lying in his palm. Somehow its even texture reassured him, smooth, soothing. It gave him a sense that things couldn't get any worse.

The harsh blare of a taxi horn wrenched his attention from the sea and the warm reassurance of the stone. The rear door of the taxi was thrust open and out rose Peter Innes McGhee like a wraith, his customary black coat dawn around him. The bad spirit at a funeral.

"Christ," Suds ran his hand over his face, a shiver running through him.

Peter marched down the slope towards Alan. Everyone else fell away from the approaching older man.

"Where the hell's ma boat?" And his fury.

Alan took a breath.

"That all you came here for?"

"Answer me."

"She's gone."

Peter scanned Alan's face, looked around for confirmation from the others, though all he was met with was confusion and anxiety. Peter looked out at the empty bay before he turned back to face Alan and Suds. Almost subconsciously, the brothers were standing together.

"The weakling and the waster," sneered Peter.

Alan examined Peter's face.

"All you care aboot is the boat. People don't matter. You robbed me, Suds and Mam, took advantage of her. You're a thief, Peter Innes McGhee."

"Thief! You lost MY boat!" rage engulfed Peter.

Erin was standing a few metres away, listening. He stepped forward unexpectedly.

"You better head north if you want to track her," he suggested to Peter, but the Scot was battling to control himself, and Erin's words did not penetrate the blood red mist that engulfed him. All Peter could taste was his black fury.

"Killybegs is your best bet, the Atlantic drift will take her north," Erin continued helpfully.

Peter was livid, wrestling to contain his raw hatred.

"You lose my boat, abandon your pregnant wife…" All this was directed into Alan's shell-shocked face. He was stunned, so was everyone else. Alan laughed in disbelief. He turned, but Abina had gone. She was already walking towards her Kombi with her young son at her heels, the waif glancing back at Alan in confusion.

Alan moved to follow her before Peter stepped in front of him. Erin studied Abina's departure and considered Alan, as Peter spoke with self-righteous venom.

"So that's how it is. Yvonne was right. You're finished. You're all fuckin' finished. Sacked, the lot o' you," Peter's spittle splattered Alan's neck and sweat shirt.

A battered one-eyed Chad, his cheek raised and darkening, limped up and spoke to Peter.

"I can take you north," he offered.

Potty spat out his baccy in disgust. Defeated on sea and land, Chad craved an escape.

The company of Irish and Scots surfers watched Peter and Chad climb into Chad's splattered car. Peter screwed his nose at it with distaste, but that did not stop him getting in. His vengeful fury drove him.

Beyond the telephone box was the Atlantic; it was the last call box in Ireland. Alan stood inside it, clutching his mobile.

He stared out at the ocean. He needed the privacy for this call, the buffeted space it offered. The telephone box provided that and shelter from the rising wind and his bitter thoughts.

As the phone rang, he focussed on the horizon.

"Hello?" Yvonne voice was fuzzy with sleep down a distant connection.

"It's me."

"Hi," Yvonne was waking up.

Alan's face was pressed against the cubicle's window, looking out to sea. He changed angle and now he could see that Abina and Jake were packing their Kombi. Abina paused as if sensing his eyes. She looked up and saw Alan's face against the glass.

"I'm in Ireland. You know. I mean, I lost," said Alan, as he pulled his thoughts and eyes away from the Irish woman.

No answer.

Abina turned away from Alan's gaze to ruffle Jake's hair before chivvying him along.

"How are you?" Alan's breath against the glass clouded it and his thinking.

"I'm pregnant, Alan."

Alan's shoulder's hunched slightly. Somehow, hearing it from his wife made it real.

"I ken."

"Arlene told you?" Yvonne sounded uncertain, lost.

"It's a women's thing."

"Aye, it is," her voice stronger.

The beach is beautiful, thought Alan: wide stretching sands, warm sun, the Atlantic surf. The sound of the muffled waves calmed him.

"We'll probably head back the morn," Alan didn't know what else to offer her.

"OK. See you. Alan, you'll make a great Dad," as a parting word, it struck its mark.

Alan's rested his forehead on the window.

"Yeah, bye," as he gently ended the call, the phone greasy in his hand.

Alan stepped out of the phone box and turned to the west, letting out a deep breath to face the future.

His crew were waiting for him.

Alan faced them. Suds's face was hard and drawn. Potty lit up, drawing heavily on his pipe.

"We could stay here, dude," Reef suggested quietly.

Arlene shook her head. That would not do.

"What aboot Yvonne and Bella?"

The crew waited as Alan stepped away from them, lost in thought. Each one doom-ladened. He walked off along the beach. The crew waited. They knew he did his best thinking alone. Walking the beach, riding the waves. It was the same in Norhaven.

He stood looking out at the waves. From the water's edge, he could pick out Abina's Kombi slowly leaving the camp. He looked back at the crew sitting by the beached life raft. He turned and headed back to them. As Alan re-joined them, Erin approached them. They were wary of each other now.

"You were quick to help," Alan made his point.

Erin just shrugged.

"I don't like bullies," it was a flat statement.

Alan studied the big Irishman.

"They're peculiar here, the tides, despite the Atlantic drift. Today, there's only one way she could have gone," Erin nodded down the beach.

"South," guessed Alan.

"South," confirmed Erin.

Suds stepped towards his brother. He put out his hand, the neoprene gauntlet hung in it.

"If we find her – I'll sign," he handed over the glove with the promise.

Erin's Kombi came coughing over the hill where it stopped with a shudder for Reef to leap out and point ahead.

Below the curving, sharply descending road, the *Sans Peur* was drifting towards the jagged shore. The hard-spiked rocks looked to him like cruel jaws ready to devour the boat.

Erin, Suds, Alan and Reef gazed down at her. Potty was slower climbing out of the back of the van.

"What now?" he asked when he reached the others.

"Now we board her," replied Suds.

Potty frowned at that, but Alan nodded slowly.

Down in the Cove, the group were donning wet suits and checking their boards. Only Potty was not active; he was busy shaking his head.

Alan made it clear, pointing to the drifting fishing vessel. "You have to. She needs you."

"O'er ma dead body," spat Potty, with feeling and phlegm.

Seawater filled his mouth and Potty was in all sorts of trouble, choking and cursing in the black choppy water. Suds reached out to help him.

They had paddled out on their surfboards, resembling members of the Special Boat Service. The thought made Alan smile, despite the exertion and anxiety.

Suds almost lost Potty, but managed to get him back above the water line. The tide was turning, which meant they had to pull against it to reach the boat before it hit the rocks. Alan redoubled his efforts to reach the *Sans Peur*.

Alan angled his board and shouted to the rest of the crew with Erin to avoid being slammed against the boat's hull. Reef was already sitting on his board in the shadow of the *Sans Peur*; he was working the board to maintain his position. Erin joined him and pointed to the remaining anchor chain. The other was lost, so the boat had dragged along the coast. It had meant that it had not travelled far, but was now in danger of being pulled to shore and dashed on the rocks. So were they, as a heavy swell slapped around them.

Erin and Reef reached the base of the chain links, crusted with rust and limpets. Reef signalled Alan, who had angled his board to meet Suds and help him drag a near-drowned Potty along with them.

Reef and Erin began to climb. It was the right decision, thought Alan, as Reef had always been a great climber. *Like a rat up a drain pipe.* Alan strained to look straight up.

Even with his natural aptitude, Reef struggled for purchase on the wet, rusted metal chain links. Its age and the sea had pitted the surface and his fingers had to work for a grip. Reef was at full stretch, pulling himself around the chain as it scored his palms like sandpaper. With every stretch, Reef felt his muscles scream. His hands burned and tore as he shifted his weight, hauling himself up with one hand, judging the next movement, before finding another secure hold with the other. He tried to steady his breathing. Taking a snatched glance downwards, he realised he was alone. Erin, for all his size and strength was still labouring below him, unable to gain any momentum in his ascent. Reef realised that this part of the rescue was down to him. With each breath, a lunge and a hold. And again. Sinews and ligaments threatened to pop as he dragged himself upwards.

Reef was making good progress, Alan was not sure how he would fare, let alone Potty, who was clinging to his board, threatening to go under with every wave.

Suds gave Alan the thumbs up, but he was desperate to hold Potty, as the older heavier man slid across his board. Potty was not going to last long. Suds lunged to reach him and in doing so, had to abandon his own board.

Alan strained back to peer upwards. Reef had reached the top. Not so Erin, who appeared to have stalled. Alan turned his attention back to help Suds. Potty clutched at them both.

"Alan! Alan!" he turned to see a rope above him. Reef had reached the deck and had thrown over the rope, tied in a sling. Another followed.

"Potts, Potty, grab the rope, the rope!" Alan cried to the older man. "We have to stay with him," he shouted across to Suds.

Climbing Reef's bowline, oily, wet and rough, was not easy, but better than trying to follow him up the huge metal links. Going up the swinging anchor ropes like ninja, they struggled aboard with difficulty, dragging the breathless retching Potty aboard. The muscle-burning, agonising, reverse abseil had taken its toll.

On deck, Suds hauled off his hood and raced to the wheelhouse. Potty was being helped by Reef, the older man coughing up water and half his guts. Alan lifted Potty up as he tried to clear his head and guided the drenched Driver towards the engine room. Potty was cursing, a breathless foul-mouthed monologue aimed at Alan, Suds and the whole fucking world.

In the wheelhouse, Suds swung the wheel around. He threw the switch, but the engine would not start. It remained still. Dead.

"Fuck!" his fist hit the wheel.

Suds peered through the wheelhouse glass; Reef was at the bow pointing to the rocks and shouting to Alan, who was urging Potty to fix the engine.

Stepping into the engine room, Potty looked unsteady. His face almost colourless. His hands were shaking. He realised his entire body was doing the same, his frame juddering. It was the cold, he told himself. Just the fucking cold, and that was not going to beat him. He hefted a heavy black spanner and started turning a gasket. Not to fix the Old Girl but to give his hands and his brain something to do. *Focus, for fucksake!*

"Come on, old girl," he spoke softly to her, struggling to summon any voice. His throat burnt raw from saltwater and swearing.

The *Sans Peur* was drifting towards the brutal, spiked rocks that hungered to impale her.

Alan stuck his head inside the hatch.

"Come on Potts, for ony sake, min," he urged the engineer.

"I need time. Tell Suds," the craggy, soaked Driver growled in reply.

Alan dashed back to reach Suds. They could see Reef dancing in panic at the bow.

"Suds," Alan was at a loss, but not his brother.

"Leave it to me!" Suds cried excitedly.

With that, Suds swung the wheel round.

"Get oot there, call the swell," commanded Suds.

Alan looked at his brother, a new man.

"Aye, aye, Skipper," Alan was gone.

Dancing at the prow, Reef was pointing to the harsh cliff face and brutal, broken-faced rocks, Alan was passing on the signal to Suds in the wheelhouse.

At the helm, Suds nodded and worked the boat over the waves.

Sweat streamed down Potty's face. He was disconnecting a nut. He wiped his face and turned the switch. The engine kicked then died.

In frustration, Potty slammed the engine with the wrench. More coarse swearing formed a kind of ritualistic chant like the weaving of an ancient spell.

In the wheelhouse, Suds's face was tense, twisted into a grimace of concentration, responding to Alan's signals from half way along the deck.

"Come on, girl."

Reef, hanging on for dear life, was gazing at the looming rocks.

"Come on, mak' her dance, Potts."

Erin, great surfer that he was, had discovered that he had no sea legs and was clinging to the wheelhouse door. His head swam and his stomach bounced and lurched as the *Sans Peur* began to surf the waves, suddenly and dramatically turning first one direction, then another.

Suds was furiously spinning the wheel. He looked up at Alan, signalling from the deck, and grabbed the spinning wheel, using all his strength to stop the spin, correct it and send it spinning again. Despite the strain and the danger, Suds felt alive, his muscles afire as he wrestled the wheel, his hands welded to it.

Potty made another adjustment and flicked the switch. The engine kicked again, came alive for an instant, shuddered and died.

"No!"

Potty hammered the engine with his wrench in frustration. The engine levelled, rallied and gathered momentum.

"Yes! Ma beautiful girl."

The sound of the engine dying had almost broken Suds's resolve, then, it kicked in again. Suds spun the wheel once more, a grin breaking out on his face.

"Sans Peur! No Fear!" he hollered.

On deck, he could see Alan and Reef dancing in celebration. A wild fisherman's jig.

An exhausted Erin sensed rather than saw the *Sans Peur* move slowly, precariously, away from the threatening rocks. The motion had forced him to his knees. He clenched his fist in triumph, but for the first time in his life the sea had sapped his strength to rise. His body was washed in a sweat he now recognised as fear.

Alan and Suds clasped hands and Reef was patting Potty on the back.

Sometime later, Reef and Suds watched from the wheelhouse as Alan and Erin, further along the deck, shook hands. An envelope was exchanged. Suds frowned, but Reef, none the wiser, scratched his shaven scalp. He was missing his hat. Naked without it.

Standing on the deck of the *Sans Peur*, Alan and Suds looked back at the shore where Erin was loading his Kombi with the boards and surf gear that had survived the rescue.

"Arlene will be hame by now," observed Suds.

Alan glanced back at the Irish shore. Unbidden, Abina's song rose up again in his mind, spilling through his thoughts, in rebuke.

Suds was still at the wheel when Alan stepped into the wheelhouse with a steaming mug. Suds accepted it gratefully.

"Have you given a thought to it," asked Suds.

Alan shook his head. He didn't want to.

"Peter, Yvonne, Mam," Suds pressed on, his own anxiety harrying him.

"Let's see what they have to say first, Suds," reasoned his brother. In truth, Alan's thoughts were fogged. They had saved the *Sans Peur* from the rocks, but there was still Peter to face.

Suds pointed to the heavily marked calendar showing surfers in Hawaii.

"Your Birthday next week, mind," Suds reminded him.

Alan just nodded absently. His lack of reaction worried Suds. It was as if his brother had lost something. *Perhaps himself.*

The wind had dropped at the Scottish Parliament where Hendoo and Watt were watching a couple of young skateboarders weave past them, undeterred by the light passing soft spits of gathering rain.

"It's them!" Watt pointed to sea, forcing Hendoo to look up from rolling his tobacco.

"Aye. So much for McGhee's insurance claim," Hendoo nodded with satisfaction, twisting Peter's surname as though it were a blight on his tongue.

The *Sans Peur* was making headway towards the harbour entrance.

The news travelled fast, so that Bella and Arlene were waiting at the quayside as the *Sans Peur* drew alongside the basin pier. Bella and Arlene could see no life aboard the vessel as it swung to the quayside. It was not clear who was piloting her. From nowhere, Reef launched himself onto land and within minutes the *Sans Peur* was securely tied up.

The crew trooped off and Bella hugged them all, even Potty, who was both embarrassed and faintly pleased. Arlene wrapped her arms around Suds.

"Mam, we're getting married," Suds held on to his mother, as she hugged him again.

Bella was ready to cry as she began hugging everyone again. However, Alan's attention was fixed over her shoulder and the others followed his pensive gaze.

They all watched Peter's black Mercedes draw up. He yanked the handbrake on and climbed out.

Bella turned to face him.

"Peter McGhee."

"Isobel Sutherland."

Peter eyeballed Alan with contempt.

"Seen yer wife, yer pregnant wife, lately? My daughter is three months pregnant and he abandoned her to chase some Irish tart," Peter stabbed his finger into Alan's chest.

Alan's eyes were on his mother, on her horrified face. Her

reaction was Peter's intention. Alan faced Peter for a moment, then glanced back at the *Sans Peur*. Without speaking, he walked away, leaving the field to Peter, but he was not finished.

Peter let him go. *Run away, you spineless shite*.

His attention fixed on Bella. Fixed on hurting her.

Twice she had rejected him. She'd chosen his best friend over him, then clung to him in desperation when Graham had been lost, only to turn away from him as he demanded more.

"Better hope he is good at grovellin', hell, we ken he is, otherwise you'll never see MY grandchild," Peter's threat was a roar, right into Bella's stark, pained face.

Alan stood outside his front door. It was his home, but there was no homecoming welcome. He hadn't expected any. He took his boots off inside the front door, then, stood in the hallway, but there was no sign of Yvonne. At his first step on the stairs, he sensed movement upstairs. Christ, he wasn't looking forward to facing her.

Alan quietly pushed the bedroom door open. That was when he got his homecoming. A man was on top of his wife.

"Give it to me. Harder. Yes."

Her voice was cut off by a rough kiss.

Yvonne's glazed eyes opened in ecstasy. She stared at Alan not seeing him at first. Then his presence reached her consciousness and her situation. She froze. Body rigid. Her sudden reaction instantly registered with the man entangled with her. Their impetus dissolved, he stared down at Yvonne, straining to follow her horrified stare. Alan's looming frame filled his vision and he started to sit up in alarm.

Alan stepped forward and hauled the naked, already scrambling, man off the bed by his hair. In one fluid movement, almost in slow motion, he swung him round and planted his fist on Chad's jaw.

The power of the punch sent the American falling back into the en-suite. He peered up at Alan, but remained slumped on the tiles, with his mouth and nose bloodied. Thick drops onto the ivory marbled floor.

Alan's eyes burned down at him. Slowly, with a growing coldness, he turned to Yvonne, who was pulling at the sheets to cover her spoilt modesty in front of her husband.

"That rough enough for ye," asked Alan dangerously, already moving from her.

Alan walked away from the house; tucked under his arm was the model of the *Sans Peur*.

She could keep the rest.

Alan stopped in the harbour to examine the sad wreckage of the decommissioned 'HOPE' lying on its torn belly. Gutted. He cradled the model of the *Sans Peur* more closely and walked on, bending into the harsh Norhaven wind, his heart pumping, but his mind finding an icy clarity.

He didn't get a warm reception when he stepped into his mother's normally cosy kitchen either, where Bella was sitting with Suds and Arlene. Her joy at their news, which she had secretly hoped for was tarnished by her other son's disgrace. Alan, she realised, was the spik of the toon. She found herself wishing Alan and Yvonne had never wed, even though she'd pressed for it, but she shook the thought away. *Be careful what you wish for.*

Bella challenged Alan even as he appeared at the door.

"Haven't ye done enough?" her voice was tired, as though further disaster was imminent.

Alan did not reply, instead, he gently laid the *Sans Peur* model on the table in front of her. His manner was purposeful, edged, coiled. Next, Alan reached up and removed the calendar from its hook on the wall. He laid it on the table, too.

"Clear enough for ye, Mam?" that quiet voice again. It reminded her of his father, her Graham. A man to be reckoned with. A man of will and substance.

Through her anger and confusion, Bella tried to fathom the heavy mass of blue 'awa' days her son had dropped in front of her. Nothing was clear to her. Alan came to her aid, gently marked two dark red stars at the weekend before the last 'Ireland' trip 'away'.

Bella looked at the two marks, then up at Alan.

"Twa?" this was still not making sense to Bella.

"Twice, a week ago, the Norhaven Open weekend," Alan confirmed, as he made another red mark on New Years' Eve, "since then."

Bella looked at the chart again, focussing on today's date October 28.

"Oh, Alan," as the penny dropped, and the proof of nature hit home.

Peter was standing beneath his new boat with Harbourmaster Salt. He turned to find Alan and the crew with Arlene and Bella ranged around him. Peter recovered from his shock, the sight of Sutherland reigniting his anger.

"What the hell? Come to see ma new boat?" he scoffed, "the *Sans Peur*'s replacement." Twisting the knife.

Alan stepped before him, his voice low, but clear.

"I declare Salvage, the ancient right to claim an unmanned vessel at sea," he said.

Peter was bewildered.

"The *Sans Peur* was adrift in Irish Waters. The owner had reported her missing and she was salvaged by Alan and Graham Sutherland, witnessed by Erin O'Callaghan," said Alan handing over an envelope to the Harbourmaster, "Here's Mr O'Callaghan's statement and the papers from the Harbourmaster at Killybegs. They've been lodged."

Peter started to laugh. *This was ridiculous.* But his mirth was cut short as Salt tore open the envelope and rapidly scanned the letters.

"Better get yourself a lawyer, Peter."

Peter and Alan stood just feet apart, close enough to touch each other. To smell each other.

"You work for me," Peter reminded Alan. His voice a poisonous hiss.

"You sacked us," accused Suds.

"Some men have dreams, others realise them," Alan told Peter.

Alan nodded at Bella.

"It's not ma child, Peter," said Alan, as Bella thrust the calendar chart at Peter. She was ready to punch him with it.

As he read it, Peter seemed to shrink, his mind spinning, whirling and shaking, as he tried to simultaneously grasp and reject the truth in Alan's words and Bella's evidence.

At the rear of Bella's house, overlooking the oncoming waves, Alan and Suds were sitting amid the washing hung out metres from the sea. Just as they had done as kids.

Alan was winding things up.

"She can keep the house. The *Sans Peur* is yours, Graham, and the licence," Alan laid a hand on his brother's shoulder as he rose.

"Alan," Suds stammered.

"I'm awa' to find her an' the boy." This said gently. Alan was settled on it.

Suds was left sitting on the back step, staring out to sea, trying to fathom his own course, as his brother moved purposefully along the shore. Ducking beneath the flapping garments on the taut washing lines, he was gone.

In the stretched diagonal shadows of the slipway, Peter was peering up at the new boat, lost in a maze of confused bitter thoughts. The breeze from the sea caught his charcoal coat, his fists buried in its pockets. Standing against the wind, he no longer seemed to fill the expensive jacket which he had pulled around him, its collar, with velvet trim turned up against an unshaven jawline. His burgundy scarf was absent. He couldn't remember where he'd put it.

The Harbourmaster and the Minister approached him cautiously and, respectfully, halted a few feet behind him. The Minister followed Peter's gaze to the glistening new boat. His voice was gentle. The weighted tone he reserved for the bereaved and the bereft.

"She's gone. So is the *Sans Peur*. The partners have agreed. It's time for you to think of your family, Peter, your daughter and your grandchild."

They left Peter staring up at the new boat, with 'Charity' newly painted on her bow.

Peter turned beneath the 'Charity' as a fishing vessel moved past the quayside. It was the *Sans Peur*.

Suds was at the wheelhouse waving to Arlene and Bella. Behind him were pictures of the crew in Ireland: Potty dancing; Suds and Arlene on the beach; Reef sitting cross-legged atop a stout bold green Irish postbox.

Potty was in the engine room with a surfboard behind him 'I'm nae mad, I'm Potty' written on it in Celtic script.

A creeping, wheezing bus, with a dated Eire number plate, shuddered and lurched to a halt. It had juddered down the winding road and was relieved to find itself on a low straight stretch of road which ran closer to the sea. The engine idled, gasping, before it groaned and moved off, leaving Alan, his holdall, and surfboard, by the roadside. In his hand was a piece of folded paper. Alan put the holdall down and, leaning against the board, opened up the creased, stained sheet of discoloured worn paper. It was the tattered Celtic Surf Flyer. He turned it over in his hands. On the back, was the schedule of a dilapidated old garage and out buildings.

A map of sorts. It had got him this far.

EPILOGUE

On the high south wall of Norhaven Harbour, a man in an oily overall was painting the hull of a small old wooden boat, a wee yawl, but he paused to watch the *Sans Peur* as it was leaving port. The trawler had been repainted, perfect pillar-box red, where once the hull had been a battered sorry blue.

Suds acknowledged Peter from the wheelhouse and, to his credit, the older man slowly raised his paint brush in return. The distant chords of Dougie Maclean's '*Caledonia*' cushioned the wheelhouse, adding to its warmth for Suds.

As the vessel manoeuvred, Suds turned to find Arlene waving warmly from the opposite quay. Suds smiled at the pictures and postcards that were clustered on a section of wood panelling in the wheelhouse: Alan, Suds, Potty and Reef raising pints of Guinness, eyes shining in the moment. The pictures were all from their time in Ireland. To Suds's mind, it was The Trip. The turning point in all their lives.

The Skipper ran his hands over his face, gathered himself, and turned the wheel to take the boat out on another trip.

The *Sans Peur* left the port and steamed north-east, heading out to sea.

Yvonne, in heels, determinedly pushing a pram, was caught in the rain. Her hair already plastered to her face. It was a long walk home, but a Volkswagen Beetle with terrible paintwork pulled up.

"Want a lift, Ma'am?" said Chad, through the open window, a note of uncertainty in his voice above the engine's low growl.

Yvonne lifted a strand of wet hair from her face and considered the American and his offer. He wasn't Alan, and, for that, she was grateful.

The car drove off with the '5' in C5AD still painted out.

He had kept it that way.

Reef was carefully painting his motif on to a surfboard. His t-shirt carried the same distinctive shaded design. Reef studied his work, checking the line. He reached across to take a draw, smoke spiralling. Reef watched it rise, almost as if comparing its path, its beauty, with his artwork. There was a composure to him, an artist without a hat.

The old garage and outbuildings featured in the schedule had been newly painted. The matt sheen was a marine tone against the stone and wooden construction.

Although the workshop was unmanned, its double doors were thrown open in welcome, wide enough to take a tractor or small bus. Sitting in the shadow was the face of a vintage Kombi, light falling across a corner of its dusty powder blue face.

The sign above the double wooden doors read 'SANS PEUR', solid white on the marine paintwork. In smaller font beneath was 'Surf Board Makers', with Reef's intricate scrimshaw-style monogram incorporated in blue and sea-green hues, with yellow and black shades for emphasis. A Longboard was propped up beside the double doors, swirling mermaids, kelpies and dolphins playing in waves across its surface.

Its owner was walking down towards the beach in the rich morning sun. Deep gold light caught the same motif on his wetsuit, dead centre like Iron Man's heart. The workshop receded behind him, while Jake skipped through the channel in the dunes ahead of him to catch up with Abina.

She paused, to look back at Alan, her heavy hair tied back, her smile wide and warming. The sound of surf and the cry of gulls became background to him. Her music was calling him. Abina's song.

THE BEAUTIFUL GAME

The pale, orange-washed, morning light had the taste of rain in it. Its crisp, low amber glow made the small, harled house sparkle, as though the modest, semi-detached box shared the optimism of the new day. The front door swung open and Dougie, slightly built for ten, stepped out, in grey trousers and a blue school sweatshirt. A boy in a hurry. Or running late. No jacket for him. None of the boys wore one. And he was determined to be one of the boys. His school bag, a branded rucksack, was slung over his shoulder, a football tucked protectively under his arm. He pulled the bag on more firmly, gripped the ball tightly and took off down the road. Slightly built, he was made for distance.

A cluster of schoolchildren were buzzing around a football, in the shadow of a wide school building, surrounded by a moat of tarmac. Grass was a stranger to the squat drab functionality of the early 1900s build. James had the ball at his feet when the bell went. He turned his foot over the ball, drew it back. Deft control. A fresh-faced boy, the best at keepie-uppies in the school. The best at almost everything. Every mother's dream.

As Dougie rushed to claim his ball from James, the bigger boy changed position and held off Dougie with ease. Next to James' sturdy, well-proportioned frame, Dougie's slightness became obvious. As Dougie struggled to regain his ball, James looked across at Robert and smiled, confident in his ability. Robert, a be-freckled enforcer, grinned back. He was one of life's natural seconds. James' lieutenant.

James feinted one way, then back-heeled the ball and strode the other way towards the low building. A captain leading his squad towards the blue double doors and the school day. James and Robert exchanged satisfied nods, leaving Dougie to scamper after his ball as it ran slowly in the opposite direction towards the school gates.

The same group of boys were tugging off their bags, jackets being thrown roughly on to pegs. Dougie had learned though; he now had the ball between his feet to stop anyone kicking it. *My ball.*

He pulled his bag strap over his head and hooked it onto a peg. The label above the peg read 'Douglas Wilson'. It might as well had 'wee Dougie' written on it in Miss Simpson's curling open script. He was 'wee Dougie' to all, even though his father's name was Alex. Dougie was defined by the prefix. He had been since he'd been wrapped in a blanket.

His class were lining up to go into the classroom, sliding and jostling on the heavily polished wooden floor. Dougie was in the line, somewhere in the middle, trying to hold his ground as he was being pushed by James, who barged Dougie again before casting a swift worried eye towards the classroom door. Safety, no teacher in sight. James gave Dougie a victor's smile. Untouchable and guileless. Dougie struggled to think of a time when James had been caught out. Primary Five. That was it. James and Kenny Parkin had broken into the Caretaker's Shed. Both of them had been hauled to the Head

Teacher's Office for the high jump, until, that is, James' Dad had arrived in his uniform. Kenny took the fall. Glancing again at his tormentor, Dougie felt a surge of helplessness and frustration. He couldn't separate James from his ever-present smirk.

The rest of Dougie's primary 7 class trooped in, watched by their young teacher, Miss Simpson. She smiled at Dougie as he passed her and took his seat. She had a soft spot for Wee Dougie, admired his nervous enthusiasm. His Mum was a nice woman; another with too much on her plate.

Robert and James were seated across from him on another table.

"Good Morning, everyone." Miss Simpson ran the school choir and her voice had an uplifting quality; Dougie liked it. She wore bright colours, too.

The class all mouthed 'Good Morning, Miss Simpson' back to her, although with mixed enthusiasm. Dougie sang it out. The school day began.

The class were shuffling at their desks, while Miss Simpson read the register. Hands went up and down; a disjointed, solo Mexican wave. Dougie was day-dreaming – his singular talent – and needed prompting to put his hand up. A heavy elbow from Sonja Cooper supplied the reminder. Beneath the desk, his feet were resting on his football. Possession was nine-tenths of the game. *My ball.*

Miss Simpson was talking, going over their tasks. Dougie was still day-dreaming. He was looking out at the tarmac pitch, greasy black from the night's steady, slanted rain.

The goalmouth was empty. Warm optimistic morning sunshine glinted off the posts, picking out the rusting, blistered paintwork. A goalframe that had never seen any netting. Or, if it had, Dougie had never seen it.

For Dougie, the goals were a symbol of hope. He could hear the commentator as the cross came in, "angled to the far post and Wilson rises to thunder his header past the outstretched arms of the visiting keeper. It's a goal and a hat-trick for Wilson!"

Dougie came back slowly and reluctantly from his triumph. He was aware of slowly lowering his half-raised arms. He was relieved to see that faces were expectantly turned upward to Miss Simpson and so his moment of imaginary glory had gone unwitnessed. Miss Simpson was writing 'Team versus Weir Street' on the blackboard. Her melodious commentary reached him.

"… and tomorrow, the school team will play Weir Street…"

James was hanging on every word. This was his curriculum.

"The following players must be at the school gate by 12noon."

Dougie's gaze came back into focus. This was the part he dreaded, a weekly ritual in failure and omission.

"James Robertson," Miss Simpson's voice sang out the names.

James clenched his fist and looked even more triumphant. Top marks for Robertson. First on the team sheet. The Sergeant's son. He got up from his seat and stepped up to take the football jersey, white with gold trim, from Miss Simpson. It was a well-worn path for him. He took it in easy steps.

Dougie allowed himself the briefest moment to imagine collecting a team jersey.

The feel of it in his hands. Telling his Dad. A man who had once had a trial with Greenock Morton. His Dad's glow of pride. Dougie tried to imagine the warmth of that glow. It was a ghost. A still-born dream.

Miss Simpson's recital and reality called him back.

"Robert Smith, George Findlay, Gregor Pirie," a litany of the talented and the blessed.

Robert, seated the other side of Dougie, nodded to himself as he too rose to claim his shirt,

"and Dougie Wilson."

It was as if Miss Simpson had hit a wrong note in her song. The entire class seemed to take a deep breath. A collective gulp of disbelief.

Dougie was in shock. So, too, were James and Robert. They were both staring at him. As reality seeped through the football at his feet, Dougie sensed his whole body beginning to tingle. He felt as if he has been picked for Scotland. He looked again out at the empty sun-kissed goal posts, then looked back at his teacher. She was writing on the blackboard:

1. James Robertson
2. Robert Smith
3. George Findlay
4. Gregor Pirie
5. Dougie Wilson

Dougie's face was shining as he mouthed his name, reading it from the board. Miss Simpson turned and smiled at him. Dougie needed another prod from Sonja to rise. His gaze was fixed on the shirt. He almost lost his footing, snubbing his toe on a chair leg.

"Well done, Dougie." Miss Simpson's voice enveloped him.

He clutched the shirt to him, vaguely sensing the hostility

as James and Robert shared a hard indignant look. The laws of football and nature had just been broken. Natural selection corrupted.

Low Friday afternoon sunlight stretched across the desks into the classroom. It was time for Art and Crafts and Dougie was painting, pausing every few strokes to clean his brush in a jam jar of murky water, the result of too many colours. His creation was an ambitious blur.

He sat back and looked across at the blackboard: No. 5. Dougie Wilson.

Under his poised brush was a picture of a football goal on a lush green pitch with a penalty being taken by a footballer with a bold Number Five on his back.

"Right. Start clearing up, please. Everything away." The teacher's words marked the approach of the end of the school day. The bell would go any minute.

Eager to share his elevation to the school team with his Mum, but most of all, with his Dad, Dougie stood and turned, holding up the cloudy jar. Bad timing, for as he moved his chair back, his football rolled out, a gentle mischievous rebound. James was holding up his school football shirt, showing it off to the rest of his table. Another weekly ritual.

Dougie turned around, his foot landing on the rolling ball. Dougie pitched and went down as if felled in the box. He lurched sideways, the dark, murky liquid spraying James and his football jersey as Dougie hit the floor.

Dougie looked up, his expression of horror mirrored James' own. Everyone could see that the shirt was ruined. Dougie struggled up to be met by James, with Robert at his shoulder, ready to meter out his Captain's justice.

Miss Simpson examined the jersey, speaking first to James,

"It'll wash out in time for tomorrow, James," then turning a darker eye to Dougie.

"And, you better take your ball home with you, and do not bring it back."

Dougie was shaking with shame; anger had displaced dismay for James. In a guilty daze, Dougie reached down to his chair, offering up his shirt to James, who nodded abruptly. Honour satisfied. For now.

"You can't say fairer than that, James," Miss Simpson said, as the shirts were exchanged. Dougie clutched the wet, stained shirt to his chest as though he might forfeit it and his place in the team.

At the gates, chatting parents were waiting for their offspring as the school emptied. The rain had stopped, although the tarmac still glistened. Dougie rocketed out of the school building, still tugging on his bag. His ball tucked under his arm, he resembled a pocket-sized rugby player as he veered left and right, around other dawdling pupils before he disappeared through the school gates. He had to tell him Mum about being in the team. He also needed to get away from James and Robert. Quick.

He ran all the way. Dougie dashed around the last corner, his home in sight, and charged into his house.

Dougie burst in, dropping his ball and throwing off his bag. Both bounced on the hallway floor.

Dougie's mum, Debbie, was in their small kitchen feeding a young baby, Alistair. She turned as Dougie rushed in, short of breath.

"Mam. Mam. I'm in the team. I'm in. Tomorrow. We're playing Weir Street. I'm playing, Mam. I'm in." Dougie's words were a rush. Delivered without a breath.

Alistair burped, cutting short Dougie's gush. Debbie wiped her younger son's mouth.

"Come on, just a little more."

"Mam. I'm in. In the team," Dougie tried again.

"I know. That's a good boy," but Debbie was speaking to Alistair, as she dabbed the infant's mucky mouth.

This was not the reaction Dougie had expected. Not the one he felt his news, his new status, merited. Dougie pressed on.

"But I need boots. Proper boots. Else I can't play. I need boots."

Debbie frowned slightly.

Dougie pressed on.

"I do. Else I can't play." The sentence tailed off.

Debbie picked up Alistair. At least, now her attention was divided. It wasn't that Dougie's announcement had half her attention, but he had some of it.

"Don't fret. Your Dad'll be hame soon," but her words failed to sooth her oldest boy and Wee Dougie remained agitated.

Dougie, Debbie and Dougie's Dad, Alex, were sitting with trays on their laps, the TV addressing them from the corner of the room. Alex was speaking between mouthfuls.

"I'll take him down to Dalgarno's the morn, the back of nine. He'll hae some boots. And shinpads an' all maybe."

"Alex, does he really need…" but, even as she spoke, Debbie knew she had already lost the argument. *Men and football.*

"Dalgarno's will have some," Alex finished his point with another forkful. His boy was in the team. This might be the start of something. Maybe his eldest was a late developer. You got those. Although, Alex already had a strange feeling that Alistair would prove the footballer. Sometimes you could sense these things. It didn't matter. Wee Dougie was in the team and he was going to back his son to the hilt.

Dougie followed the conversation over his chips, his eyes darting between his parents as if watching a tennis rally, as his fingers tightened on his utensils.

The day was a chill slate. Dougie and his Dad were standing at the window of Dalgarno's, the town's long-standing general store. Sunlight blanking out the entire window. Dougie's eyes were on his father as Alex flicked his cigarette, stamped it out and moved towards the door. In Dougie's eye, his dad's movements blended into the grace of doing keepie-uppie's, the cigarette had become the football and his Dad was the star player. Left Fullback, that was his position. Dougie remembered his Dad telling his Uncle Steve one Christmas.

Dougie was hurrying to keep up with his Dad, a shoe box in his arms. Excitement in his steps and his chest. He could still feel the squeeze of his Dad's hand on his shoulder as he stepped forward to try on the boots.

Dougie was sitting in front of the fireplace and reverently opened the shoebox. He slowly drew aside the delicate tissue paper. The boots were new. Black with blue stripes, shiny plastic.

Debbie looked in from the doorway, but her son was oblivious. He was entranced. Real boots. His boots.

"Dougie! Come here, son," Alex voice echoed from outside.

"Dougie, Dougie. Your Dad's calling you," Debbie gave her son a nudge.

Dougie came out of his reverie and jumped up.

Alex was squatting, carefully laying out newspapers. Dougie, against the doorway, watched him intently.

"Where are you playing, son?"

"Weir Street."

Alex laughed.

"No. What position?"

Dougie shrugged.

"It disnae matter. Even if they stick you in goal you'll need these."

Dalgarno's hadn't had any shinpads. Auld Dalgarno had shrugged when asked. Since the shop had been out of stock, Alex found himself revisiting his own childhood. A private pilgrimage. It gave him a warmth to be passing this impoverished gift to his son. His son the footballer. Alex's Dad would have savoured this passage.

Alex had formed inch-thick piles of newspaper. He cut out a thick oval shape. He put his cigarette down, resting the smoking stub on the stone step. Reaching for the tape, Alex bit off stripes with his teeth. Dougie watched mystified. Alex continued with his labour, breaking off to take a breath of nicotine.

"That's aboot it," as he studied his handiwork. Satisfied, he held them out to Dougie.

"Now you'll be able to tackle anyone."

Dougie reached out to take the two oval saucers of newsprint and tape; his first shinpads. Made in Norhaven. Made for him by his Dad.

Just before 12 noon, Dougie and Alex walked through the school gates. Other members of the team and their parents were gathered around the school minibus. Miss Simpson was at the wheel talking through the open window.

Robert and James watched Dougie approach. Alex nodded to one of the other parents, but he was not fully at ease. Neither was his son. Dougie glanced across at James and Robert. They glared back.

An athletic male teacher in starched whites pointed down the corridor as Dougie's team trooped in to the Weir Street PE department, lugging their bags.

"Visitors on the right." His voice gruff and unwelcoming. This was the opposition. He didn't want them to feel comfortable.

The boys trudged down the corridor with Dougie bringing up the rear. As he approached it, the door closed in his face forcing him to look up at the small plaque on the door – 'Girls'. He pushed the door open to find his team were already getting changed.

Dougie was completely ignored until he took out his boots. Robert stopped lacing his own sleek leather boots to stare at them. James put his hand out, demanding the Dougie boot. Dougie meekly handed one over and James, taking his time, studied it in exaggerated fashion. James turned the boot over, inspecting the clean moulded studs. He handed it back. Dougie took the boot, considering its weight in his hands, realising that somehow, he has failed the first test.

Dougie pulled on his shirt. The ugly dark stain was still clearly visible. Last night, in his excitement, he had forgotten to ask his mum to wash it. The team, all four of them, stared

161

at him in his discoloured shirt. Robert looked to James, who had clearly not forgotten, nor forgiven Dougie. The shirt had become Dougie's badge of failure. Its soiled dampness clung cold to his skin.

The team, except Dougie, trooped out. He waited until the door closed behind his teammates. He reached into his bag and pulled out the shinpads. He was learning. He hesitated. His resolve strengthened. *This is my chance.* He rolled down his socks and carefully put the shinpads in place. They felt strange and itched, but his Dad had made them.

At the side of a bleak dipping field, in the grey light spitting drizzle, a bewildered Dougie was standing uncertainly. Alex sensed his son's nervousness and ruffled his hair.

"Don't hold back, son. Man and ball," he coached encouragement," make it yours."

Dougie nodded, but his eyes were on the goals with netting sharply pegged back. He'd never played on a pitch with actual netting before. The playing field sloped away, running down to the far corner.

It had rained overnight. Alex dug his heel into the turf. It was sodden.

"You've got pace, son, but everyone will be slower today. A boggy pitch is a great leveller."

He'd heard his Dad say that before, watching matches on TV, except he didn't know what his dad was speaking about. He was the slowest in the team. By miles.

He felt the turf give and squelch as he followed his dad across the park. He was already cold and wet and he was going to get filthy on this pitch.

Dougie trotted on to the pitch. James pointed towards Robert in the goal. Dougie looked across at his Dad. Alex looked proud, his collar turned up against the increasing rain, as he pulled out a cigarette.

"Make it yours, son."

The whistle went. The teacher in white from Weir Street was the match Referee. The Weir Street players were in blue; Dougie could see them encouraging each other. He was in the school team but he was alone.

Then the game reached him. Dougie looked unsure as the ball bounced near him.

"Get in there!" Alex's voice barked across the pitch, 'Make it yours!"

Spurred on, Dougie stepped forward and punted the ball out of play.

For Dougie, the match was a blur. A confusion of angry shouts, lost footing and missed tackles.

A hefty Weir Street player, their striker, burst through, brushing off Dougie and pumped the ball into the net. Dougie's flank and arm were coated in mud; cold and clinging. He watched as Robert, in goal, picked the ball out of the netting and scowled at him. 1-0.

The parents were balling at the teams. Dougie could pick out Robert's mother, Mrs Smith, her shrill voice challenging every whistle. Alex thrust his cigarette away and turned up his collar further, as though prowling the dugout.

They were only a goal down. Dougie was determined that would be Weir Street's only goal with 'Make it Yours!' spurring him on, Dougie ran across to make a tackle, but he slipped, his feet spraying from under him. He regained his feet to see Robert picking the ball out of the net. 2-0.

By now the paint stain on Dougie's jersey had been completely replaced by mud.

The Referee blew his whistle and pointed the other way, towards the centre spot.

Dougie was trying to keep pace with a Weir Street player, a sparely built, zippy winger. Dougie matched him for size, but not for speed. While in his mind he made the crucial tackle to clear the danger at just the right moment, perfectly timed, the striker eluded him. Alex was beside himself. He was screaming from the side-lines. "Get in there!"

Robert picked the ball out of the net. The teacher blew his whistle again and turned back to the centre spot. 3-0.

From the restart, Weir Street poured forward. Skill, territory, possession, they had it all.

Alex threw up his hands and Miss Simpson cast him a dark glance. If he used more words like that, she would have to speak to him. Not that he was the only one, as Mrs Smith waved her fist at the Referee and loudly questioned how he came into the world.

Robert lined up a goal kick, but the ball barely cleared the 18-yard box. Glued in the dubs. Dougie and the Weir Street striker raced in. *My ball.* Dougie gritted his teeth and lunged. *My ball.*

In near slow-motion, Dougie drew on his reserves and beat his opponent to the ball. At full stretch, he won the race, only in his haste, his foot went from under him and he pumped the ball straight at the goal. Robert tried frantically to stop it, but the ball crashed into the back of the net. It was a peach. 4-0.

Alex put his head in his hands. Other parents were starting to look at him. Miss Simpson put her hand to her mouth. *Oh, Dougie!*

Wee Dougie Wilson had been her selection.

Robert glared at Dougie. He hated him now. Behind Dougie, James was gesturing at him in disgust and despair.

Alex strode back and forth along the touchline. He was no longer with the other parents. Like his son, he was not part of the team.

A corner for Weir Street. All Dougie's team were back defending. They had to be. Robert was shouting something at him, but Dougie was too dazed to take it in.

The ball came over. Pumped high. Robert was still shouting. Dougie could not hear him. He could spy his Dad on the far side. He was shouting too. Everyone was shouting. The world was shouting.

Dougie focused on the ball; only on the ball. *My ball.* Robert jumped. Dougie leaped. Dougie soared. His header was perfect.

THWACK!

A clean contact. A beauty and Robert was beaten. The ball crossed the line. Dougie landed. He began to raise his arms in triumph, a dreamlike smile on his face. It dissolved as he saw his Dad. Alex's arms fell to his side and so, too, did Dougie's.

Dougie turned to see Robert. The goalie wanted to kill him now. Dougie stood forlornly. 5-0.

Alex ran both hands through his hair in exasperation.

In the minibus, no one spoke. The final score killing any conversation. Four members of the team were sitting on the back seat. Parents occupied the rest. They were all going for a carry out, a post-match ritual. Dougie, Alex and Miss Simpson, who was driving, were crammed in the front seats. Alex stared fixedly ahead. Miss Simpson glanced nervously across at the father and son. She noted the distance between them. Dougie, sandwiched, looked from one adult to the other, but there was no response. Rather than contemplate his failure, Dougie looked out of the window.

Alex and Dougie turned into their narrow garden. Alex was walking ahead. He had done all the way from the school. Setting the pace and the mood. His collar up, he discarded his tab. Dougie, his bag weighing him down, struggled along behind him, side-stepping the flicked missile.

Debbie looked up from her magazine, as Alex stalked in.

"You're back," but there was no answer from either her husband or her son.

Dougie was sitting on the back step. He was unlacing his mud-caked boots. His fingers were numb white with the cold and the laces waterlogged. The back door to the kitchen was open.

"How'd you get on?"

Alex unzipped his jacket.

"It's just boiled."

Dougie pulled off a boot weighed with mud, their voices coming to him, like a post-match radio commentary. A lament.

Alex opened the biscuit tin.

"Murdered. Eleven nil.

Dougie's second boot came off. Mud heavy.

"But your son scored. Twice. Aye, beauties."

Dougie stopped picking at the mud on his boots and peeled back his sodden socks.

Debbie's magazine rustled as she put it down to take in what her husband was saying.

"Oh, well, at least he scored."

Somewhere upstairs in the house, baby Alistair started crying.

Dougie's shinpads came apart in his hands. His fingers were covered in papier-mache. Pieces fell to the concrete floor, crumbling in sodden, discoloured clumps.

Friday morning a week later, the Primary 7S were working. All but Dougie, he was looking outside through the greasy rain-washed glass. He had dreaded Monday, but like every other day of the week, he had been ignored. In a way, the reaction of his team had been a relief. A confirmation of his failure. Not just on the pitch, but his inability to be one of them at any time.

The goalmouth was empty, gallows with a large dark puddle in front of the sticks; a symbol of doom.

Dougie was peering at the blackboard.

"This week, the school play East Park at home."

Dougie was staring at the blackboard: No1. James Robertson; No. 2 Robert Smith; No. 3 George Findlay; No 4. Gregor Pirie; No 5 was blank. Dougie's name had been wiped off. He became aware of James and Robert's scrutiny and their blatant smirks.

"… George Findlay, Gregor Pirie…"

Dougie slowly began to raise his hands to his ears to block out Miss Simpson's warm melodic chant.

"Robert Smith and Johnny Brown."

Dougie's head sank further. He wished he was just a piece of furniture. His eyes rose reluctantly from the desk. James was watching him. An ambush in waiting. Beside James, Robert was patting another boy on the back. Normal service resumed.

James, careful to angle his body to shield his actions from Miss Simpson's line of sight, gave Dougie the thumbs-up sign, and graced him with his victorious team captain's smile.

THE SCURRY

"Kick it. Fuckin', kick it!"

The hoarse command echoed around the garages, bouncing off the battered pulled down doors.

"Kick it." A dull cushioned thud. A cut-off half cry. Not human. Not mammal.

There were three of them, Malc, Spaz and Brucie. The feathered victim was sent into the wall. Again.

They had cornered the scurry. A gull, still brown-flecked, still unable to fly. The chase had been short. The bird's dash a death sentence, wildly heading to a dark corner where the garages halted with a wall.

"Kick it."

The blur of a trainer lifting the feathered victim into the wall. Again.

That soft sound of impact.

Peter stood ten feet away, wiping his eyes with the back of his hands.

"Come on, guys," his plea weak and fearful. For the gull and himself.

The kicks went in. A flurry of wings, flapping tracksuits and a cry. A desperate, hopeless screech; the high notes clashing against the deeper, softer, heavy thuds.

Peter stood. His school bag at his feet.

"Kick it. Get the Bastard."

The kicks had become stamps. They died away. The carcass mashed into the wall.

The trio paused, Malc breathing heavily from exertion and exhilaration.

His trainers smeared with giblets.

"Fuck it. Ma Mam'll kill me."

Malc's mother had bought him the trainers. She was the one person he was scared of.

Peter had already turned away, dragging his bag over his head, speeding up along the alley. Keen to reach the road and cleaner, unsullied air.

'Peter. Wait up, you arse." The guiltless call of a smalltown killer.

Peter speeded up. His trousers and feet at least were clean; his conscience less so. He'd have to stop walking from school with Malc.

His mam had warned him. Malc was a nutter.

ALL IN A DAYS WORK

Hamish turned over an egg timer. The timer was a new gadget out of place in the small pine-panelled kitchen.

You couldn't beat an egg for breakfast, he smiled to himself, as he took out a slice of bread and began to butter it.

A young man, Pete, was standing outside a corner shop. He was dressed ready to labour, clutching a pint of milk and with a paper tucked under one arm. A couple of cars passed. He was looking at his watch as though waiting for a lift. They were always late, especially when it rained. The wind rained a lot in Norhaven.

The egg was scooped out of the boiling water and placed into a china eggcup. Hamish lifted them on to a tray.

The tray was meticulous, arrayed with a small china teapot, a cup and saucer, a napkin and a side plate with soldiers neatly cut. Hamish valued precision; a job well done. He hoisted the tray and carried it out of the room.

He balanced the tray along the corridor. He stopped and knocked gently, pushing open a door.

"There you are, Mam. Nice and runny. Just the way you like it."

Pete was still waiting, head down and collar up against the rain. He looked up as he heard a vehicle approaching. A battered working lorry pulled up. Two older men, Ron and Alan, were inside. Ron was at the wheel.

"What time do you call this, like?"

Ron scowled at him.

"Shut up and get in."

"Where's my Record?" demanded Alan.

Pete, climbing in beside him, waved the damp paper at him.

The lorry turned into a small entrance a line of garages. It pulled up in front of a small ramshackle bowling club, an old building in need of some repair.

The sign, which needed repainting read, 'Norhaven Comrades Bowling Club'.

"Is this it?"

Ron switched off the engine and gave Pete a dismissive look. It wasn't so much that youth was wasted on the young, Ron thought. It was wasted on Pete.

A net curtain flickered. Someone was watching the workmen from across the road as they stepped down from their truck.

The three workmen start lifting scaffolding and ladders from the back of the lorry. Alan lit up a cigarette and nodded to Ron, who turned and looked across the street. The net curtains of a small cottage were swaying as through someone had been watching them. Ron studied the cottage. It was out of place amid the council estate, as though it had outstayed its welcome. When it had been built this had all been farm land, thought Ron, turning back to the job in hand.

Ron and Alan were putting up the scaffolding. Pete was already on the roof.

"Cold enough like," he shouted down.

"You the weatherman?" Ron threw the question back at him.

Pete looked down at Ron and then beyond him causing Ron to turn and follow his gaze.

Hamish was approaching them from across the road. Even crossing the road looked like an effort for him, as though it was a river he had to overcome.

Ron stepped forward to meet him.

"Fit like?"

"Nae bad. You here to do the place up, like?"

Ron nodded, indicating to Alan and Pete to keep working.

"Didn't expect you to start so soon. I'm the caretaker, Hamish Paterson."

Ron raised an eyebrow and offered his hard hand.

"Nobody tells me nothing. You'd think they'd tell me, the caretaker.

"I ken. That's committees for you.

"Careful with them tiles," Ron yelled as Pete dropped a slate.

"He's shite. It's the haircut." Ron jerked his thumb at Pete.

Hamish looked slightly embarrassed by the language.

"Do you want the keys, then?"

"What?" Ron is still scowling at Pete and the broken slate.

"The keys. For the Clubhouse."

"Oh aye. Ta. Won't get far without them."

"See you later.

Hamish waved and headed back across the road. Beyond him the curtain twitched.

177

Ron was standing at the doorway from the corridor into the main room of the bowling club, looking up scrutinising the work overhead.

"How's it doing? We haven't got all day!"

"I ken. It's heavy gear, like." Alan shouted back.

Ron grunted and turned around. He was stunned. Before him stood Florrie, an old lady with a faded blue rinse. She was holding a large tray with an enormous tea cozy, with a china tea set and a plate of fancy pieces. It was a magnificent spread.

"Morning, ma loon. Thought you might be needing a cup o' tea."

Ron, giving her a dazzling smile, ushered Florrie back along the corridor and out of the Clubhouse. Florrie was slightly flustered at having to move backwards and slightly put out at the manoeuvre.

Florrie retreated out of the building, struggling to keep the tray upright.

"Thanks, but we've …" Ron waved at the work behind him.

"Oh, but you must. Ma loon Hamish said you're here tae mend the roof." Her smile was firm.

"Well, that's affa kind of you. Boys! Tea break! Tea!"

Ron smiled and Florrie beamed back at him.

Pete was on the roof. He stopped and moved to look down.

"Tea? What the f…" He stopped himself in time.

Hamish was setting out brightly coloured deckchairs and a table. Pete and Alan were sitting uncomfortably in their working clothes. Florrie was already settled and in her element.

"The rain's been affa coarse. It's been needing doing for years. Sugar?

Pete shrugged, unsure if it was a trick question.

"Ham in, ma loon."

Pete looked at the other two, selected a piece, paused then took a second.

"Gets so damp the pictures keep falling off the walls.

Ron, Alan and Pete nodded with their hands and mouths full.

"Will you be doing the painting and all. Needs a bittie brightening up kind? It used to be so bonny."

Ambushed by sandwiches and fancies, Alan and Pete looked to Ron, who took a gulp of his tea.

"Not today. We've too much to do. What colour would you like?"

Florrie was flattered and delighted.

"Blue would be bonny."

Alan and Pete sat back and nodded. Ron made a point of studying his watch then began to rise.

"Well, um, that was affa fine. We'd best be getting back to the job in hand. That was affa fine."

Pete offered his thanks too.

"Aye, affa good."

Alan grunted his agreement. He and Pete stood up, stretching.

Florrie was even more delighted.

"Nae bother, ma loons. Nae bother. My pleasure."

Florrie beamed up at the workmen and smiled broadly at her son. Hamish smiled back as he began to clear away the cups and saucers.

The five deckchairs and table were still clustered on the verge. The workmen were lifting down the scaffolding.

Ron was growing impatient.

"What are you doin'? We haven't got all day."

Ron came out of the front door of the Clubhouse. Alan and Pete were standing recovering from their labour.

"Finished at last, like?"

Alan lit up, while Pete examined a damaged finger and looked across at Ron as though it was his fault.

"Don't forget to clear up, Haircut."

Pete looked as if he was going to speak, but Alan defused the impending clash.

"Nae bother," he took another drag.

Ron emerged from the Clubhouse, closed the door and locked it carefully.

He turned towards the lorry. Pete and Alan were already in the cab, grateful for its warmth.

He looked across the road as Hamish lumbered over. The curtains flickered and Florrie's face appeared.

"All done. Locked up and all."

"Nae bother. I wanted to have a quick look like. See how you've done it. It'll make a difference you ken. No more water running down the walls."

"Aye. Aye it will." Ron dropped the keys into Hamish's hands.

He looked across at the house to where Florrie was watching. She waved happily and Ron returned the wave like a cavalry officer about to ride out on patrol. Ron walked to the cab and climbed in. Hamish was stacking up the deckchairs against the Clubhouse wall.

The lorry moved off. The driver tooted the horn. Hamish turned from waving at the lorry and looked up at the Clubhouse. He looked pleased with an air of expectation. Good to have it done. The committee had been arguing about it for ages. *That's committees for you*. He struggled slightly to unlock the door.

Hamish looked down at the dirty boot marks and tutted to himself. More work.

Remembering what he had come inside for, he pushed open another door and looked up.

The caretaker's face was rigid with incomprehension and disbelief. The ceiling has been replaced by the sky. The entire roof has gone. It started to rain again.

Hamish stepped away from the Clubhouse, shell-shocked. He fumbled with the key.

As he crossed the road, his head was shaking from side to side. The curtain flickered across the road, where his mother was watching expectantly. Her expression changed. Bewilderment. Concern. A worried frown, as her son retreated to the cottage.

THIRD TIME LUCKY

It was quiet in the Horseshoe Bar. A late afternoon stillness.

The barman, Paul, was polishing glasses. Rodney should have done it last night, but that was nothing new. Since he'd started seeing Anna, Rodney's outlook had become very limited. He dragged his mind back to the present. That was the trouble with quiet days in the bar, he thought. He needed a few regulars to slide in.

There was just a solitary customer in the Horseshoe Bar, Frank, who was tending his pint. He looked as if he had come to the bar straight from work. He was a plasterer, and considered a good one in Norhaven.

A hand-drawn poster behind Paul read:

'New Local Lottery Card'

Mammoth prizes

Three x £1,000.

DON'T MISS OOT.

Paul had put the poster up this morning. He was pleased with himself. He had stolen a march on the other harbour bars, getting this lottery thing set up. He was convinced there was only one place for it: here, at the Horseshoe Bar. George Masson had once quipped that it must have been a damn wee horse. That had been before Paul had banned him. *Cheeky shite*. Drank in the Schooner now, boring everyone arse-less about when he had a trial for Inverness Thistle. That team didn't really exist anymore, now that all the Inverness teams had merged.

The door opened and in floated Janey.

"Guys! What a day! Frank, how's you?" Janey was a force of nature. Bubbly, bright, in your face. That was Janey. That she made the Horseshoe her first port of call gave Paul a small glow of pride. Her grandfather, Auld Joe, had been an institution here. He'd propped up the far corner of the bar for decades. Grouse and a half. Janey had called in with her pals to check up on him, buy him a nip and pass on the same message every time from her mother, Auld Joe's daughter. To behave and not to come home the worse for it.

Not that Auld Joe had paid any heed. He'd have died in the Horseshoe if his heart hadn't given out one night as he climbed the back brae after closing time.

Janey had come straight from work. She dropped her shoulder bag on a stool and selected another one to sit on. Paul put her drink in front of her without even a single word.

"Thanks, Paulie." She pulled herself up onto the stool.

Another man entered, Tall Alex. He sat down next to Frank, who indicated to Paul that Alex needed a drink.

"Just a pint," muttered Tall Alex.

"Nae Bother," replied Paul, "that's all you're getting." He was known for being droll.

Janey smiled and acknowledged Alex. She sipped her drink, as Paul served Alex his pint. His job done, Paul turned his attention to his customers, to Janey in particular.

"Fancy a shot on the new lotto, Janey?" A polite pitch.

Janey shook her head.

"No way."

"Give it a go, ladies first."

Janey shook her head and took another determined drink from her vodka and lime. Paul frowned in disappointment.

Janey dug in.

"Never a gambler nor a slapper be," she quoted archly. Paul didn't know where that crap had come from.

He persisted. He needed to, he'd bought the package from the bloody rep.

"There's a £1,000 jackpot. Three of them. It's for the new club house," he added, meaning the Norhaven Bowling Club. The old one had had its roof stolen, the lead stripped away in broad daylight. Rumours abounded as to who had carried out the daring theft. Right under the caretaker's nose. And he still had the job, thought Paul.

Frank took pity on him.

"I'll take one."

Franks handed over his money. The pound rolled across the bar in a hurry to leave Frank's hand. That was the story of his life.

"A fool and his money are easily parted," sang Janey from down the bar.

Paul frowned at her and passed Frank his scratchcard.

"So's a whore and her knickers," came Frank's retort. Janey cackled. The crack. That's why she still called into the Horseshoe. Still sat in Auld Joe's old perch.

Janey scoffed as Frank fished out a coin and started rubbing his scratch card. Tall Alex's eyes widened as he peered over Frank's shoulder.

"No way!" Tall Alex breathed out.

Frank held the card aloft.

"A grand, I've bagged a grand," Frank was in shock, mainly speaking to himself, "Christ."

Janey's face was a mix of shock, disbelief and envy.

Paul shook his head, too, took the ticket and inspected it. Inside, he was swearing his head off.

"Does he get cash?" asked Tall Alex.

Paul tried to look positive and happy for Frank, and nodded.

"Mo will write you a cheque when he gets in."

Christ, Mo was gonna go ape. Paul just knew it. First ticket out of the pack. *Shit.*

Janey stood up on her bar stool.

"I'll have one of them tickets, Paul!" she called down the bar. Frank wasn't getting one up on her. Oh, no.

Paul grinned at her and passed a scratchcard over, as Janey dropped her £1 coin on the bar. Hers did not run anywhere.

Janey challenged Frank down the short, curved bar.

"Luck be a lady tonight!"

The men watched as Janey rubbed on the scratch card for all she was worth, muttering a low incantation.

"Come on, ye beauty, come on, ye … Knickers."

Janey tossed the card away. The men laughed, with a strange sense of relief. No one likes to see too many people win. Janey scowled good-naturedly at them.

Paul moved to take advantage of her frustration.

"Want another?"

Janey shook her head.

"You've got to be joking," she said, taking another mouthful of her vodka and lime, to numb her disappointment and sense of injustice.

Tall Alex volunteered. He was not known for his bravery.

"I'll take it." He put his arm up, almost as if he was still at school and uncertain of the answer to the question.

Paul looked again at Janey, offering her the chance to change her mind, but Janey just focussed on her drink. Paul shrugged. He had played the gent.

Alex handed over his money and Paul threw him the card.

"Let's have a drink from you, Paul. Janey and Alex an all." Frank was conscious that this was the least that was expected of him with a grand coming his way. He wished Mo, the bar's owner would wander in now.

Alex scrapped away at the card furiously. A zealot. Alex threw his hands in the air, thrusting the scratch card at Paul, who struggled to reach it as Alex tottered back off his stool and had to put both legs down to maintain his balance. In truth, Tall Alex's balance was gone. Paul grabbed the offered card and took a double take. And another. He felt a rising taste of bile as the cruel reality stared up at him. He was stunned.

"£1,000!" Paul felt as if he was struggling for breath.

Tall Alex and Frank shook hands. They were ecstatic. Janey thudded her drink down, spilling it.

"I canna fuckin' believe this!" She wasn't sure who she was most angry with, the two celebrating men, who were now doing a little jig, or herself for missing out. Or Paul for witnessing it all.

Paul had other worries.

"Neither can I. Three tickets and only one jackpot left. Mo is going to kill me." In part he was talking to himself.

Tall Alex broke off from his jig, bowing to Frank

"Get everyone a drink, Paul."

Paul started pouring the drinks, but his worry was growing. Mo was going to go ballistic.

Janey was shaking her head, struggling to see the funny side.

"I turn doon twa tickets and then you twa lumps take them and win. There's just nae justice," she protested.

Alex and Frank were both laughing. Paul glanced at Janey with some sympathy.

Paul handed over the drinks.

"On Alex," pausing in front of Janey.

Tall Alex and Frank both toasted Janey. They had the look of men at the start of an adventure. She smiled back in twisted, sour resignation.

Paul leaned forward, a scratch card in his hand, offering it to Janey. He smiled at her.

"Third time lucky."

Laying down the challenge.

Janey's smile froze as she sucked on the ice from her drink.

THE BID

The fishing trawler was called the 'Star o' the West'. A wooden hulled veteran of the Norhaven fleet. The boat negotiated the mouth of the harbour. As it the entered the port, it swung round. The name 'Star o' the West' was beautifully painted on its bow. The early light picked out the precision of the ship's painter's skill. The boat was a vivid deep blue, its name carved out in white. The morning air held a dampness, a taste of saline at the back of the throat.

The vessel manoeuvred to a berth on the quayside directly outside the Fish Market as the dawn thickened and brighter, bolder light reached over the warehouses that lined the port's southern edge. A young man named Davie launched himself from the boat to the quayside. He landed like a cat, sure-footed and poised, even in heavy rubber boots, and turned to catch a rope thrown by another crewman, Big Alex. Davie tied the heavy rope around a squat stanchion. Steam rose off him in the morning chill.

A winch hoisted two boxes of fish and ice from the hold of the boat. Billy was standing on deck steadying the pallets as they came up, guiding them with an attached line. George, his brother and the boat's Skipper, was standing with him.

Billy's shout carried across the quayside,

"Fish!"

The load rose unpredictably upwards and across. Davie, on the quayside, was waiting with a trolley he'd requisitioned for the fish boxes. As the fish boxes landed, he steered them gently to the ground. The plastic blue boxes were almost indestructible, but their contents were easily damaged and that affected the price at market. He unhooked the grapple and tossed it back. He looked around to see if any lumpers, were around to help. Lumpers were the market porters. Having a tea break as usual, he thought.

Davie ran his rubber-gloved hand across his face. The men were working at speed.

"Fish!" Billy's voice boomed again.

Davie quickly positioned the trolley for the next load. Rob and Ali joined him. They were both lumpers and of an age with him.

"Fit like, Davie, min," greeted Rob, "Ye enjoying yer berth, aye?"

About fucking time, thought Davie, but said,

"Aye, it's nae bad. Hard graft, like."

Davie felt he had to make the point with this pair of skivers.

Four boxes curved up and over this time and Davie quickly undid the hooks and hauled the boxes onto a half-stacked pallet a few feet away. Rob and Ali had dragged it over.

From the deck, the two older men watched his labour. They were both in their forties, well-built and heavy-muscled. It was their boat. Davie was the newest addition to their small, tight crew and still on a form of probation, although so far he seemed to be working out.

"Fa's he speaking tae? Tell him to get a jildy on . . ," George threw away a cigarette stub to finish his sentence.

Billy hauled the winch line.

"Ali Mackie, his cousin."

George shook him head in a form of dismissal and contempt.

"Aye, I ken him. His faither an a'. A fuckin' waster."

In Norhaven Harbour, reputation was all.

Norhaven's Fishmarket was a long low building. Granite walls and a low sinking roof. The lighting gave the white painted walls a cold cast. The only warmth was men's breaths as they bid for the fish. The fishermen and the buyers were pressing the Harbour Master for a new market, but they couldn't agree on the design. In fact, they could hardly agree on the day of the week.

Rows of plastic boxes, crammed with fish and packed with ice, lined the cold floor. More boxes were being hauled into single tiers.

Men in gumboots trod over the boxes to inspect the fish, mobile phones in one hand, burning cigarettes in the other. Ice was swept away to get a better look as the salesmen talked into their phones.

A small group gathered at the head of one of the lines of boxes. The salesman stepped onto a box of fish.

George, Billy and Davie were standing watching the sale. They had pulled insulated jackets over their oilskins. It was one thing to work in the cold, different when you stopped moving. Davie offered his cigarettes to the others; an offer of heat.

A man standing among the buyers' huddle looked up and acknowledged George.

Billy shook his head in resignation.

"Bob Muirhead."

George nodded in agreement.

"Aye."

Davie glanced across trying to catch their meaning. He knew Muirhead's daughter. Same age as his sister Susan, but a menace with a drink in her. He had only been with the brothers and the 'Star o'the West' for three months. Best to say nothing.

Billy made things plainer for his benefit.

"Norhaven Fisheries. Only buys at our expense, like."

Davie nodded and adopted a different posture towards the fish buyer.

George was more direct.

"I was at sea with him years ago."

With that, George threw his cigarette out of the market door as the auction started. That said it all. Davie got the message. A dispute between crewmates that had never ended. Something he'd better remember.

Billy turned his back on the bidding. He had done his job.

"Young George's Birthday the morn," he pointed out.

"Aye. Aye you're richt, Brud," his brother nodded, although his hooded eyes were stilling trailing Muirhead and the auction party.

"A swally the nicht," suggested Davie.

George and Billy laughed at Davie's enthusiasm.

"Used to play for the Rangers, the boy like," Davie ran on in his excitement, but the other two were lost.

"Some player like. The boy. Speaking the nicht," Davie waited for confirmation. Football was his passion. In particular, the Rangers. A passion shared by his Skipper. It had helped get him a chance shot on the boat and cement his berth.

"Aye, he was ma loon," agreed Billy, catching something of Davie's energy.

The entire crew were going to the Norhaven FC fundraiser that evening. Davie was buzzing with his own excitement. It could have been his birthday rather than that of young George, the Skipper's son.

The fish auction moved along a tier. They watched as a young man, James, flowered the boxes in front of them with small paper tickets with Whyte's Fisheries boldly printed on them.

"Fuckin' fishmeal," George looked fit to spit, "fuckin' Muirhead."

The large, dated ballroom at the Victoria Hotel was being prepared for a function. Waitresses were setting out places on the large tables.

Hayley, a young woman with untidy dyed hair around a tired face, was working behind the bar, lifting bottles of spirits on the long strip of mahogany, while a younger waitress, Morag, filled a tray and carried the bottles of whisky, vodka and mixers to a nearby table. She placed the bottles in the centre of the table, before picking up the tray to make another ferry run to the bar.

"Fa's in the nicht, like?" Morag rested her arms on the bar.

"The fitba club," answered Lisa, as if it were a disease.

The younger girl looked at the clusters of bottles still on the bar.

"Oh," was the best Morag could muster. It was going to be a long night.

Early evening and the ballroom was now crowded. The only women were waitress and bar staff, including Morag and Lisa.

The event was a formal footballing dinner. Men and whisky only. Drinks were being bought accompanied by laughter from clusters of men as introductions were made.

At the bar, a group of six men were gathered; the atmosphere was friendly, almost self-congratulatory. The 'Star' was doing well and so was its crew.

"Brud, what are you for?" Billy called across to the bigger man.

"A Vod. Cola. Nae ice." George replied like a well-learnt scorecard.

Billy to the rest of the crew

"Davie?"

"Vod for me an al'."

Billy signalled the barman

"Twa mair vodkas."

As Billy handed out the drinks to the others, he looked across at George, who took his glass and nodded.

"To our new crew member. Welcome aboard, Davie!" Billy raised the toast as the others joined it.

"Star o' the West!"

Davie looked around the group, pleased with the impression that he has made. It would be a share now, a full berth.

"Star o' the West!" he raised his glass higher.

The M.C. coughed slightly into his microphone:

"Gentleman, Gentleman, please. Can I ask you to take your seats!"

George nodded at Billy as Davie was being slapped on the back by the others. Billy took his cue and pulled out a brown envelope. He put his hand on Davie's shoulder and quietly handed him the envelope.

"The first of many, ma loon."

Davie looked down at the envelope. It was a wage packet, a mighty one packed with heavy notes. He smiled to himself and knocked back his drink.

The group were sitting at the table. The meal was over. Bottles of vodka were still standing on the table. The men's ties were loosened and faces flushed.

Billy, George and Davie were sitting with a man each

between them; Big Alex, Zander and Cruz. They had worked together for years. The kind of closeness and awareness that made them an efficient unit at sea. Davie knew he'd done well to gain acceptance and a measure of respect from these men. They each had their place. Zander was the Driver, the boat's engineer, Cruz was the cook and the best at splicing nets when they needed it. Big Alex was a Norhaven phenomenon, built like a shed with an engine.

Billy was still laughing even though the comedian had stepped away from the small stage.

"The man was funny. Affa good speaker."

"Aye, funny as fuck." Davie's voice has risen pumped by the vodka.

George and the others nodded in agreement. Davie poured himself a large measure.

The evening had moved on. The M.C. was now standing in the middle of the throng, clutching his microphone. It was the salesman from the morning's fishmarket; same job, different product.

"Gentleman, next we have …"

The M.C. looked around, lost for a moment. He too, has had a drink. A football shirt was held up.

"Awa' the Gers!" a voice washed down from a table at the back of the hall.

The M.C. was not put off.

"Signed by all the team. By all the mighty Gers," he added, by way of a sales pitch.

On Table Five, Bob Muirhead and his son James looked at the up-held shirt. Bob, already glazed, took a heavy slug and reached for the bottle, unscrewing the cap with one hand. He needed a cigarette and a piss, but his eyes were on the shirt. James poured the drink for him.

James leaned in towards his father.

"Dinna even think on it, Dad."

Bob considered his son, smiled and patted him reassuringly on the hand, then reached for his glass again.

Six yards away, on Table Three, Billy leaned forward to fill his brother's glass.

"Your loon's birthday, aye?"

George nodded, a thought he'd already had. Sitting across from them, Davie's eyes were fixed on the shirt.

"What am I bid, Gentleman? Do I hear fifty?" The M.C. started the bidding.

"Fifty," George's voice was commanding as if still on deck.

Billy was sitting back, both pleased and sated.

"Sixty!" The voice from further down the hall.

"Seventy."

George sat back confidently.

Bob looked across at George. He glanced at his son and nodded drunkenly to himself. It was time to have some fun.

"Eighty."

James looked at him sharply and shook his head.

George's reply came straight back.

"Ninety."

Bob looked across at James, who mouthed the words 'No, Dad, dinna," but Bob waved the words aside.

"One hundred."

James' growing anger was met by Bob's mean drunken smile.

Davie watched the bidding with mounting excitement, as Billy turned from looking at Bob and looked at his brother.

"Bob Muirhead."

George nodded impassively.

The M.C held his position between the two tables. The winner would come from here.

"One hundred pounds, Gentleman. With Bob Muirhead."

Davie looked across at George and Billy. George nodded at his brother.

"One hundred and ten!" a new younger voice.

George and Billy stared across at Davie. George nodded as if it was bit of a joke. Zander sitting next to Davie cast the younger man a quick warning glance. Zander still had his wits about him. Further along the table Cruz was resting his head on the table. He needed a timeout.

"One twenty." George's tone was confident. Laying down his marker.

"One fifty." Davie was at the Races.

The M.C. helped matters on.

"One hundred and fifty pounds, Gentleman!

Billy gave a slight surprised frown.

Bob was struggling to stand.

"Two hundred!" he cried almost toppling.

James reached out to steady him or give me a shake.

"What are you doing?"

"Two hundred pounds. This shirt signed by the Rangers. All the money raised this evening goes to your club," The M.C. was on a roll.

George's face was set.

"Two hundred and fifty." His voiced edged.

Billy looked across at his brother, as the first hint of danger brushed him. Billy took a breath as the two bidders were wrapped up in their arm-wrestling pride.

Davie, unseen by the others, slipped out his envelope of cash and started a quick count. He took a quick drink.

Bob Muirhead was on his feet, in drunken challenge.

"Five hundred," his words were disjointed, undone by drink, as he slid back into his seat.

It failed to hold him properly; Bob was swaying in his seat, "Five hundred," a whisper to his drunken self.

"Five hundred pounds I am bid by the Gentleman at the back from Norhaven fisheries," The M.C. was moving in for the kill.

James grabbed Bob by the shoulder.

"What are you doing? You stupid fuckin' bastard. Stupid." His face inches from his father's.

George turned from watching Muirhead. He and Davie looked at each other. Billy looked between them. Davie was smiling, his Skipper was not.

Davie raised his hand, he was swept away by the evening's tide.

"Six hundred, yes, yes, six hundred pounds from the young man on the table to my right," a note of amazement in the M.C.'s voice.

"Seven hundred and fifty." George cracked out his reply.

"Eight hundred."

George looked across at his brother and Billy stared back, faintly worried.

"Eight hundred pounds, Gentleman. Do I hear anymore?" The M.C. was only speaking to one man in the room.

All eyes were on the Skipper. Slowly, as if pulling himself back from the brink, George shook his head, acknowledging defeat.

"Eight hundred pounds to the young Rangers' fan. Give him a big hand, Gentlemen."

Davie jumped to his feet, upending a bottle as he did so.

"Yer Beauty! Away the Gers!"

The older waitress, Lisa, moved in to mop up the mess. Her expression was washed with barely disguised distaste.

Davie toasted the Skipper. He was flush with success and drink. The men near him patted him on the back. Davie stood and counted out his money before handing it over. Full of bravado, he waved the remaining flimsy couple of notes.

"Plenty mair where that came fae."

George was also being congratulated, the gallant loser, but Billy was studying his brother, a warning knot forming in his gut. George watched Davie showing off his prize.

Davie turned to the Skipper, holding up the shirt and his Skipper nodded and accepted Davie's outstretched hand.

"Loon."

A very drunk Bob was still being harangued by his son.

"You stupid fuckin' bastard. Can you hear me?"

The drunk waved aside the words. He was too happy to care, a fixed satisfied smile on his face.

Men were beginning to leave, rising slowly, unsteadily to their feet. The final auction the slurred talking point. It had been like being at a match, a sporting contest. A wee piece of Norhaven folklore had been made and they had been there.

George gave Davie, now draped in the Rangers shirt, a final clap on the back as he left with his brother, Billy.

At the door, Billy and George looked back at the young man nodding to people as they went.

"He's a cheeky little fucker 'at," commented Billy drily.

"Tell him to pack his gear." The words are flat, brutal and final.

Billy looked at his brother and Skipper and nodded.

A semi-conscious Bob was half carried out by his son. George and Billy watched them contemptuously.

James was speaking to the man helping him carry his father out.

"If Mam finds out, she'll fuckin' kill him."

Davie was left with the shirt he has bought, with only the unconscious drunk, Cruz, at his table for company. He looked at the shirt, then at the unconscious figure next to him. Davie shook his head and crumpled the empty brown wage packet.

The waitresses were already cleaning nearby tables.

The hall was a mess, so were most of the men trailing out of it, leaving a scent of sweat and alcohol.

The two waitresses exchanged a shared look; sour and dismissive. To their eyes, Davie looked abandoned. Condemned. Beached.

ALL FOR CHARITY

Sunlight crept into the bar in ordered stripes, falling across the wooden floor in a pattern dictated by the angle of the smoke-yellowed blinds.

The barman, Alex, was pouring a pint, his face split by the bands of light and shade as he squinted across the two feet of mahogany that dominated the Crewman Bar. It was reputed to be the oldest in Norhaven, a claim disputed by all the rest of the motley crew of salt-weathered drinking dens that crowded the seafront along Shore Wynd. The dark water of the harbour was a short stagger from their front doors.

Two customers were already sitting on stools at the bar. Old Albert sat with a half and an unfinished game of cards in front of him. Derek was flicking through a paper, which he affectionately referred to as 'The Sleaze'. He spent much of his time in the Crewman Bar slagging off the paper. Yet, like millions of other moaners, he kept buying it, shelling out his hard-earned coin. The opinionated rag fed and soothed his dissatisfaction at the state of the nation, Scottish Football and the rising cost of a pint. He wore the face of a man accustomed to working outside, carried a small paunch and a considerable chip on his shoulder. But his money was as good as that of everyone else who stepped over the threshold. That was enough for the landlord.

Derek stopped at the centre pages, marvelling.

"Fuck me. Will you check that oot?" blowing air out of his cheeks for attention.

Alex put the pint down with a slight smile and a hint of mischief. The barman was a slim figure, with dark wavy hair, greying in the curls. A hint of the rogue about him. Derek reached out for the pint without even taking his eyes off the page. He licked the froth from his lips.

"Fuck me. Charity Chancellor."

Derek whistled to over-emphasis his point, as the door opened and the wind outside gusted in a third customer. Pete fought to close the door behind him as Alex reached for a glass and poured without a word.

"She's coming here," Alex was deliberately casual, flicking back his wayward parting.

"Who?" Pete asked, leaning forward on the bar with his question.

Derek's eyes came off the page. He looked at Alex, who was enjoying himself. The bar-keeper pointed at the paper.

"Her. Miss Charity Chancellor." Alex placed the pint deliberately in front of Pete. He was a tall man with an extended neck. His hair cropped close to his skull in a style that had once earned him the by-name 'Bald Eagle', but that was a long time ago and the name hadn't stuck.

"Awa' and fuck." Derek was dismissive.

Alex smiled as he took the money from Pete.

Alex's smile and confidence grew. He was enjoying the game. It livened up the length of a day in the bar.

"Bottom of the page. Read it yersel. Little box, it says…"

Derek was incredulous as he read it.

"The lovely Charity will be showing her generosity at the Crewmen Bar, Nor'haven, on Monday, July 4, as part of her nationwide 'Good Look, Good Cause Tour'.

Derek's face, staring over the edge of the paper, was a struggle of cynicism and lechery.

"They canna even spell Norhaven, like." He spluttered to make some sort of point. Alex peered over.

"Aye, well, that's how it used to be spelt." He wasn't going to allow a prune like Derek spoil his entertainment.

Old Albert climbed down from his perch and, fumbling with his glasses, stuck his nose into the paper. Pete also edged in next to Derek; expressions of wonder, disbelief and delight.

Alex was triumphant. Word would spread now, he knew it. This trio of sweetie-wifies would ensure that.

Two young boys with an old shopping trolley were pasting up a billposter outside a boarded-up shop. The poster was a cheap photocopied A4 sheet, with 'Charity gives it all away at the Crewmen Bar' and a banner with 'Censored until July 4' slapped across it. The picture gave little impression of what Charity looked like. In fact, she could have been anyone's Mum.

They stepped back to admire their handiwork a few inches from a sign reading 'Bill Posters will be prosecuted'.

"It's nae straight," observed Rob, shaking his head.

Mikey thumped him on the arm.

"Shurrup."

The Crewman Bar was busier that night. A dozen or so men were drinking. Alex and Lisa were behind the bar. They were an occasional item. Gravitating to each other at Christmas Parties, then spent the year wondering and drifting, until another event in the calendar; a blackening or a wedding.

Pete pointed towards one of the blurred posters that had somehow crept inside.

"Is it true, like? Is she really coming?" Pete's nature was such that he still questioned whether Celtic had won in 1967. He worked for the Council and doubted everything he was told there.

Derek had no such illusions.

"I ken someone else who will be an all!"

This pearl was greeted with expected male laughter, while Lisa gave a quiet shake of her head. Derek sneered across the bar at her.

"Bit of competition for you like, Lisa."

Lisa offered him an empty smile, her assessment of him confirmed.

Derek turned his attention to Alex.

"We'll need a photographer ye ken and charge the boys a pound a strip."

Derek laughed at his own joke. No-one joined him this time.

"I've asked Blinker to do it."

"Blinker? That pervert."

"The hairdresser boy?" Pete chipped in.

"He's doing it." The landlord was adamant.

Derek shook his head.

"I've never liked the boy. He's always been an erse," Derek didn't like that many people. If there was a bad word to be said about anyone, he could usually find it.

"Blinker's doing it," Alex wasn't going to give any ground. Lisa recognised that tone and smiled at their muttered protests. A small dreg of comfort.

Lisa was clearing the empties. She moved to the table where two women, Frances and Alison were having a news. The pair were slightly older that Lisa, comfortably into their forties.

"Getting a wee bit steamed up, are they?" cackled Frances, nodding towards the male gathering at the bar.

Lisa smiled and shrugged.

"Boys will be boys."

"Dicks will be dicks, you mean," Frances waved a dismissive hand towards the group.

Lisa's smile broadened as Frances leaned forward.

"Will you be there, Lisa? On the nicht, I mean?"

"Oh, aye. I'm not missing the circus. Not with these clowns."

They all laughed. The men at the bar turned at the sound, as though the woman have committed an unspoken offence. Intruded in their bar. Frances laughed louder and signalled the men.

"Did you hear that ye clowns!"

The Big Night. The bar was filling up. Alex and Lisa were working the shift again. Lisa has dressed to show a little style. She stood back to take in the scene.

Derek was holding court on the same bar stool, while Alex was speaking to a small man with a goatie beard and nervous air, Blinker the hairdresser.

"You ken what you're doing, Blinker?"

Blinker nodded.

"Aye. They pay a pound. Get their picture taken with Titty Chancellor."

Alex frowned slightly. Perhaps asking Blinker had been a mistake after all.

"Aye, that's aboot it. Dave'll take a pound off them at the door.

Alex indicated an imposing doorman, who has dressed for the event, in a Tuxedo and a Dickie Bow.

At the door, Dave the bouncer was collecting tolls, when Blinker appeared at his elbow.

"Any sign of her yet?"

Dave looked down at him and dismissed the smaller man. *Annoying wee shite.*

The bar was hoachin; an atmosphere of excitement, expectancy and bravado.

Dave the Doorman was the first with the news.

"This is her."

This was it. Nervousness quietened the bar, seeping in like a haar rolling in. Pete took a hasty swallow. Old Albert polished his lenses. Blinker checked his camera. Faces turned towards the door.

When the door opened, Dave became a Hollywood minder; a blocker with shades. He did a good job. All that could be seen of Charity was a cowboy hat and boots. With her was a tall sun-tanned geezer with a ponytail and flash suit. A gold tooth somewhere in his fixed smile.

Dave took charge.

"We've got a room where she can change."

The man with the tan nodded.

Derek had not moved from his perch.

"What the fuck does she need to change for?"

Lisa, standing behind the bar, rewarded him with a dark

disgusted stare. *In this day and age.* She took a sip of her diet coke and thought she might need a dram later.

The door to the ladies' toilets opened.

The men all stared. They started to cheer, but more out of obligation than conviction. Lisa was watching them from the bar.

Blinker was lining up a picture.

"Check oot that camera shake."

Blinker ignored Derek's jibe.

"Come on boys, make a wee bit of noise," Blinker said trying to inject some sense of theatre.

They started cheering. All eyes torn between the lens and the attraction.

The two small bill-stickers, Mikey and Rob, hesitated before pushing the Crewman Bar door open a couple of inches. They nodded at each other ready to advance a bit further in, when Dave's eye appeared in the gap.

"What do you think you're doin'? Fuck off."

A night of flushed faces: old Albert toothless and lustful, Pete transfixed, others a mix of guilt and sheepishness. Charity floated among them. Flashes bounced around the bar, illuminating her cowboy boots and a red stetson hat.

Pete was standing at the urinal when Derek sauntered in.

"I didn't ken she was blonde," Pete confided.

Derek was in a dream-like state and not really listening.

"It's nae real, man."

"Looked real to me." Pete zipped up, leaving Derek clutching his dreams.

Derek and Alex were watching proceedings as Alex rinsed glasses.

"I thought she'd be a bit bigger."

Alex looked at him as if he was crazy and Lisa pursed her lips in ill-disguised disdain. Christ, she needed a smoke.

Derek left his perch and was shuffling around the crowd waving a collecting tin in people's faces. He was desperate to be a part of his event, this piece of Crewman history.

"Put your pound in, you tightarse."

Derek was drunk. Smashed.

He turned his attention to Lisa.

"Your turn like, Lisa."

This was met with silence. Everyone heard the remark. Lisa looked at Derek and then beyond him.

Charity's hands appeared, and her long, red painted nails tugged at Derek's shirt.

"I think it's your turn, sweetheart." Her voice was a rough south of England new town drawl.

Charity's fingers started to peel off his shirt. Derek's pale aging torso was revealed, a swollen gut hanging over his belt.

Pete decided to join the party. He hadn't believed the night would happen. He decided to make the most of it. Get into the spirit of the event.

"Get 'em off!"

Others took up the refrain.

"Off! Off! Off!"

They started to clap. Behind the bar, Alex and Lisa passed a quick glance. Lisa realised that she, too, was clapping.

Derek scanned the faces of the crowd. Full of drink and bravado, he started to undo his trousers.

His britches hit the floor and Derek raised his arms aloft as though he has scored a goal. In a way, he had.

"For Charity!" a crazed, strangulated, triumphant cry from Derek.

Across the crowded bar, Charity nodded to Lisa. A small half smile from an unexpected ally. *No cigarette needed now, sister.*

A sunny morning with a slight nip in the air and Derek was walking to work, taking a short cut to the harbour. As he passed a figure busy welding a railing on a fishing boat stopped, and lifted his mask to acknowledge him. Derek checked and walked on. He didn't think he knew the boy.

A woman's hands, strong with short nails, picked up an ashtray and dumped its contents in a bin. The newly washed bar floor was still shiny. Lisa walked around the bar past a small notice board. Charity's blurred poster was still up. Lisa picked up the mail and paper. She propped open the door. The Crewman was open for business.

Derek was approaching the slipway, with boats resting high on cradles. Painters rolling on bright blocks of colour: lipstick red, ice blue, bumble bee yellow. Derek was a mite late, but he felt he'd earned it. Wait 'til he told the boys about last night. They'd never believe it.

Lisa was smoking, the paper – 'The Sleaze' – spread out on the bar. She should have been washing more glasses, but in a small way, today was a special day. She took a long slow drag and nodded gently. Tapping off the ash without looking at the ashtray. *In this day and age.*

Derek was at the harbour yard when he was greeted by his grinning workmates. Their Prodigal Son. They nodded at him, patted him on the back, offered the thumbs up sign.

Derek was pleased, but unaccustomed to this warmth of reception. He knew enough to realise that both his humour and his face were tolerated. It was amazing what a spot of sunshine could make.

He nodded, arriving in the middle of them. A paper was presented to him. Laughing his colleagues moved away, as if he has just been given the Black Spot.

Derek looked at them retreating from him, then down at the paper, his own read, 'The Sleaze'. Realisation began to dawn as he pulled with frantic dread at the pages. A full spread. His dazed sweaty face. His modesty spared only by a small unfocussed overlaid circle. An Editor's kindness to the nation.

Blinker was sitting on a chair in his hairdressing salon, its walls populated by pictures of 1980s television stars' hairstyles. He lifted the open paper. This morning he'd bought ten copies of 'The Sleaze'. Worth every penny. He started to laugh, spinning on the chair as it picked up speed and his laugh with it.

THE DATE

"She said 'yes'." Ted's voice was incredulous.

He was speaking to himself. Preparing himself.

His hand ran down a record collection. A finger ran along the titles. One record selected. The hand changed its mind and selected another, a romantic crooning record. The hand moved the needle across, the music rose in volume.

He was alone in the small dated bathroom except for his reflection in the cabinet mirror. His hand reached out to turn on the taps of the bath. Hot water coughed out. The hand moved to pick up a bottle of bath foam, shaking a liberal amount of the coloured liquid into the water.

The bath was a three-quarter size. Not common now. Ted was submerged, water lapping his chin. Well, not completely. The bubbles lapped the rim of the bath. A pair of pale bony feet protruded from the water and rested either side of the taps as the steam rose.

"She said 'yes'." Hope has become belief for him. The water was up to Ted's neck.

"Yes." Whispered with the possibility of passion.

His toes tapped out a tune on the taps, amid the bubbles.

Ted, with a towel wrapped around his waist, stood at the wash hand basin. He was a rugged man fraying around the edges. A half century on the clock. He rubbed the mirror in front of him, peered at the image facing him, his dark wet hair swept back.

Ted rubbed the mirror again and looked down, looking for something, a shaving stick. He started to lather up. He picked up a bulbous, dated razor and began to shave, gradually moving to the rhythm of the crooner. A careful shave to avoid nicks, done with precision and artistry, a hint of a flourish.

Ted studied himself in the mirror. He applied deodorant, sniffed under his arms and applied more deodorant. Ted reached for some aftershave. He unscrewed the bottle, sniffed that, put on a dab. Having second thoughts, he splashed on some more, reacting to the sting of the alcohol. Ted smelled his hands, looked concerned, and hastily splashed water on his face to dilute the scent he had just applied. He swilled out his mouth and put his toothbrush back into a small glass on the wash hand basin, and ran his fingers through his hair.

In his bedroom, Ted began to work on his hair. Gel rubbed in, he used an enormous 1960's-style hair drier, which resembled a blow torch. Slowly the quiff took shape – a flamboyant 'Duck's Arse'. He sat on the edge of his bed, the towel still wrapped around him, and opened a shoe box. Tissue paper was carefully, almost lovingly, removed to reveal suede shoes. He sat with his feet wide apart as he blew away imagined specks of fluff.

Ted put on his shirt, tucking in the tails, and buckled his belt. He sat again to pull on his socks and shoes then moved to the door, where his jacket, a long frock coat, was hanging. He brushed off a couple of specks of dust.

Ted stood by the old tiled fireplace in his compact lounge. He checked his pockets: a packet of mints, a comb in his top pocket, a wallet. Ted checked his money in its clip. He walked across to the record player and lifted off the needle. He bent down to pick something up and turned around. He has glasses on, old brown NHS specs. He smiled.

Ted emerged from a small door next to the entrance to a shoddy burger bar. The faded sign read 'Ted's Diner'. He locked the door, turned and studied his watch. In good time. A small band of young girls ran past him.

"Ted! Ted!" Their giggles followed them down the street.

The girls ran on. Ted pocketed his keys. He walked away, with a spring in his step, as if singing to himself. He crossed from one side of the road to the other. A young woman pushing a baby buggy crossed from the other side. Ted stepped aside theatrically to let her pass and gave her a dazzling smile. A gallant.

She looked up at him and glanced back as he sauntered past her. She shook her head.

Ted walked towards the bus stop. Over his shoulder he could see a bus coming. He quickened his stride and hurriedly flagged down the double-decker. He bounded on, fumbling for change as the bus doors closed and the vehicle edged off. Ted strode purposefully up the stairs, smiling almost foolishly at the other three passengers. Ted sat in the front seat and looked like a king surveying his kingdom. He beamed across at a young girl sitting in the seat opposite.

"It's a great nicht," he said. The girl looked blankly at him and turned away. Ted shrugged, fished out a mint, and leaned forward to offer the girl one. She refused to look in his direction.

"Please yersel," he popped the mint into his mouth, put his feet up in front of him and sang quietly to himself. Nothing could deflate his optimism.

"Get your feet off there! Now!" the driver's amplified voice boomed over the bus intercom. Startled, Ted swung around, quickly moving his feet.

"He can see you through the periscope." The woman sitting to the left behind him indicated a slab of thick glass by Ted's side.

Ted nodded, his self-image slightly cracked, and sat back. He leaned forward and peered down the periscope.

A distorted fish-eye view of the driver and his big wheel stared upwards. A grotesque inverted gargoyle.

Ted sat back quickly, rattled. He worked to regain his composure and darted a look quickly across at the other passengers to check they had not noticed him. They had. His polish was fading faintly.

The bus turned into a wide street and halted at a bus stop. The driver gave Ted a sour look as he left the bus. It moved off. Facing Ted on the opposite side of the street was a Picture House. Ted walked towards the cinema. He stopped in front of it and looked at the building, his anticipation building, savouring the moment. Ted checked his watch and walked to the doors. He looked up at the cinema listings, scanning the choices. Ted found the one he wanted to see. He was tense with anticipation.

"Yes," he breathed. He ran a comb through his hair and joined the small queue.

"Aye, aye, Ted?" said a man, looking back in the queue.

"Nae bad, pal. Yersel?" asked Ted.

The man nodded a fraction.

Ted was now second in the queue. He stepped forward eagerly. A woman with a jaded expression stared back at him through the glass panel.

"Twa for number four, please," said Ted, holding up two fingers.

"Twa for number four. Eight pounds," a mechanical echo with the price added.

The machine spat out two tickets. The woman snatched Ted's proffered note and dropped two coins on the tickets. She scowled at him suspiciously.

Ted came out of the cinema, holding his tickets and put his change in his pocket.

"Sorry," Ted stepped out of the way of a pair of foursomes trying to get in. He looked up and down the street. His hand drew back the cuff of his jacket, exposing a watch face. The time read 7.06pm. Ted studied the time for a second longer. He looked back at the queue that has started to form outside the cinema.

"Good job I got ma tickets," he muttered, congratulating himself on his foresight.

Ted considered the couples in the queue. A couple of people nodded to him in recognition. He allowed himself a slight smile. Less confident than earlier beamers.

Ted stood tapping his foot. He sneaked a look at his watch again. The queue behind him had started to go in. He looked at his watch again.

"Quarter past. I need a pish."

Ted looked towards the cinema doors. He moved from foot to foot, as though faintly uncomfortable.

Ted was undecided.

"I might miss her."

Ted looked up and down the street, looking for a face. He was beginning to feel vaguely concerned.

The queue had gone. Ted walked up to the listings board. 'Programme starts – 7.20pm.'

Ted turned to look hopefully along the street. He looked at his watch. The watch face read 7.28pm.

"Come on."

His face was more tense.

Ted stood with his hands in his pockets. Behind him a young male cinema attendant was taking the bollard marked 'Screen Four' inside. The young man shook his head slightly on spying Ted still loitering outside.

Ted stared at his watch 7.48pm. Ted shuffled uncomfortably, his expression now one of impatience and disbelief. The watch face read 7.59pm. It changed to 8.00pm.

"An hour. I need a pish."

Ted shook his head and walked towards the cinema door. The same woman who sold him the tickets was there having a sly fag in the shadows.

Ted showed his tickets.

"You can't come in now. The show's started." She handed back his tickets.

"I just want tae use your toilet," he said.

"You can't come in."

Her face was set. Dark, resolute, with a hint of contempt. A large young male attendant moved to stand beside her. She took another drag. Her face hardening.

"You can't."

Ted was beaten, he turned away.

The young attendant looked at his colleague with a slight frown. The woman shrugged, acknowledging her harshness.

"I ken. I'm just scunnered with him hanging aboot."

Her colleague nodded sympathetically and pursed his lips.

Ted walked to the edge of the road. He looked along the street in both directions, shaking his head slightly.

He was angry, hurt and bewildered.

Ted studied his watch again. It now read 8.17pm.

He looked at the tickets, which were still in his hand. He held them to his chest.

Ted was standing with his hands in his pockets. His head lowered, feeling uncomfortable.

The cinema began to empty. Ted saw couples laughing, discussing the movie, their eyes acknowledging him still standing there.

"See you, Ted," said the man from the earlier queue.

Ted nodded slightly at the greeting.

Ted waited directly in front of the cinema. Flanked by posters. He took a deep breath, a sad pensive expression forming. Taking a last look at his watch, Ted turned away towards the bus stop. At the door way, the two attendants watched as Ted trudged away. The woman slowly exhaled, blowing a line of smoke. The two exchanged a look. Bemusement, sadness and contempt. She shook her head slightly and flicked her tab outside. He pulled the doors closed.

Ted, hands in pockets and head down was studying his feet. Two women were walking arm in arm towards the bus stop. They shared a distinct family resemblance. Mother and daughter. A striking pair. The mother, Dorothy, noticed Ted first. Her expression changed abruptly. Annoyance and exasperation. She changed their direction, guiding her daughter away, her eyes on Ted, yet avoiding him.

"We'll walk, Ellen."

Ellen, her daughter, checked her stride. She gave Ted a bright smile.

"Hiya, Ted."

Ted looked up and was briefly illuminated by her stunning smile. The women walked on, Ellen setting the pace.

"Why do you not speak to him, Mam? Surely you can do that? Poor soul."

Dorothy quickened her stride.

"Because I don't."

Dorothy speeded up further.

"I've told you before, Ellen. I'm past feeling guilty aboot it. Think if you'd had him as a father."

Ellen gave her Mother a tight smile and threw a glance back at Ted. He watched them pass; hurt, lost and abandoned.

Ted climbed onto the bus, weary and slightly bowed. He paid his fare and sat in the first seat available. Downstairs. The bus started off. Ted looked at his watch again – 8.45pm.

He glanced across at a middle-aged lady sitting opposite him. She was surrounded by her messages.

"I wonder if she's ever been stood up?" he thought.

The woman smiled at Ted. He smiled back crookedly.

Ted turned back over his shoulder at the cinema. There was no one stood waiting. There never was.

The sound of a key being turned. The door opened quickly and Ted charged in. He turned rapidly into the bathroom. He unzipped and urinated. A sigh of relief.

"Miserable… sour… faced… She could have let me go… all I needed…" Every word was despair, the words washed away by the flush.

Ted was sitting directly in front of the small black and white television, his feet propped up on a small table, a bottle of Newcastle Brown in his hand. Three empty bottles lay by the side of the armchair. *Sportscene Match of the Day* was on.

"No score so far," intoned the commentator.

Ted took a slug of beer, his gaze fixed and unhealthy.

Soon he was asleep. By his bedside he has emptied his change and the two tickets for the show.

In his dream, the theatre is dark. A channel of seats leads down to the bright screen. The melody of "Kissing in the back row of the movies" plays in the background. A couple are sitting in the last row of seats. He has his arm around her. His feet are perched on the seat in front of him. His face is in shadow. He looks across at her and smiles. Triumphant. Cocksure. Her smile eclipses his. Ellen's dazzling smile beneath a beehive hairdo. Dorothy in her youth. He is still smiling as he turns to watch the couple kiss on the big screen. Above the film stars' embrace, the screen reads 'THE END'.

After the credits, comes the subscript.

SUBSCRIPT

Dedicated to Dorothy – in her absence.

HOMEWORK

Period 4. Class 2E. Friday afternoon. The last and longest period of the week. Jo, Miss Kindness to the class, was handing out homework.

"For Monday. On my desk." There was no point being gentle with this lot. Show and tell. They knew it was the last period too.

One boy, Robert, exchanged a sour glance with his mate, James, His mouth curving down.

"Eneugh tae mak ye demented" keeping his moan below the classroom hum, and the teacher's radar.

A sea of pupils poured out of Norhaven Academy. Jo was heading out of the school with the surge, carried along by the eagerness of the coming weekend.

It felt like the end of the school week, her bag heavy with work for the weekend, pupils skipping ahead of her. The bag gave her a slight list as she tried to avoid the quick-stepping kids. Their only burden was to escape, reach the school gates and leave education behind. Another young teacher, Lynne, waved across at her.

"Have a good weekend!"

Jo nodded back. Lynne was a glamorous new addition to the Physics Department, if that wasn't a contradiction. Jo tried to remember where she'd parked her car. Its MOT was coming up and after this morning's carry on, she was worried that it might not get through it. Still, in the scheme of things, as her dad would say.

Jo was asleep, head tilted back, when she was gently, but persistently, shaken awake.

"Jo, get up. Jo, I need tae finish ma homework." The voice was gentle but insistent. Jo struggled to sit up, brushing the duvet aside to reach her alarm clock – the luminous dial said 4.10am.

Jo was helping Michael, a much older man, to do his homework. They were perched at a kitchen table beneath a dull light fitting. Jo watched as Michael worked through his assignment, pursing his lips in childlike concentration.

Ten minutes later, Michael had fallen asleep. He was ranged on a camp bed in the lounge. It was a small room with the armchair and settee pressed together to accommodate the narrow bunk. Jo pulled the duvet up around his neck and studied his face for a moment. She was too tired to concentrate. This was an erratic routine. Sometimes it was his homework, other times, he'd mis-placed something. An item vital to recover in that instant.

Jo was sitting finishing Michael's homework for him, as he slept a few metres away. The kitchen clocks all read 5.15am. She sipped from a chunky 'Alton Towers' coffee mug as she made another correction.

Clusters of slow-moving pupils were heading into school as Jo made her way towards the building. The reluctant Monday morning surge. Lynne, with not a hair out of place, caught up with her, smiling. Monday to Friday, Lynne was inch-perfect. At one time, Jo might have resented such a model young colleague or even a young colleague who looked like a model.

"Must have been a good weekend, you look shattered. Hope he was worth it?!" Lynne turned away laughing.

She had obviously had a good weekend. Jo wondered with whom and offered a resigned, tired smile as they headed into the school.

Monday, Period 3. Friday's class were back. Class 2E, whom Mr Graydon had labelled 'Twa Eejits' and laughed at his own wit. His brand of staffroom banter.

Jo was sitting at her desk, as the pupils, including Robert and James placed their homework books on a pile at the corner of her desk. She watched them settle with deliberate slowness and sighed. The arm-wrestle that was modern secondary education.

A rare free period and Jo was marking the homework. On her desk was a small, framed picture. Jo and Michael beamed out of it, a rollercoaster ride in the background. The words 'Me and ma Dad' carved into the frame.

"He is."

Jo's smile grew stronger, resolved, worth it. She opened another homework book and continued the marking.

WHERE

It is wooden, the bench. It sits, quite comfortably, on a slight rise just off the centre of a wide park. Common land.

Hands, young and strong, already accustomed to work, turned the small metal band over and over, his fingers sensing the smooth metal ring.

Slim feet, in heels, were perched at the other end of the bench, a bold flash of colour and youth.

The arm of the bench is weathered by the wet, the wind, the heat of the sun.

She was sitting on the bench, waiting.

Her hand was wearing the slim wedding band and placed delicately, deliciously close at the nape of his neck. *They were kissing*, the bench their theatre.

The bench is squat and soaked in the rain. A downpour.

They were holding hands. A glint of gold. His and hers.

The bench is drenched in sunshine.

Heavy feet. The shoes were a sensible uniform, an old man's fashion with scant room for vanity. Dull practical garb.

Old hands. Strong worked veins, a man's, slowly turning over a shrunken gold band.

Both palms are open to the dying light.

Two rings. A set. One larger than the other. A man and his wife's.

The bench is alone, a plaque still bright.

'Where Ann met Tom'.

HOGMANAY

Hogmanay. Scotland's night. Scotland's party. Scotland's almighty, bloody swally.

Makar lit another cigarette in a futile attempt to ward off the cold. It came in with the wind, off the sea, the tide carrying it in with the icy tang of salt.

Crossgate, the broad main street of Norhaven, was crowned by a wide Square. A simple stage of scaffolding had been erected at one end. A Christmas Tree threatened to list beside it. Makar stood in the lea of a large freight container, a giant skip, that looked as if it had simply landed there. It was even painted a dark Martian green.

The biggest party of the year. Hogmanay. How did I ever agree to this? Makar wondered.

This is it. That's what he'd said.

It could be the best Hogmanay ever. He'd said that, too. And was it? Makar wasn't convinced. It was fucking baltic. That's what it was. Makar lost his train of thought for a moment. Monotony could do that to a man. Unman him, so to speak. Here he was, a fine strapping loon, Hogmanay stretching out before him with all its potential. And here he was. Standing freezing his nads off like a tube, dressed in a white boiler suit, blowing up balloons. Thousands of them. Still it was only 4pm. The darkness had already crept in. The night was young. It hadn't even arrived yet.

Move about, he told himself, and he set off to walk a few lengths across the square and back. A lone figure, all in white.

Like a splash of paint amid the darkening grey granite on which the town was built. As Makar completed his first length, a coughing van turned into the Square. On its side read the words 'Scott & Son Joiners'. The vehicle stopped with a sullen grate of an objection.

Two joiners, Scott and Mikey, jumped out, blowing on their hands to acknowledge the chill. Arses. Makar wasn't sure what they were trying to prove, they'd just got out of a warm cosy van. The pair began to haul wide areas of chipboard off the truck.

"Will ye be doon the nicht?" asked Scott.

Mikey nodded.

'Aye, I'll be out wi' him.'

Mikey indicated the figure in white, seemingly loitering over the other side of the Square.

"What about yersel?" Mikey returned the compliment.

"Aye, I'm in the band, min." This was said with a touch of pride by Scott, but there was a sour taste of resentment in his explanation. He, too, had been press-ganged by Iain into helping celebrate the New Year in Norhaven. Hadn't they all?

They hauled up a board. Stencilled on it in red was 'Scott & Son'.

Two women, Pat and Jo, scuttled across the Square. Pat, a striking woman in her early fifties with a mischievous glint, usually sauntered everywhere, but not in this weather. Not on Hogmanay. A girl had a lot to do. Both women were well-wrapped. Pat paused and nodded at the joiners then to the younger woman Jo.

The joiners hesitated. They both knew her and what was coming.

242

"Think you boys will manage to get all this done in a day?"

The tone was arched and provocative. A cat toying with mice.

Scott and Mikey looked at her, neither one wanting to risk a retort. It wouldn't be worth it. Jo smiled in spite of herself and the cold. Pat considered their blank faces and was pleased with herself.

One-nil.

"I'll see ye twa at the bells," with that she departed, Jo trailing in her wake. Two–nil. Now, they'd both be nervous. Pat was a tigress.

Pat turned to Jo, a conspiratorial sharing, "Plenty of overtime for that lot." Just loud enough to provoke the boys. They both shrugged and let out their breaths in relief.

Jo glanced back at Scott and Mikey. She liked both of them; Scott had a good voice and Mikey was a likeable chancer. She also suspected that overtime didn't come in to it.

Jo turned to find Pat had changed direction, charting a course for Makar. She quickened her step to keep up, not wanting to miss more banter.

Pat stopped dramatically in front of Makar.

"Many mair tae dae?"

Makar nodded hurriedly. He didn't want to risk speaking in case his teeth started chattering again.

Pat nodded, satisfied, "At least you're here, doing yer bit, min," Pat let her meaning sink in.

Makar and Jo shared a glance and a recognition. Pat's message had been delivered. Aaron's absence had been noted. Sourly.

Pat set sail again, and Jo, with a small sympathetic smile for Makar, trotted after her.

The women paused to view a news hoarding which read 'MBE for Scott'. Two shops along another shouted, 'Norhaven man honoured.' They both smiled.

"About time someone fae Norhaven got one," declared Pat.

Jo nodded, "And we ken him'.

Pat snorted, "I ken a'body."

Aye, intimately, thought Jo with devilment, although she hoped she would look half as good as Pat did when she was whatever age Pat was. Her Uncle Bob had once remarked that Pat Walker could have been Norhaven Gala Queen for decades if the rules had allowed such a monopoly.

Standing beneath the stage, Makar was sticking to his task, the one Iain had set him. He was blowing up balloons. When he had filled each balloon, he stuffed it into the large tarpaulin-covered pallet parked behind him. A bleached Santa, he rocked from one foot to another in a white jump-suit, talking to the tall gas cylinder. It had been his only company for most of the long day.

A monologue in two voices.

"How many balloons is that, Cyril?" Makar asked, waving a balloon.

Makar took a big gulp of gas, turning the nozzle of the cylinder as he did so. Gas cylinders talk in a fast high-pitched tone.

"Too fucking many, pal," squeaked Makar under the influence of Cyril the cylinder.

Scott trotted across the square to speak to Makar.

"Fit like, Makar?" he called.

"Aye, aye, Scott," from Makar the pale Santa, still a squeak for a voice.

Makar launched into his party piece, a song from 'The Proclaimers', high-pitched and off-key, another mouthful of gas enabling Cyril to provide the high notes. A disjointed harmony.

"You're a boay, Makar. See you, the nicht," said Scott heading, back to his task.

After a cold afternoon with only Cyril and balloons for company, Makar wasn't about the let Scott go just yet.

"How many mare of them have ye got tae dae, Scott?" Makar finding his voice again over Cyril's.

Scott paused, did a quick calculation.

"That's aboot all o' them done now, onyway. Just a couple on Shore Wynd."

Makar nodded. They had been busy.

"Scott, mind to be doon early. It's Iain's last," Makar had now regained his voice.

"Aye, I ken. Nae news of Aaron?"

Makar's face darkened slightly. Scott hurried his next sentence. Best not to trespass. The last thing he needed was a pissed-off Makar.

"Dinna worry, I'll be doon the back o' seven. See ye the nicht."

Scott walked away. Makar lit another cigarette to sooth his annoyance. First Pat, now Scott.

It wasn't Scott's fault. He ought to remember that. It was Aaron's choice not to be here. He realised that he hadn't completely forgiven his best friend's absence. He suspected others hadn't either.

Makar laboured on, busy in his balloon production. A few feet away was the large metal pallet, with tarpaulin taut over it. Makar popped each balloon he made into a small aperture at one corner, where the cover has been tied back slightly. He was absorbed in his task, drawing on his cigarette against the cold. He'd need another pack for tonight at this rate.

Makar heard them before he saw them emerge out of the gloom of one of the narrow arteries that ran from Crossgate to Shore Wynd and the harbour basin. He glanced up. A couple in their thirties; he clocked them straightaway. Kenny and Stella were heading towards the Victoria Hotel. He recognised them.

The sparsely built Kenny was in a suit, with a scarf for warmth and a nod to fashion; Stella was in her Saturday night best.

The Victoria Hotel was built to celebrate a monarch and named for her. She was an old lady, a dowager hotel, that was now struggling to accept change in a state of faded velvet and brocade. Remnants of her former majesty remained; the spirit of the hotel clung to them, refusing to abdicate. The dark wooden rotating door guarded her main entrance with watchful frosted carved glass panels.

The couple's destination, however, was the stunted public bar slumped on the side of the once grand dame. But the public bar kept the money coming in, and the old lady needed its tenure to survive, to ward off the chill of old age and the bludgeoning cost of repairs that came with it.

Kenny raised an arm in recognition and greeting.

"Coming in for a wee nip, Makar?" a warm invitation on a cold night. The best kind.

Makar smiled, but shook his head. Kenny gave him a final salute as he steered Stella into the bar. Its entrance a narrow hole lit only by the red glow of the 'T' sign. Makar smiled. Locally, the bar was known as the 'Regent' after Victoria's German prince.

Makar watched them disappear into the welcoming warmth.

Makar knew their story. Kenny had been going to leave Stella since their wedding day. The entire town was still waiting for that event and the fallout.

His mood was lowering with the temperature. It was going to be a cold one. But dry. That was the key. People would turn out. As long as it didn't rain.

The five o'clock bus drew up in the Square. Three people clambered off. Makar watched to relieve the boredom.

Sandra, a startling girl in a belted overcoat, with a shop assistant's uniform beneath, noticed the snowman at work and meandered over to him, curiosity getting the better of her.

"Nice work if you can get it," she said, cocking her head at one side.

Makar scratched his head at the innuendo in her voice. Her lipstick was a match for her deep scarlet knee-length coat. Set against her jaunty black beret, it gave her a timeless quality; she was like a star of the silver screen. Even the wave of her hair underpinned the sense of Sandra being of a different era. Looking at her warmed him. His day was getting better.

Makar vaguely knew her granny and realized that he had just glimpsed what Auld Jeanie would have looked like in her heyday.

"Does the suit come wi' the job?" Sandra was still looking for a reaction from him. Makar smiled and offered her a balloon. That caught her by surprise and pleased her.

"Ma lucky day," Sandra laughed, but she didn't take the balloon.

Makar watched her skip away laughing.

Suddenly, Sandra stopped, spun round, and stepped towards Makar, snatching the balloon and, with an impish grin, walked away with her film star sway.

"It's nae flowers, but it's a thought," this parting shot thrown out over her shoulder.

Makar smiled crookedly, then looked down at his own uniform, another balloon with its limp tag still in his hand. Air was escaping from the balloon.

"This is the last time I'm dein' this," Makar reminded himself, before taking another gulp of gas.

"Good job, ye dinna mind making a dick of yersel," observed Cyril, his high-pitched friend.

That restored his humour.

After all, if you can't laugh at yersel, who can you laugh at? He clapped his hands together, in part to ward off the creeping cold and to raise his spirits. When Iain had talked him into this, Makar hadn't considered the weather. With Aaron away, Makar had felt vaguely flattered to be asked to fill his best friend's shoes. What he needed now, though, was a pair of boots. Fucking fur lined or something. He stole another glance towards the Regent. That was another thing on his wish list. He didn't normally feel the cold, but spending the day, the whole day, mind, filling balloons had left him cold and a mite resentful.

Makar patted the huge pallet beside him. When he had started this afternoon, he'd been determined to count them all. A small matter of pride to keep a tally of the balloons he had filled. He'd lost accurate count around 1,800 and the will to live somewhere near 2,000.

He inflated another, tied it off, made sure the tag was attached. The tag with the winner's name on it. Well, someone had to win the balloon race.

As his fingers numbed, Makar realized that he was getting slower. That wasn't the plan. More of the inert gas enlarged the thin rubber skin, before the supply died. Not completely. Two half-hearted spurts and the cylinder coughed up its last breath. *Shit*.

He shouldn't have wasted so much time speaking with Cyril. But Makar needed company and Cyril, his buddy for the day, had been his sole companion.

He'd have to let Iain know.

Makar cast a quick furtive glance towards the Regent. It was a friend calling to him. The heat, the welcome, and the glow which that first sip would bring, but Iain would crucify him if he arrived reeking of drink. Aye, with bad news to boot.

Makar patted Cyril goodbye, then checked. On second thoughts, best to take the evidence with you, he thought. Especially when delivering bad news to Iain. Drawing the creaking Cyril along behind him, Makar started to trudge towards the Scotts' house. It was Norhaven's unofficial Hogmanay Headquarters. They'd be busy getting ready for tonight and Makar hoped they'd lit the fire.

He arrived to find Jackie and Rob tying even more tags on to flat balloons. *More balloons*. Iain Scott, Chairman of the New Year Committee, the NYC, was counting piles of coins with one hand, a mug in the other. He ran his own joinery business, but his focus was the town. Norhaven. In particular, his focus was making sure it celebrated Hogmanay. Did it justice.

Makar had heard Iain's impassioned speech on Hogmanay many times, even in the middle of June. How Iain told it, Cromwell was to blame, him and his parliament banning Christmas. The Scots, not to be denied the chance to party, claimed New Year.

The history might be debatable, but Iain's passion for Hogmanay and what it meant was not.

"There's nae mair gas, Iain," announced Makar. He knew how to make an entrance.

Iain put down his coffee and looked up.

"Fit?" Iain hadn't taken that in.

"Nae mair gas. The cylinder's empty. Thought ye ought tae ken," Makar grinned. A substitute for a shrug. He had everyone's attention now: Jackie, Iain's wife, and their other son, Rob, Aaron's younger brother.

"That canna be richt," Iain said, refusing to accept this.

Makar nodded and waited. The peat fire cast a friendly glow around the Scotts' living room. Makar was glad to be in the warmth, walking from the Crossgate had warmed his feet, but his fingers felt as if they were fused together with cold. So numb that he'd had a struggle opening the Scotts' front door.

"Must be the valve." Iain was talking to himself. He looked up, focusing fully on Makar, the bearer of the bad news.

As he listened to Iain, Makar gravitated towards the flames, toasting his hands above them. Studying the rosy excited faces around him, he realized he'd definitely got the shite job this year. He wondered if he should dare sneak into the kitchen. There would be mounds of food ready for midnight. Should he risk it?

"Must be the valve." The thought was a comfort. A dummy. Jackie lit up between laughs.

"Just great. Just great. You know, there's always something gings wrang," her humour was legendary. Every setback was sidestepped or brushed aside with a wisecrack. Armed with it, she'd held her family together and gloried on.

"Must be the valve," Iain was plainly at a bit of a loss.

Heap's head rounded the door as the doorbell died.

"There's nae mair gas," he confided in a sympathetic whisper, as if someone they knew had died.

"We ken," Makar and Rob in unison. Heap was always behind the play, although he had a tendency to catch people out.

"Oh, right. Scot's doon with the band," Heap added, wanting to convey some breaking news.

Heap could have owned his by-name for any number of reasons. He was hefty. He looked like a heap. He was untidy. He just kind of arrived. He usually ended up in one after a few drams. Take your pick. Heap was all that and more.

He was universally liked because of the size of his heart, his care for others. One and all. Perhaps that was the real reason he was known as Heap.

Jackie gave Iain's arm a quick squeeze.

"We'll just have to have a draw, that's all, if we havnae got enough balloons.

Ian turned to Makar.

"Have we got enough? Balloons?"

Makar nodded.

"Hundreds, thousands, millions!"

Jackie laughed and clapped her hands together. Makar looked at her in gratitude and smiled.

"Empty. Must be the valve," Iain was shaking his head in disappointment, but it was a small one. Makar's confidence reassured him.

Behind him on the mantel above the fire was a small picture. As Makar looked at it, the photograph was pulled into focus for him. Iain, Jackie, Rob and another youth, Aaron, caught in the moment, a minute after midnight, all with arms aloft, laughing. On the frame it read 'Happy New Year'. Makar couldn't remember what year it had been. Not long ago. He'd have been there somewhere, in the same room. Or in the kitchen, chatting up Sandra? It could have been that year. He spent a lot of time at the Scotts'. It was an open house. His second home. The warmest hearth in Norhaven.

It was different tonight though. There was no avoiding it. There was no Aaron. It was the first year that he was absent. Going to varsity was all very well, thought Makar, but you should be with your own people on the night. He looked across and realized that Iain was offering him a drink, proof that this was Norhaven's beating heart. For him, anyway. Suddenly glad he hadn't given in to temptation and nipped into The Regent, Makar raised his glass to them all: Jackie, Iain, Robb and Heap.

"Slàinte!"

"Cheers!"

"Here's to us," began Iain.

"Fa's like us," said Makar, saying Aaron's line in his absence.

"Damn few and they're a' deid!" the chorus.

Makar took the glass of Malt to his lips, his eyes on Aaron's face grinning out of the picture. *Here's to you, bud. Have a good one.*

The city bar was packed. The post-work crowd were taking in a final spirit of the season before wending their way home, or on to another favoured watering hole. Aaron, the youth from the picture, was behind the bar. Slim and tall with a warm smile, he leaned forward to hear an order, gave a nod. The female customer was flattered. She turned to her mate and raised her eyebrows. Aaron was a natural.

"Two gin and tonics," she had to shout to compete with the music being pumped out. Aaron nodded his understanding and reached for two glasses, cupped in the ice, reached for the gin bottle and free-poured two long measures over the ice.

Sue watched him performing the order. There was no other word for it. It was a performance. Fluid and agile. She'd noticed him before, although she'd only been in here a couple of times. She hadn't had a drink yet, but what the hell.

He placed the two tall highball glasses on the bar's smooth surface and, almost simultaneously, a couple of tins of tonic. Perfect, Sue thought. Yes, it was his gracefulness that did it.

"Are you working all night?" she asked.

"Eight pounds, please," he smiled.

"No. Ok. I said are you working all night?" Sue raised her voice above the din. At that moment she hated Big Country. Aaron checked. This time he had heard her, or thought he had.

"What? No, thankfully not," he smiled.

Sue was trying to find her tenner. She held on to it as she tried again, a flag for parley.

"We're going to a party after. If you want to come, like. I could give you the address and my number," Sue was suddenly conscious of her friend Mandy staring at her. *God, this was so out of character.*

She handed over the tenner, feeling like a pure idiot and now scared he'd say no. Scared he'd say yes.

Aaron took the tenner offered and considered the invitation.

He was due at Kevin's when he finished his shift before heading across the city for a party at some mate of Kev's.

Aaron realized her hand was on his. Aaron took a breath. This kind of thing didn't happen to him. Well, it did tonight.

"OK," he stuttered, "I'm supposed to be meeting friends, so I can't promise."

He thought he was being fair, plus it kept his options open.

Sue was already writing on the receipt he had handed her. She was beaming. So was her friend. They were both cute. He accepted the receipt and tucked it into his hip pocket, turning to face the next customer.

His gaze settled on the balloons tied up around the bar. You couldn't really escape them. He knew Makar or Rob would be standing in for him at home. Hame.

As he poured the next pint, he looked across at the large industrial-style wall clock. Thoughtful.

Makar had left the Scotts' house and dashed to Mikey's place. A quick shower and a pizza and now they were jostling in the bathroom, vying for a reflection in the steamed-up mirror. Simple Minds' '*Forget About Me*' poured in down the landing. Both were trying to shave. They moved around each other. Mikey rubbed another spot the better to see. Makar edged left to avoid cutting himself. The excitement was building.

"A rare nicht, the nicht," Makar announced. He was warming up now. The Malt had helped and the shower had sealed it.

"I'll only be a mintie," said Mikey, trying to get the better position, but Makar was wise to him and refused to move.

Makar was getting reflective, running over the possibilities the night, this special night, could bring.

"Fiona will be oot. And Sandra."

"Aye, Sandra'll be oot. She's still seeing Rob Bruce though," Mikey reminded Makar.

But Sandra had made an impression on his friend that afternoon. Not for the first time.

"That's what she says. She was supposed to be with him in the Zulu on Saturday," Makar pointed out. Mikey thought this was just a case of Makar justifying his interest. Mikey tried again.

"She's still nae over Aaron. Never will be, like. Rob Bruce is wasting his time an' a'."

Was it the lipstick or the elegant tailored coat? Or just something about her voice? Perhaps all three.

For Mikey, there was something old-fashioned, homely, about Sandra. For Hogmanay though, he was thinking glam. Aim high: Leona Kirby or Isla Gammack – Norhaven first division, to Mikey's mind.

"Handsome bas," this was Mikey addressing the mirror. Satisfied with his new look, Mikey left Makar to his fantasies.

By the time Makar emerged from the bathroom, a towel wrapped around him, Mikey was already dressed.

"What time are we meeting Martin?" checked Makar, as he started to button up his shirt.

"Echt. At the Zulu," confirmed Mikey.

Makar nodded, judging how much time he had to get his arse in gear.

"I'll get a swally."

Mikey returned with two cans. They posed in front of the bedroom mirror and Makar raised a toast. A click of Mikey's mobile for posterity.

"Hogmanay and Sandra."

"Aye, and Sandra. Rob or no."

They both knew Rob Bruce, but it was Hogmanay.

"Aye and anyone else. I'll be using my tongue the night," Mickey stuck his tongue out at the mirror. Mikey laughed loudly, although he couldn't understand his friend's interest in Sandra. She was alright, but that was the sum of it.

Rob was sitting with a drink watching TV and pulling on his boots. From what Maker had said, he'd need them if he was marshalling later. The living room door opened and Cal wandered in, already opening a tinnie of Tennents. He brought a cold draft in with him.

"Where's Jackie?" he said, closing the door behind him with his foot.

"In the back room. They're getting dressed." said Rob.

"Fa?"

"Mam, Pat, and Jo. Elaine's late. Jo's just arrived," Rob thought Cal should have heard them all laughing when he came in.

Cal nodded during a deep swallow.

"They still need two stewards to close up Jubilee Street," Rob pointed out.

Cal was already shaking his head.

"I'm nae doing it. Get some dick deciding you're his punch-bag for the nicht."

Cal switched into Glaswegian. Or his take on it.

"Steward, eh? Big Man, eh? Stitch that, pal," he said, miming an exaggerated headbutt, "Nae chance. The lights are up. I'm done."

Cal plonked himself down in an armchair and drew on his tin. Cal's task had been to set up the lights on the Christmas Tree and a couple of spotlights for the main stage. Rob gave him a disappointed look and hauled himself out of his chair. Rob pulled on his jacket. He knew that Calum wouldn't have turned Aaron down. He tried to keep the annoyance out of his voice.

"Dad needs some help. He can't do it all." With that, he left Cal to his drink and black humour.

Cal sat scowling. He turned in his seat to shout.

"Aaron's not here though, is he!"

A door slammed. Rob had gone.

Cal reached across for the remote control and changed the channel. "Dick."

Not everyone loved New Year. He'd done his bit, what his Uncle Iain had asked him to do. Feet-up time.

The fire was now a deep red-orange glow. Costumes were draped over the chairs, sitting in piles, each with a labelled collection bucket standing beside it. Jackie ushered in Pat and Jo.

Pat was quick to make her decision.

"Oh no. I said nae teddies," as she darted to grab a clown outfit. Jackie had set up a tall standing mirror which Pat used to assess whether the costume would fit her.

"This should just about dae," said Pat. It was not the kind of fancy dress she favoured, but it was for a good cause and she couldn't wear any of her own stuff. At least, she smiled to herself, not without being arrested.

Jackie had also opted for a clown outfit, while Jo was contemplating a teddy bear all-in-one. Ever practical, she thought it might be the warmest option.

Jackie and Pat helped each other into their clown aprons.

"Watch the pin," warned Jackie.

Pat nodded – a row of safety pins for teeth. Jackie passed around the white wine.

"Ta. Where's Elaine?" Pat took a good swig, one hand on her hip, the other waving her glass.

"She said she'd be a bittie late," said Jackie.

Pat lit up a cigarette. Elaine was always late. You could set your watch by her.

"She'll have to have the teddy," said Pat firmly. Being late always cost you, and Pat would make sure that she paid.

When Elaine arrived, all the others laughed and pointed to the teddy.

"Shit. I'll just have to look a neep, and hope no one will recognise me." Elaine was not impressed, but knew better than to argue. You're always at a disadvantage if you are the perpetually late friend.

"Come on, Pat, we're to be starting in the van at ten," Jackie waved her glass at Pat.

With an exaggerated shrug of resignation, Pat downed her drink. The others were ready. A bucket apiece, they set off laughing. Aye, thought Jackie, two bears and two right clowns.

Huddles of people drifted along Crossgate, pressing towards the stage.

A small pack of youths strutted, laughing and joking, high on expectation. They turned into a bar. A small crowd had gathered, predominantly families, the Christmas lights providing the downward sparkling illumination.

Charlie the Clown was performing on stilts for a cluster of families gathered beneath him. Grandma Margaret knelt beside a young lad, her grandson Bobbie.

"Do you like the clown, Bobbie?", she asked the small boy.

"He's a tall mannie, Nana," observed the small figure.

His grandma nodded, "Aye, he is."

Bobbie pointed at the clown.

"A tall mannie," shouted the wee boy at the man on sticks with the garishly painted face.

Bobbie pointed upwards.

"How tall are you, mannie?"

The clown paused, putting on a thoughtful face, started to answer, then theatrically stopped to think some more. He scratched his head. Thinking was hard work. Bobbie scratched his head too as he waited for the answer.

"Taller than you," said the clown finally, pointing back at the wee boy.

The chic city bar was still busy, but the crush had died.

With work matters washed away, the punters were now looking ahead to their Hogmanay. Aaron handed over a brace of beers. He couldn't see the girl and her friend who had invited him to the party. Perhaps he'd imagined it, but patting his pocket he felt the thin trace of a piece of paper, the receipt for two gin and tonics with her number scrawled across it in her flowing curved script.

He took the money and turned to open the till. As he did so, he glanced up at the clock. He caught his reflection in the mirrored bar. It was, he realised, the face of a man who would rather be smiling elsewhere.

Iain hurried along Crossgate, a 'Happy New Year' sign under his arm. Heap, bearing the other end, scurried to keep up with him.

"The hotel disnae board up their windows. It's their policy. Touch wood, it's worked so far," Iain was pointing to the Victoria, as if somehow the old hotel was above such frivolity.

Trotting along with him, Heap looked doubtful.

"That'll be richt," he muttered, but he knew it to be true. The modern world didn't dare intrude on the Victoria, unless she permitted it.

The crowd had thickened. A handful of youths, cans aloft, jigged and lurched around a litter bin to the strains of '*Loch*

Lomond'. Their empties fell to the ground. One of them bent to pick them up, worried that a relative might have spotted him in this company of litter louts.

The first brave clambered up onto the top of the bus shelter. A follower joined him. A third, too drunk to manage, fell back before his mates pushed him up. The lads, wearing their Saturday night finest, showed off in lager-fuelled bursts.

A Police Sergeant and Constable moved in, the crowd parting for them.

Two women, clutching their kids' hands, provided a frank, sour commentary.

"Last year mind, a young loon fell off there and smashed his heid." The sentence ending with a tut.

"Serve him richt." A dose of seasonal sympathy.

The gloved hand of the law clamped an ankle as another lad tried to climb aboard the party. He just made it.

The Sergeant's restraining hand landed on the shoulder of another adventurer. The young man, arm back, swung round, set for confrontation. His face fierce.

Shock washed his features as he mumbled an apology, moving away amused at his own reaction and his lucky escape.

His mates jumped down, a couple landing badly. There was a last arm-raised show of defiance from the pack leader before he too hit the concrete. The Constable waved him on.

The queue to the portable toilet lengthened. Desperate dashes for early relief left gaps in the line.

Light spilled out from the small food van, where Jackie and Pat were serving a queue of customers, their breath visible despite the warmth of the small van.

"No, we don't sell hamburgers," explained Jackie.

"No, no burgers," added Pat.

"No. Sorry, just soup and pies. And sausage rolls," Jackie added.

"No, no burgers," from Pat again.

"No, we haven't," Pat repeated, "Read my lips."

She offered another full exaggerated pout.

A lull in the orders followed.

Jackie poured another tea and served up a couple of sausage rolls.

"How many times do you have tae tell some folk?"

"I ken." Pat agreed scanning the queue, daring anyone else to raise the subject of burgers.

"Can you cope?" Pat asked Jackie. "Time for me to walk the streets and rake in the cash."

Jackie laughed, glad she was staying in the warmth of the van, even if they didn't have any burgers.

Pat, the most glamorous clown in town, cigarette in one hand, bucket in the other, moved through the crowd, shaking her bucket.

Elaine the teddy stalked behind her.

Young children were given change by parents and sent the few steps to drop it into the buckets.

"Ta," said Elaine, crouching down to the small figures, "thanks, guys." The children smiled back shyly and trotted back to their families.

Pat shook her bucket in front of a man in a hurry to get past her. He dropped something into the tub.

Pat looked at the tub then at him.

"Fit do ye call that?" She was close to his face, "Put yer hand in yer pouch, min!"

Backpedalling, he fumbled for change, cast a handful of silver and copper into the bucket and made a dash for it.

"Tight-arse," said Pat. Elaine the teddy bear grunted in agreement.

Pat was still shaking her head.

"Tae think that I once agreed to a date wi' that creep."

Elaine's bear face was blank.

"Older and wiser noo, Elaine," Pat gathered herself, shook her bucket and sallied forth.

Rob appeared by Heap's side. He nudged him to indicate the hotel bar door. The uncertain Heap consulted his watch. The two of them edged towards the door.

On stage, Scott was singing his heart out. *'Handbags and Gladrags'*, his favourite Rod Stewart number. This was a gig where Scott got to choose the songs except for three requests from Iain. He'd get to them later. Aye, but Techno was banned. Iain could nae abide it. The band thumped out the beat. The makeshift stage was bouncing. Scott prayed it would hold. He watched Rob and Heap weave their way across and push into the dim doorway of the Regent.

Rob and Heap toasted each other. The bar was crammed. In the corner, Kenny and Stella had been joined by friends. Kenny was telling a joke; their laughter was loud and harsh. Heap and Rob give them a glance. The duo downed their pints. Heap consulted his watch. Rob signalled the barman; if they are going outside again, they'd go fortified.

Rob pointed to a vertical bottle on the optic.

Aaron pushed the glass up against the optic. The swish city bar was emptying of customers. Aaron had a white tea-towel slung over his shoulder. He shifted glasses from the bar counter to the washing machine. He looked at the clock and frowned.

Heap was standing with Makar when Libby strutted up to them.

"Hiya, Eddie," she addressed Heap. Makar raised an eyebrow.

"Oh, hiya," from Heap, a tad self-conscious to have Makar as a grinning witness.

"You helping out tonight?" somehow Libby was now between the two men. Makar wasn't quite sure how she'd got there. Neither was Heap.

"Aye, I'm doing the balloons," said Heap.

"What?" Libby wasn't sure what her target was talking about. She moved closer for more clarity.

"The balloons. At 12 o'clock. Midnight. They're in the lorry," Heap thumbed to point at the lorry pallet.

"Oh, right," Libby sounded a mite disappointed.

Heap turned to Makar, as the girl's friends waved to her and, distracted, she glided away.

"What do you think? Aye?"

"Aye, nae doubt," said Makar. He wouldn't have let Libby wander off.

But he, too, was distracted, looking elsewhere as a couple walked past.

"Fit like, Sandra?" said Makar, stepping forward to greet her.

Sandra was drunk and vaguely flirtatious.

"Hiya, Makar."

Some boy had her by the wrist. She was led away. Makar tried to figure out who the boy was. It was still early. Whoever he was, he wasn't wasting anytime.

Abandoned, Makar turned to Heap.

"You think?"

Heap shrugged.

"Aye, nae bother. What do you think?"

"Nice to have a fan club, Eddie. Heap's Harem, eh?" Makar mimicked his friend's shrug.

"Aye. I like her," confided Heap. Makar wasn't sure if he meant Libby or Sandra. Probably both.

Hemmed in, Mikey turned in panic from his cluster of mates, barging past his pals.

"Sorry," he mouthed.

He bumped his way through other groups. The bodies thinned. He reached out for a wall to give him balance and safety. Cold, rough support.

The first heave.

"Fuck. Shit."

More waves.

"God."

He looked down. His shoes had not escaped the splattering.

The last few spits. He straightened up with a wipe of his mouth, relieved that no one nearby knew him. Deep breaths. He pushed back through the crowd and re-joined his mates, taking an offered tin to drink away the sour taste of puke.

A lad tapped a girl on the shoulder. She turned and nodded. They kissed. Restrained. Polite. A bit formal. An early evening kiss.

"Oh yes! My first New Year kiss!" Sandra laughed to herself. It was a bit early, but who cared.

She hugged him. She was talking to herself, her own delight. He was forgotten. His mates moved him on.

Sandra checked, faced with another entangled couple. She hesitated, ambushed by thoughts of last New Year's Eve. Images of Aaron and the following months. Damn. The couple were still hamming in. Sandra scolded herself, damned Aaron again and sidestepped the amorous pair.

The station concourse was wide, cold and deserted. His footsteps echoed as Aaron, still in his work gear, a jacket hastily thrown on, ran towards the platform, but his train has gone. He stood catching his breath. A few feet away a lone couple embraced, their evening's journey at an end.

Aaron paused, calculating. His decision made, he turned and started to run again, leaving the station.

Iain was standing feeling pleased with how the evening was going when Makar arrived at a trot.

"We need a ladder, Iain," he said.

"A ladder?"

"Aye, for the balloons," said Makar, pointing towards the large shadowed pallet by the stage.

"Damn," muttered Iain.

A pause.

"I ken far there's a ladder," said Iain, inspiration coming to him as took off down the Brae, kilt flapping and arms pumping. Makar followed.

A youth was urinating in a discreet corner, his back to the other revellers. Makar barged him out of the way, reaching for the ladder. The youth was left swaying, facing the crowd, flies down and white-faced, fumbling to salvage his dignity.

The two men heaved the ladder out. Moments later, the ladder-bearing duo reappeared at the bottom of the Brae, a silent film comedy partnership. Watching their progress, Jackie and Elaine the teddy bear started applauding.

With Makar on one side, Heap and Rob on the other, the tarpaulin was edged off pull by pull, yard by yard. From below, Iain watched in anticipation.

Up went the first balloon, a red one, peeping from the top of the green transport container. Another, a third, two more.

The tarpaulin pullers waited. The tops of the balloons peeked over the rim of the fish lorry. None rose further. Iain's smile slipped, dipped and fell.

"Shit," said Heap.

Heap and Makar looked at each other. A blank exchange.

Makar clambered into the truck. Heap climbed the ladder as Rob steadied it.

Balloons began to appear, edging their way upwards in ones and tangled twos. Makar and Heap pushed, punched and kicked the balloons aloft.

Rob, perched atop the ladder, one foot on the lorry, helped the balloons along. Bunches of tangled balloons were pushed skyward. Makar fanned the balloons. Heap kicked and shouted at them.

In bundles, the balloons rose only a few feet before easing on to the wet tarmac.

A young boy spied them and charged towards them.

"Balloons!"

A girl followed his movement.

"Mam, look. Mam, balloons."

Other bundles of balloons drifted around the lorry container.

Makar and Heap sweated, forcing the single balloons up and the entangled clusters over the edge. Iain tried to encourage the balloons to rise higher, flapping at them.

Kids trailed around the truck, handfuls of balloons bobbing along with them. Iain's smile was back. Simple and satisfied.

A stout woman with cropped, dyed-blonde hair stepped forward with two young children. Shaking off her charges, she approached two lads, one collecting, the other holding a huge continent of balloons.

"You've got mair than enough. My bairns ha'e nae got ony."

She divided the balloons between her children in front of the shell-shocked victims of the balloon theft.

The band were banging out *'Loch Lomond'* again. Scott, his arms aloft, could have been playing a stadium to thousands. This was his Hampden.

Beneath them, people were doing wild jigs and unsteady flings.

The band made way for Iain Scott MBE.

Iain Scott stepped up to the microphone. He tapped it.

"Fit like? Hello. Hello. Are ye dein' a'richt?"

He was answered by the crowd.

"Iain! Iain!" A rising wave.

"The whole point of tonight, the whole point of this year was for folks to enjoy thirsels."

Iain raised his arms, a minister to his congregation, "Did ye enjoy yersels?"

"Aye!"

More voices from the crowd.

"Iain Scott MBE!"

"Well done, min!"

"He's done nae bad."

"The mannie deserved it, like."

"I hope you have enjoyed yersels. That's richt. Enjoy

yersels!" Iain stepped forward, arms wise embracing the audience. "Five!"

The crowd took up the cry. "Four! Three! Two! ONE!"

As Iain left the stage, Slessor the Piper stepped forward. Expectancy from the crowd.

He started to play *'Flower of Scotland'*. Norhaven joined in. The Bells. Drowned by the cheers.

Iain was standing at the side of the stage. He was searching the crowd. Makar noticed and patted him gently on the arm.

"This'll be the first. . ." Iain said softly.

"He'll make it." Makar didn't know where the words came from. Or if they held any truth. But it needed to be said, and Iain needed to hear it.

People cheering. Hugging friends.

A Police Officer at the side of the crowd was being coaxed into a dance by a couple of women.

Elaine and Pat, the bear and the clown, were hugging each other. People were spotting and waving at friends. Hands primed a tin of lager, shook it, and pulled back the pin. People shaking hands.

The lager erupted.

Someone tapped Elaine the teddy on the shoulder. She turned around. Struggling, helped by the other's hands, she tugged off the teddy's head. Elaine and Rob kissed.

Groups of lads were singing and spraying the nearby crowd with their beer.

The Constable was now being draw into a kiss. Well, a polite police peck.

Children were hoisted onto their parents' shoulders, partly to keep them out of harm and also to see the few balloons rise steadily above the town. Bobbie was one, pointing to the sky. A lone pale balloon was on its way to the dull moon.

Girls moved arm in arm, singing, and stopping for kisses.

The Police Officer was now being offered a drink. He was tempted, but sheepishly declined.

Bobbie, at the centre of his family, was being given a close hug by his Nana.

Drinks were being offered; people were toasting each other.

Iain pushed through the crowd. He reached Heap, who was wondering where Libby had disappeared to. Or who she'd disappeared with, if he was honest with himself.

"Far's Jackie?"

Heap pointed back towards stage. Iain patted him on the back and turned around in search of his wife.

Moving through the crowd. Iain reached Jackie.

"Happy New Year, wifie!" he shouted over the cheering.

Jackie smiled. They embraced.

"Alright, hun?" she whispered as she held her man tight.

Iain nodded unconvincingly.

"It's going well, Iain. It is. I'm feeling it too. I'm sure he tried." She gave him another squeeze.

Iain nodded and held her.

Rings of friends and strangers formed.

The band were singing *'Flower of Scotland'*. Again.

The crowd members were singing along. The whole Square was singing.

Iain met Makar amid the crowd.

"Happy New Year, ma loon."

"Happy New Year tae you, Iain Scott," said Makar.

They shook hands. Makar reached into his coat and produced a tinnie. He offered it to Iain.

"Cheers!" said Iain taking the can and a mouthful of goodwill.

The band started *'Auld Lang Syne'*. Scott looked euphoric, standing above the crowd.

People formed small circles to sing 'Auld Lang Syne'.

In the crowd, couples formed private islands, mouth to mouth, limpets without a rock.

Deep in the crowd, Libby moved from passing male to passing male, a bumper car ride of kisses. Some were hurried and slurred, others over-long, drawing out the last alcoholic breath from her partners. Although young, she tottered with the grace of a matronly ballerina, a face filled in by makeup, bouncing from breathless embrace to buffeted rejection. Her unfocused eyes were triumphant, as only a drunk can be with a good snog. Hazily, Libby wondered what the hell had happened to Heap.

Makar and Rob had witnessed the entire series of snogs. They exchange a mingled look of amazement, amusement and admiration as Libby swayed, assessing them.

They moved off laughing, making a mutual escape.

Aaron was thumbing a lift beneath the sign that read 'North'. He knew he was going in the right direction. He just wished a car would stop soon before he froze to death. Another car whizzed past, refusing to stop. The wind cut through him again. He was drenched with cold. Perhaps he should have thought this through. Rung that cute girl. Gone to the party.

It was Hogmanay – surely someone would stop for him?

The crowd thinned. Couples wandered off arm-in-arm.

Children were led away by their grandparents, leaving parents to greet friends.

Bobbie was in his father's arms, asleep against his shoulder. His grandma checked his gloves were secure, brushed his cheek, and on this night offered up a silent prayer for his future.

Couples clung to each other, staggering on with their own celebrations.

The band started to unplug their equipment between toasts of Export.

Scott was still hyper from the gig. What a night: Elvis, Midge Ure, Rod. All his heroes. He had been them all.

"Shit, I was nervous. It was great. Just great. I'd have done it for free," he said.

The guitarist nodded between swallows. Iain emerged, smiling from the shadows.

"Next year, we may ask ye tae," slapping them all on the shoulders.

The two toasted him. It was a running joke – no one got paid. No one ever had.

In the corner of the stage, Rob and Makar were taking down the lights.

"Bloody tight these. Nae need to hae them this tight," said Rob, suspecting his cousin Cal had done this deliberately. Aaron had spoken to him about it after last year.

Makar looked up.

"Dinna worry, if you fall, I'll catch the spot," he laughed. Rob joined in, as he passed the first one down. Where was Cal? *Useless shite.*

Hands were cutting a large slab of cheese into cubes. Jackie tipped the pile of cubes into a bowl. Jo skewered the cheese and pineapple chunks with cocktail sticks. Jackie made the finishing touches to a platter, with sections of small pickled onions, crabsticks and plain cheese. On the kitchen table was a vast array of similar snacks and nibbles. A Hogmanay Festive Board.

Jackie halted her labour and raised her glass to Jo, who took her cue and lifted her own drink. They toasted each other.

Jackie finished her drink. She hastily reached to pour another. Jo giggled, returning to her chore. The boys would be back soon.

Country music crowded the cab. Aaron and the heavy-set driver were singing. Murdering '*Galvaston*', in spite of Glen Campbell. A small Netherlands flag hung from the central mirror, a nodding Johan Cruyff on the dashboard. The music and the small overworked heater took Aaron's mind off the time and the stale impregnated reek of old cigarettes. And the miles still to go.

Only one clump of revellers remained in the Crossgate. They were taking the last swigs from their bottles, prolonging extended New Year kisses. Next to them, Iain Scott MBE was sweeping the streets.

Rob and Makar paused between spotlights and watched him.

Iain halted at a bin and opened it. It was nearly empty. Iain started again. The preoccupied party-goers were blind to his efforts.

Makar and Rob were caught in the moment of watching Iain sweeping the street.

"He's some boay," declared Makar.

"Aye, I ken." Rob felt the pride and love for his father build inside him. Only his brother meant more to him.

Iain swept, oblivious to his audience.

The Police Sergeant was joined by a Constable beneath the front of the stage. The last strand of drunken stragglers approached, girls leaning on their men, hands outstretched.

"Great night. Just great. Cheers, Pal," gushed Mikey.

He pumped the Sergeant's hand.

"Nae bother," mumbled the officer.

"Great," said Sandra, hanging off Mikey.

The Constable listened to the same record, shook the same hands. Then he stopped, looking around to see if anyone has seen him shaking the hand of the pisshead.

From the scaffolding, the grinning Makar gave the policeman the thumbs up. The policeman nodded back, a wry acknowledgement.

Makar took in that Mikey was with Sandra. His friend gave him a wide open-armed shrug. They were mates after all.

Makar swallowed his disappointment – it was not as if it was the first time she'd gone off with the wrong bloke. The thought gave him false comfort.

Sandra waved, drunkenly, but slightly embarrassed just the same. She pushed her thoughts away.

Makar nodded and raised his tinnie in a mocking toast. That's what comes of supporting the community, he thought. *Shite to it.*

A taxi came down into the square, cutting into the evening's debris. Crossgate was officially closed until 6am. Rob had gone over the licence paperwork with his brother before Aaron had gone away. The taxi driver was a Chancer.

The back tyre blew out as the taxi swung around the corner, back end hanging out like a heavy drunk. The car did not stop.

On the stage, Makar and Rob stood shaking their heads.

"Arse."

"He didn't need to come through this way," said Rob in disgust.

"He's always been a dick," added Makar, making a mental note to have a quiet wee word with Kenny Barclay, who owned the taxi firm, next time their paths crossed.

The crew were lifting down sound and lighting equipment from the stage to the ground. There were four of them: Rob and Makar on stage, Heap and Iain below. A generation separated them, but Iain could still hold his own. Years of joinery work had granted him forearms that Popeye would envy.

"This one's heavy," Rob breathed.

"He's nae jokin'," said Makar, strain in his voice.

The four men struggled with the huge awkward black boxes. Keeping a grip was the key.

"This one's heavier," warned Rob.

"Christ," groaned Heap.

A breather.

"Squat. Bend your knees," said Rob.

The instruction came too late. One of the four groaned, clutching a tear. It was Heap, the largest of them, biting back the pain.

"This one's very heavy," Rob giving more instruction.

"Shit," Makar gave a pained breath, "I could do myself a mischief here."

"Squat," ordered Heap.

"Why do we do this?" Makar said finding air between lifts, "Every year, min."

"It's Hogmanay," this from Heap, rubbing his bicep.

"We're Scottish, ken," said Rob, taking a new grip. He straightened, "It's part of who we are. It's ours."

Deep breaths and sore arms. Fingers numbing and failing to grip.

"This one's extremely heavy," more commentary from Rob.

Makar was getting irritated.

"'Extreme' the boay says. The last one was just 'very heavy'."

They took the strain.

"He's nae joking," gasped Heap.

"Shit," Makar moaned.

"Christ," said Heap as he took the strain. Heap had huge heavy arms, but even he was struggling.

Mouthfuls of relief.

"Everyone celebrates New Year." Makar wanted a cigarette. The heat, the comfort of it. A break from the labour too.

Rob straightened, "Not like we do."

"How many more of these are there?" said Makar.

"Four," said Rob doing a quick count.

"Four?" Makar couldn't believe it.

"Quit girnin'," said Rob, "let's get this done."

Slow progress.

They lowered another to the ground.

"We invented it. Best thing we ever did. Ever gave the world," Rob added with passion.

"Aye? Fit about whisky? Golf?" Maker raised an eyebrow.

"The kilt?" this from Heap.

"Billy Connolly, Sean Connery, Archie Gemmill," Makar recited, "aye, Andy Murray."

"James Bond," Heap again.

Makar frowned at him. "Bond?"

"Aye, OO7 – Scottish." Heap was adamant.

Makar shrugged. Heap knew some strange shit.

"Better. Bigger than them all," Rob was standing firm.

Makar had one last go. "Tunnock's Teacakes?"

Rob laugh was a terrier's bark.

"I love 'em, but aye. It's a new start, with the people ye love, or thinking of them. Wishing them the best. It's hope, it's ours, it's a gift and that's what makes it great."

Makar and Heap looked at each other.

"Fuck me, Rob. Some speech," said Makar, slapping Rob on the back.

Rob took the compliment from his brother's best friend and smiled back. "Squat. Lift, yer bass!"

They almost dropped it with laughing. Then Heap took the weight and it was done.

"Tunnock's gets ma vote," the voice was older, deeper, wiser.

Iain had been a smiling, silent witness to their discussion, but had said nothing. This was his last Hogmanay, he was passing on the baton to these younger men. It reassured and warmed him.

"That's it," announced Iain, beaming at his protégés.

"Thank Christmas," said Makar, stopping himself from saying worse. He knew Iain didn't approve of coarse language. Makar had never heard him preach, but with Iain you just knew. Swear words had no currency.

The four stood, chests working, grateful for the relief of the cold air in their lungs.

Iain was next to the 'Scott & Son' van with the unloaders. He pumped each of their hands.

"I just want to thank you. It was tremendous. Made all the difference. Thanks."

Makar, left to struggle alone, almost toppled a rebellious amp. "Christ."

The amps were shifted onto the van parked behind the stage. Steam was rising off the figures despite the close midnight chill.

"Good job these things have wheels," said Makar, pushing them towards the van, "even if they are wilful."

"Aye, too richt," said Rob, speeding up to race him.

The last amp was lifted into the van, which creaked in protest as it took the weight.

"You lot can go on up tae the house, I'll just finish up here," said Iain.

"You're sure?" asked his son. Part of Rob wondered if his brother would have insisted on staying to clear up until the end. He looked about. They were almost done and his dad meant it. He always did.

"Ok," he nodded.

But Heap was already swinging round. "Ok, cheers." He knew Jackie would have a banquet prepared and he needed the consolation of a real feed after losing track of the lovely Libby.

Rob, Eddie the Heap, and Makar made their way down the Crossgate.

"Now for some serious swallying," sang Rob.

He theatrically rubbed his hands together, mimicking downing a jar.

"Aye, too richt," said Heap, his New Year just beginning.

Makar was still obsessing about the amps.

"Like the way each one got heavier as we went along."

Rob knew that when Makar came to recount his part in proceedings, the amps would have become half-tonne bisons. Makar's was a fertile mind. His prowess in exaggeration was legendary.

Makar lit a cigarette, equilibrium restored.

"Shame aboot your brud." A fag always made him thoughtful.

"Aye. Thought he'd mak' it," said Rob, looking back towards his father, who was shifting bins back into place further up the street.

Makar followed his gaze and his thoughts.

"Rob, alright to leave your dad?"

"Fit?"

"Your dad."

"He'll be alricht," decided Rob. He knew his Dad wanted some time to himself to savour the night and take stock.

Makar shrugged, then brightened as if remembering something profound.

Like a conjurer, Makar produced another tinnie from his coat.

"Cheers Rob, Heap. Happy New Year tae yous," he said, holding his trophy aloft.

Makar took a swig and passed it to his mates. They responded with grateful grins. The trio walked on with lighter spirits.

The lorry pulled up. A figure jumped down and gave the driver the thumbs up sign before swinging the door shut and stepping back. Aaron moved into the neon light and raised his thumb again. The Dutchman had given him an old pair of gloves, a gift on Hogmanay. This was the magic his father believed in, the kindness of strangers. Iain did not believe in barriers. He was with the Bard: all are equal.

The lorry, with the address of an Amsterdam flower wholesaler written with a flourish on its side, moved off with a last yell of the horn.

As Aaron braced himself against the wind at his back, he

could see lights approaching and prayed for further festive kindness.

A drink was being poured, ice cracking. Pat passed it to Jackie. Elaine and Jo were there. So too was Cal, eyes still fixed on the television which was showing some tribute to Scots funny men. Elaine was changing the music.

Makar, Heap and Rob strode in. Jackie got to Rob before Elaine and hugged him. Rob had tears in his eyes.

"Happy New Year, Mam!"

Jackie gave him a quick kiss.

"God love you, son. Where's Dad?"

"He'll be here in a mintie."

Elaine, now out of her outfit, tugged Rob in her direction.

Heap and Jo were looking at each other. Jo made the first move. Heap did not complain. Makar looked bemused.

"What aboot me?"

Pat winked at Jackie and theatrically put down her drink.

"Come here, tiger," Pat growled, shaking her cleavage at him and sassying towards Makar.

Makar blanched, then laughed.

"Happy New Year, Pat. Jackie." He got to kiss them both, "Whey Hey!"

Cal looked on sourly. New Year. He didn't see what all the fuss was about.

Iain directed the band in the small joiner's van to his house.

"Want a lift?" asked Scott, leaning out of the passenger window.

"No, I'll just check o'er a few things," Iain shook his head.

Crunching over scattered glass, the van headed off slowly. Iain watched it go.

Iain was alone. He looked around the deserted Square, taking in the entire scene. The noise and merriment of earlier came back to him. He smiled. You should start the year well. He had always believed that. He still did.

He looked up towards the stars before picking his way down a silent Crossgate. He looked back down the road, took two quick steps and leapt upwards punching the air.

"Yes! Yer beauty!"

Gas cylinders lined against the front wall outside the Scotts' house. Some of the youths seen earlier climbing on the bus stop were standing around the scattered metal tubes.

The group huddled in the shadows, taking turns to suck in a breath from the empty cylinder to make silly voices, recruiting others as they arrived to have a go.

"Don't you, forget about me. Don't you . ."

"For Auld Lang Syne, my dears . ."

"My name's Mr Spock!"

"Exterminate!"

"I am Spartacus!"

"I am Groot!"

They evaporated into gas-induced giggles. A cocktail of youth, alcohol, and helium.

Giggles. Aaron was crammed in the back between three girls. They were loudly dressed and loudly drunk. Aaron smiled, but his eyes were fixed on the taxi's progress, mist drifting in from the fields. Every now and then he had to shift position to avoid the hand of the girl on his left pressing his thigh. He avoided eye contact, staring fixedly ahead. She didn't need any encouragement. She'd kissed his neck twice already.

The Scotts' living room was now filling up. Jackie was handing around one of her famous platters. Jo was sitting on Heap's knee. Makar was ridiculing Cal for being a miserable git. Cal was enjoying the role. It gave him a part at the party. As far as Rob was concerned, his cousin didn't merit one.

"Forecast's good for the morn, Makar. Beach'll be bonnie for you," Rob's humour carried across the room. A yearly ribbing on the way.

"Aye, yer annual pilgrimage," scoffed Cal, trying to score a point back.

Makar considered the cousins, Rob's bonhomie and Cal's scowl, "Each to their own, min. And I'll keep mine."

On the sofa, Sandra turned back to Mikey and spoke quietly, just for him.

'It's nae gonna happen.'

Mikey gave a mechanical nod, his hopes stalling.

"What happened wi' Libby? Why didn't you just ask her here?"

Mikey was still nodding, accepting the expected. He had no idea what had happened, where Libby had gone. One minute he'd been snogging Libby, the next, he was holding hands with Sandra. How had that happened?

"Aaron invited me here last year, to the party. You could hae brought Libby."

She was trying to help Mikey. Being kind.

"A'hm nae Aaron." Mikey stopped his head nodding. An admission. An apology.

Sandra caught herself, her breath and herself. Mikey could see right through her. Perhaps they all could. But he wasn't looking at her; he was studying his drink. Why did lads always do that? No answers there, thought Sandra.

Mikey had hit the nail on the head. He wasn't Aaron. Aaron was . . what was the word . elusive. Hedging his bets. One eye always on the door. The next best thing.

But Aaron was hundreds of miles away. Aaron was last year. Sandra surprised herself by smiling. In fact, Aaron was the year before. Long ago.

Sandra kissed Mikey's cheek, hugged him and decided to change the music. There's only so much of Bay City Rollers a girl can take.

Makar standing a few jealous feet away, noticed her disentangling herself from Mikey.

"Are you away?"

Sandra cast him a glance.

"Off to see ma Grunny."

"Bid Auld Jeanie, a Happy New Year fae me."

"Come along and do it yersel."

Challenged, Makar's uncertainty hobbled him.

"Nay, you're alricht. I'll bide where I am at."

"Please yersel."

"Creature of habit me. From here to the beach the morn…"
Makar's explanation faded in the face of Sandra's gaze.

Then she was gone. Makar and Mikey looked at each other. Friends, but not comrades.

"What the hell was all that aboot?" Mikey looked up at Makar.

"I dinna ken. But somethings going on wi' her."

"I didnae even get a proper snog," Mikey's disappointment was clear.

"Glad to hear it," Makar almost added an insult. His annoyance at Mikey was dwarfed by the anger he felt towards himself. Had that been an invitation from Sandra? 'Creature of habit, me.' What an arse! And now she was gone.

As the door opened, Pat took the platter from Jackie who rushed to embrace her husband. Makar raised his glass to the main man. Others gave small cheers and one or two clapped.

Iain faintly embarrassed, but pleased, nodded back before scanning the faces. Jackie gave him a slight look of reproach. Rob thrust a glass in his dad's hand and raised his own. Iain seemed to wake up and enveloped his son in a hug. Jackie had to turn away to hide her own emotions. The three were embracing. Pat pointed the camera. They took a hundredth of a second to pose. The flash went off. A trio of smiles. Minus one.

Auld Jeanie's front room was dimly lit, a standing lamp competing with the three-bar fire. Jeanie and Sandra were on a small sofa. A small table was piled with cheese cubes and fruit cake chunks. Sandra topped up her Granny's glass: gin competing with Crabbies.

"I see your mither didnae see fit to call in by. You should have better things to do tonight than keep the company of an auld woman," Jeanie offered this welcome every time Sandra visited. Every week.

"I'm here noo." It was a ritual and a test.

"Still pining o'er that boy that's gone away to university?" Auld Jeanie only knew direct. Her Highland charge.

"He's awa' and I'm, well, I'm a small toon girl," it was the best Sandra could offer after a few drams and escaping from another complication at the Scotts'. She thought it had a certain ring – small town girl; it could be a song title.

Jeanie didn't give her any credit.

"Stop feeling sorry for yersel. He's gone. Tak it fae me, if someone disnae want you, then they're nae worth havin',"

Jeanie knocked her drink back to underline her point.

Sandra took her cue and topped them both up.

"Grunny, what do you think of Makar?"

Jeanie watched the drink poured and settled back.

"Aye, well, let's face it, no other toon would hae him. Maybe, no other lassie would either." Her eyes on her second favourite granddaughter. She only had the two.

"He makes furniture. In his spare time. I like his hands," said Sandra, trying to explain it to herself.

"Hum. I'll let you into a secret. He made the chair you're sitting on. That's a start. That and his fine hands!" A pinch of salt in her cackle.

"But is it enough?" Sandra whisper shouldn't have reached the old woman, but there was nothing wrong with Jeanie's lugs when it suited her.

"Why are you asking me! You're the modern woman. It's a new year. Ging and find oot," Jeanie raised her glass in challenge.

Sandra considered this wisdom, accepted it and jumped up.

Sandra bent down and gave Jeanie a wee kiss.

"Thanks, Grunny."

"Awa' with ye. But that Makar, get him tae come and fix the chair afore you're done wi' him – it shuggles!"

Iain was nodding in his armchair, a glass of whisky on the small table in front of him. The fire still offered up a little heat. Jackie had stoked it before turning in. This was her husband's time to reflect, the whisky and the glowing peat for company and inspiration.

The first hint of January filtered into the living room. From an old record player, at a crackling 33 rpm, Dougie McLean's *'Caledonia'* welcomed the sense of pre-dawn and the hope for another year.

"Can a man nae get a drink here, even on Hogmanay?"

Iain's eyes opened. Delight. He leapt up. The mirror above the mantle piece watched father and son embrace. Iain picked up another glass, shook it out, poured in the Malt. The two chinked glasses. Cal, still dressed, was asleep on the sofa, with an old baby blanket thrown over him, a yellow tin still held upright on his chest. A reveller at pray. He stirred, but settled again.

Iain and Aaron's smiles mirrored each other. *Hame for Hogmanay.*

It was New Year's Day. A deserted Crossgate, morning sunshine greeting the new year.

A couple, not dressed for the wind, staggered across the road. They were wrestling with each other. Neither was young.

"Richt. That's fuckin' it. Fuck off," Kenny swayed. His hand clutching his suit jacket closed. His scarf missing.

He stumbled away from the woman.

"Dinna leave me, Kenny. Dinna fuckin' leave me. If you fuckin' leave me."

She tried to reach him, but her footing and focus failed. She fell.

"Kenny. Dinna fuckin' leave me," this from the ground on stocking knees.

"Shurrup. Fuckin' hell. Jesus."

He lifted her up.

"Kenny."

"Shurrup. Jesus. Gerrup."

They shambled on, only to start rowing twenty feet on.

Kenny made his annual New Year's resolution. *This year.*

Makar became Kenny's witness. Cutting through Norhaven Square, on his way to the beach, he saw Stella fall. He watched the pair struggle out of the Square. The sea was calling him, an annual ritual to welcome the sun and the tide. That was where he made his resolutions. This year he had just one.

He reached Norhaven's wide arching beach to find his resolution ahead of him. A figure in scarlet flirting with the water's edge. The dawn's reflection made her glow. A shimmering crimson beacon.

Makar gathered a breath of resolve. His new year started here.

Makar stopped a few feet away from her. He sensed she knew he was there, that there was a purpose in her gate-crashing his annual custom. He could sense it.

"Happy New Year! How's Auld Jeanie?"

"Bedded. Gin and Crabbies," Sandra threw a smile over her shoulder. Lipstick to match the coat.

"This is the time I like best. Better than the bells. Like I own the world. The future, it's mine," it was the best he could muster.

"Don't be so selfish," she replied, then relented, "Care to share it?"

"Aaron's back."

"Aye, but he's not one for staying nor sharing."

Sandra fished out a hipflask from her coat pocket. She waved it at Makar. A peace offering. Perhaps more than that.

"Ma kinda girl."

Sandra looked away from him, out over the grey-green waves to the pale washed sun.

"I think I probably am. Gin and Crabbies."

"How mony have you had?"

"Not as mony as Jeanie!"

Makar took the flask offered.

"Here's to Jeanie!"

"Slàinte!"

"Here's tae us, Fa's like us, Gie few and they're all died!"

Sandra waited patiently for him to finish and took the flask back off him. There was always the risk with Makar that he'd start reciting poetry.

"It's a bit late for the bells," Sandra turned to face him properly for the first time.

Makar took it all in. The moment. The girl. The kiss.

"That was a rare screen kiss!" His wonder made her laugh. And hope.

Perhaps coming to the beach might turn out to be one of her better ideas.

Makar was studying her. The kiss was one thing. He took a small step from her, but held out his hand.

"You coming?"

"What about your resolutions?" Sandra waved at the beach curving into the distance.

"I'm working on that."

She took his hand.

ACKNOWLEDGEMENTS

For their help on land and sea –

The fishermen: Andrew Ironside, Gary Milne, George Sutherland, Willie Tait, Robert Wiseman.

The surfers: Malcolm Anderson, Mark Cameron, Scott Main, Iain Masson, Jill Noble, William Watson.

The friends: Bing, The Navigator, Mannie Glennie, Glenn Gibson, Ged and Janet Keilty, Main Man, Danny Masson.

The readers: Brenda Clark, Paul Main, Alison Noble.

The support: Alison, Presch and Humph.

 Matador

For exclusive discounts on Matador titles,
sign up to our occasional newsletter at
troubador.co.uk/bookshop